Books by Elisa Braden

RESCUED FROM RUIN SERIES

The Madness of Viscount Atherbourne (Book One)
The Truth About Cads and Dukes (Book Two)
Desperately Seeking a Scoundrel (Book Three)
The Devil Is a Marquess (Book Four)
When a Girl Loves an Earl (Book Five)
Twelve Nights as His Mistress (e-Novella – Book Six)

∞

There's much more to come in the Rescued from Ruin series!
Connect with Elisa through Facebook and Twitter, and sign
up for her free email newsletter at www.elisabraden.com,
so you don't miss a single release!

When a Girl Loves an Earl

ELISA BRADEN

Copyright © 2016 Elisa Braden

Cover design by Kim Killion at The Killion Group, Inc.
Couple photo by Period Images, Inc.

For more information about the author, visit www.elisabraden.com.

ISBN-13: 978-1-54-087967-7
ISBN-10: 1-5408-7967-4

Dedication

For all the girls who have stared intractable adversity straight in the eye and said, "There must be a way." This one's for you.

Chapter One

"Use your colossal head for more than hammering stone, boy.
Must I think of everything?"

—THE DOWAGER MARCHIONESS OF WALLINGHAM to the Earl of
Tannenbrook in a moment of perplexity at said gentleman's
unyielding nature.

∽∞∽

June 4, 1802
Netherdunnie, Scotland

"YER HEID BE HARDER THAN THAT BLOCK, LADDIE," GRUMBLED
Mr. McFadden, slumped and weathered against the rough-
edged door. "I told ye tae leave it fer me. Auld I may be, but
these bones binna dust yet."

Jamie paused as he straightened with the block in his arms.
Even at sixteen, he could carry twice what other men could

with half the effort. Of a certainty, he would not leave a man forty years his senior to lift such a load when he could do it without losing a breath. He raised a brow at the iron-miened stonemason who had honed him like a fine block of granite these past five years. "Shall I set 'er doon here, then, rather than upon yer bench?"

McFadden grunted, glanced at his own gnarled hands and the heavy downpour beyond the windows of his workshop, then sighed into a frown. "Dinna be daft."

Keeping his expression carefully neutral, Jamie moved the heavy sandstone block to McFadden's workbench, bending his knees to set it gently upon the scarred wood.

All day, he had battled a grin. Everything delighted him. McFadden's false gruffness and stubborn pride. The smooth-planed surface he'd achieved on his own block of stone—the beginnings of a set of corbels for a grand house between Netherdunnie and Edinburgh. Even the thick, constant rain turning the roads to a muddy stew.

Today, everything shone to a high polish.

Because of her.

Today, she would agree to marry him. He could feel it the same way McFadden's knuckles could sense a coming storm.

"What the devil has ye grinnin' sae, laddie?" McFadden grumbled, whisking away a bit of dust from the block and scowling in Jamie's direction.

Instantly, Jamie reined his mouth back into line.

"Gie's the mallet," the old man said, nodding to the tool near Jamie's hand.

He handed his former master the mallet and watched McFadden begin boning in the edges of the block with emphatic strikes against the head of his chisel. Chips of sandstone flew, striking Jamie's leather apron.

"Ye might as well gae'n see her. Seems that's where yer heid be anyhou."

The grin broke open again. "Thank ye, Mr. McFadden."

Jamie stripped his apron with sharp tugs, flinging it at the peg on the wall before rushing to the workshop door.

"Slow doon, ye fool. She'll be there whither ye tear that door from its frame wi' yer great, muckle fist or no."

Jamie scarcely heard the caution, but it was unnecessary. When he'd sprouted to his current size, towering over everyone in the village, he'd dented more than a few lintels with his skull before learning to duck when he passed through a doorway.

He'd also required only one instance of accidentally shoving his sister to the ground with a playful swat of her shoulder before realizing his new strength required great temperance, especially with women. Now, despite a drumming heart demanding he rush to meet his bonnie love, he paused long enough to snag his hat and plunk it upon his head before striding out into the silvery deluge. He felt not a drop upon his skin. Heeded none of the shouted greetings as he strode purposefully down the muddy lanes of his village, past the smithy where his father had labored until his death, beyond the small inn welcoming wayfarers on the road to Edinburgh. He started across the expanse of the green with scarcely a thought ... apart from one: Alison. She would be his wife.

An apprentice no longer, he was now worthy of a journeyman's wages, and while his mother might think him a lad, he was in every measure a man: He had become a craftsman, perhaps not yet of similar renown as McFadden, but one who worked and earned his way. He could support a wife. Perhaps a bairn or two.

Additionally, lads were small. He was taller and larger than anyone in the village—anyone he had ever seen pass through the village, for that matter. The width of his shoulders forced him to both stoop and sidle through narrow corridors.

And last, but by no means least, he had already lain with a lass.

His lass.

Three times.

He'd not torn her asunder, as he'd feared. No, he had found pleasure beyond compare. And his saucy, earthy Alison had found her own as well, if her moaning and carrying on were an indication.

His smile returned. He could not wait to see her again.

The shorn grass had gone flat and soft beneath the onslaught of rain, making the ground slick and slowing his progress. Urgency thrummed in his blood. Perhaps Alison would let him touch her again. His palms tingled with the possibility.

"... Jamie!"

He would start by kissing her. If he hurried, he would no doubt catch her behind her father's dairy, waiting for him beneath the stout oak tree, her ready smile gleaming a welcome.

"Slow doon," a feminine voice echoed behind him. "I canna run in these skirts."

He glanced over his shoulder to see his sister straining to catch up with him, the brim of her bonnet a nearly solid fall of water. "What are ye aboot, Nellie?" he called across the thirty feet she struggled to close. "Ye should be helpin' Mam prepare dinner."

Finally, she reached him, one hand settling on her abdomen as she struggled for breath. His only sibling was two years older, tall for a female, and while they shared the same dark-blond hair, her features were thankfully much more pleasant to look upon than his.

Only recently, Patrick Abernathy had come by the workshop dressed in his humble finest, asking permission to court her. Jamie had scoffed at the man's lofty airs—Patrick was a blacksmith's son, just as Jamie was, not an Edinburgh knab with a fancy neckcloth and false courtesy—but Patrick had insisted Nellie deserved such consideration.

Right enough, he'd thought dryly. *Nellie is surely the finest flower in the field with her blunt mouth and managing ways.* Although he had granted his permission, he'd struggled to keep from rolling his eyes at Abernathy's earnest regard.

Jamie's delicate rose petal of a sister now slapped his upper arm with her usual hard blow. "Mam sent me to fetch ye. I've been chasin' ye through this accursed rain since ye left the workshop. Did ye no' hear me callin'?" Her straight, blond brows lowered in displeasure, Nellie craned her neck and tilted her round chin.

Shrugging, he replied, "Nae time fer a chat."

"Blethers. Ye've more important matters tae tend than meetin' that dairyman's daughter again. I warned ye that one'll spring her trap sooner than ye can—"

He sighed, irritation slithering down his nape like relentless rain. "What dae ye want, Nellie?"

"A man has come tae see ye. Mam wishes ye tae return. Now."

"What man?"

"His name is Mr. Hargrave. From England. Insists on speakin' wi' ye."

The chill of Jamie's rain-soaked clothing saturated his skin. He'd been hoping for an hour in Alison's arms to warm him, but it appeared no such comfort was imminent. *Bluidy hell.*

"Come now," Nellie said, her voice edged with mockery. "Yer dairy lass will be waitin' again tomorrow, nae doubt."

He scowled his annoyance. But she had already turned north, striding toward their cottage. Glancing briefly eastward to where his bonnie Alison waited beneath a sheltering oak, he followed his sister's sodden-hemmed skirts, his steps considerably more plodding than before.

In minutes, they came within sight of his family's stone cottage, stout and gray upon a small, green rise on the outskirts of the village. On either side of the red door, his mother's delphiniums had not yet bloomed. Spring had soaked the spear-shaped plants until their leaves drooped, sparing and despondent. He wondered how an Englishman would view his tidy but humble dwelling.

"What does he want with me, Nell?"

His sister cast him a brief glance from beneath her bonnet and shrugged. "Canna say. Perhaps he wishes tae hire ye."

Doubtful. Jamie had not the reputation yet to attract inquiries from wealthy Scotsmen, much less a knab from south of the Roman wall. Automatically, he bent his head as he followed Nellie through the red door and into the darkened interior. Since one entered directly into the parlor, his first glimpse of the Englishman was the man's narrow back clothed in refined, blue wool and a head of brown hair heavily salted with white.

"Jamie," Mam said, her blond brows arched into the ruffle of her mobcap. Her hands smoothed her apron as she stood. "Mr. Hargrave has come with news fer ye."

The man turned, a black hat in one hand and a thick bundle of papers in the other. The bundle was contained inside a leather cover bound with twine. His face was narrow, his nose sharp, his chin long. "James Kilbrenner?"

"Aye."

Bending at the waist, the man presented Jamie with the top of his salted brown head. Jamie blinked, wondering if this odd, narrow Englishman had dropped something. Then, he watched as the man straightened and met his eyes.

"Allow me to be the first to greet you properly," Hargrave said quietly, his speech cultured and discreet. "My lord."

If Jamie had not glimpsed his mother's face in that moment, he would have taken a handful of Hargrave's blue wool coat and promptly tossed him out into the squall. But Mam's eyes were deadly sober and leveled on Jamie. She'd worn the same expression the day his father had been burned badly enough to produce a lingering death. Bess Kilbrenner was not one to raise a hue and cry unless the matter was grave.

"I fear ye've the wrong end of things, Mr. Hargrave," Jamie replied. "I am nae more a laird than ye're a sheep."

Hargrave cleared his throat and waved his hat toward the chairs near the fire. "Perhaps we should sit."

Jamie crossed his arms over his chest. "Nae need." He nodded toward the bundle of papers clutched in the man's hand. "Whatever ye've brought wi' ye, if there be a claim that I am anythin' other than a blacksmith's son, ye're best off tossin' those papers intae the fire."

"Are ye daft, Jamie?" hissed Nellie from behind him. "Listen tae the man. What will it harm?"

Serious eyes above a sharp nose met Jamie's gaze. "You will wish to hear what I have come to say, I promise you."

Jamie glanced to his mother then briefly to Nellie, whose jaw remained agape, her gaze fixed upon Hargrave as though the man would soon perform spectacular feats with his fancy hat.

"Verra weel," he said, gesturing to the rough wooden chairs his mother had covered with neat green pillows.

Mam cleared her throat and muttered something about preparing dinner. She grasped Nellie's arm on her way to the kitchen and dragged Jamie's sputtering sister from the room. Thankfully.

Jamie hung his hat on the iron hook beside the door and ran a hand through his hair before striding slowly to the bigger of the two chairs. He sank down into a sit, all the while eyeing Hargrave's careful motions as the Englishman placed his hat upon the plank floor and loosened the twine on this bundle of papers.

"Your father was a blacksmith, indeed, my lord—"

"Dinna call me that."

Hargrave paused and nodded solemnly. "I understand. All of this is rather ... unexpected."

Jamie simply held the man's stare for long seconds, waiting for him to come to the point.

A narrow throat rippled on a swallow. "As I was saying, your father was a blacksmith. John Kilbrenner. His father was James Kilbrenner, a ship's captain in His Majesty's navy."

"Till he lost an arm. Then he was a sour old sot who drank half my father's earnin's." Jamie gripped the sides of his chair and leaned forward. "Why have ye come, Mr. Hargrave?"

A lean hand settled atop the papers. "Your father was a blacksmith. Your grandfather a naval captain. But your great, great, *great* grandfather was an earl, my lor—er, Mr. Kilbrenner. An English peer. Specifically, he was the first Earl of Tannenbrook."

Cold seeped from his sodden shirt into his chest. A shiver blew over his skin, despite the low fire. He curled his fingers into his palm. They'd gone numb. "What should it matter now? Sae a man long in the grave was a lofty lord. I am a stonemason. Just completed my apprenticeship. Yer fancy title means nothin' tae me."

"I am afraid it does."

Jamie glared at the narrow man. "Why?"

Hargrave held his gaze, steady and plain. "Because my employer, William Kilbrenner, the fifth Earl of Tannenbrook, has died. And his only son unfortunately preceded him in death. Which means the title now must ascend the first earl's lines to that of your great-grandfather—"

"Nae."

"—of whose progeny, you are the sole surviving male."

"Ye've made a mistake."

"There is no mistake, Mr. Kilbrenner. You are the rightful heir. The title and the estate in Derbyshire are yours."

"I hammer bluidy stone. My place is here. *No'* bluidy England."

Now, it was Hargrave's turn to lean forward. The blue wool tightened across the man's narrow shoulders, but the finely sewn seams neither puckered nor strained. "Apologies, Mr. Kilbrenner. But you are, in fact, the sixth Earl of Tannenbrook. Whether you accept it or not, that fact remains."

"Find somebody else."

Hargrave shook his head. "There is no one else, but even if there were, the only way he would inherit is upon your death.

You cannot simply hand your title to another. It is yours by right and by blood, as it will be your son's."

"I havnae any bairns."

"Yet. Your eldest living son shall one day inherit both title and estate. To marry and beget an heir is the duty of every—"

"Duty?" Jamie squeezed the wood of his chair until he heard it begin to crack. "My duty is tae care fer my mam and sister. Will this bluidy English title help me dae that?"

His lips tightened, his eyes dropped briefly, and he released a breath. "The scope of your responsibilities must necessarily expand, Mr. Kilbrenner. There are people whose lives depend upon your direct involvement in the estate."

Jamie frowned. "Who?"

"The villagers who live near Shankwood Hall. Servants. Tenants. Many have dwelt upon Tannenbrook lands for generations. Should you shrug away your obligations, the consequences would be dire for them."

Jamie's response was a single word, but it emerged as a contemptuous grumble: "Sassenachs."

"They are English, yes. English women. English children. English farmers who work the soil as hard as your fellow Scots."

"No' my people."

Jamie's gaze was fixed upon Hargrave, so he was startled to hear his mother's voice, gentle and firm, from the doorway to the kitchen. "It appears they are, Jamie."

His eyes flew to hers. "He would have me leave here, Mam." He swallowed. Leave Alison? Leave the bairns they would have together, the cottage he had dreamed of building for them after their marriage, the workshop McFadden would pass to him once the old mason realized he could wield a chisel no longer? No. Jamie's life—his future—lay in Netherdunnie. He would not toss it away for a title he'd never wanted. "Who would care fer ye while I am in bluidy England?"

Mam moved several steps toward him, her eyes calm, her brow crinkling. "Ye know yer duty, son. In life, our plans can last only sae long as they make guid sense. Yer faither's death should hae taught ye as much."

Hargrave stood and cleared his throat. "Funds will be provided by the estate for the care of your mother and sister, Mr. Kilbrenner. Whatever your earnings as a mason might have been, they cannot match the living you may now provide as the Earl of Tannenbrook."

"Ye maun gae, Jamie," Mam said quietly.

He shoved from his chair. Approached his small mother. Grasped her roughened hands in his. "I dinna want this, Mam," he murmured desperately, feeling like a wee lad again, begging her permission to go fishing rather than sweep floors at the smithy.

Her answer, as it had then, shone in her steady eyes, the relaxed, unsmiling mouth. She accepted what life demanded of her, and he must do the same.

He let her fingers slide through his, feeling his future crack along a fault he'd failed to see. In the space of seconds, the life he'd been carving for himself split open and crumbled into something unrecognizable. Unwanted. Unavoidable.

"We should depart as soon as possible, Mr. Kilbrenner. The fifth earl suffered a long illness, and the estate has fallen into some disrepair. Many critical matters require your attention."

Gritting his teeth, he dropped his eyes to his boots. Curled his fingers into fists. "Weel-a-weel," he muttered. "In the mornin'. First light. Ye may stay fer dinner if ye like."

"Oh, but—"

"I hae matters of my oon tae attend, Mr. Hargrave." He did not care that his voice emerged as a bark or that Hargrave was twenty years his elder or that his mother was frowning at his rudeness. "An' that is how it shall be. Ye ken?"

A brief silence was followed by Hargrave's reply, muted and respectful—disturbing to Jamie's ears. "Yes, my lord."

SHE WAS THERE, WAITING BENEATH THE EAVE. WHEN HE descended the last hill on the road to her father's farm, sodden to the bone and hollowed out until he echoed inside, he saw first the flowered cotton of her skirts, then the wisps of her hair, a shade darker than wet sandstone.

"Alison," he murmured, seeing her bonnie face peeking around the corner of the stone dairy barn, her smile welcoming and relieved. He loped the remaining fifty yards, ducking past a low-hanging oak limb. He swiped at the wet leaves with one hand and reached for her waist with the other, swooping in to take her lips with his.

Husky, feminine laughter greeted him. Strong, feminine hands snaked beneath his arms to clutch his back. "Jamie," she mumbled against his mouth as her firm bosoms pressed into his chest. "I wondered if ye'd come."

He loved her voice, low and brambly. He loved that she was tall and robust, her muscles sleek from tending cows and wringing laundry and hauling water. Whenever her thighs squeezed his hips, their strength left him little fear that he would break her.

And now, he must leave her behind. Although it would only be for a short while, the ache of their parting sliced sharp and cold.

"Ah, Alison," he groaned, dropping his forehead upon her broad shoulder, feeling her stroke his back in long, soothing motions.

"Where hae ye been? I waited an hour longer than I should hae. Mam will be wonderin' why it takes sae long tae milk four cows. What kept ye?"

She always smelled the same, like grass and earth and milk. Not sweet or flowery, but good. Just good. He breathed her in, hoping he could hold a bit of her inside him while he was gone. "I've news," he rasped. "I dinna like it. But I must leave fer England."

Her muscles tensed against him, freezing in place. Her cheek was warm against his ear. "England?"

He pulled away long enough to explain about Mr. Hargrave and the bloody English title he did not want. He watched the color fade from her cheeks as he described his new circumstances. "There be an estate, one I must see tae straight away. But I swear this tae ye, my bonnie Alison: I shall return here. And when I dae, we shall marry. Nothin' shall stop us. Nothin' has changed."

Eyes lowered to his chest, she idly plucked at his shirt's ties, her body terribly still.

"Luik at me," he demanded.

She complied, but eyes typically as warm as fresh-brewed tea shone flat and solemn. Wide lips that usually tilted with a crooked smile now wore a bittersweet curve.

He squeezed her shoulders. Ran one hand over the soft, straight hair she wore in a plait. "I intend tae marry ye, lass. A Sassenach title changes nothin' of my plans fer us."

Shaking her head, she stood on her toes to lay a gentle kiss upon his lips. "Ye'll hae much tae worry ye withoot frettin' over me, Jamie. Ye're a lord now. Take care of what ye must."

He was losing her. He could see it, feel it, hear it in her voice and her posture and the way she avoided his gaze. "I shall write ye. Letters upon letters. Every day. And ye shall write me back."

She patted his chest. "Weel-a-weel."

"And when I return tae Netherdunnie, ye shall become my bride, Alison. Ye shall become Lady Tannenbrook. Our bairns shall live grand lives."

Her crooked smile reappeared, displaying the chipped tooth he so loved. But her eyes remained quiet. Sad. "Grand indeed, Jamie. Grand indeed."

He held her tight, then, feeling her arms around his waist, her cheek against his chest. She doubted him, obviously having the same thoughts he'd had upon hearing Hargrave's news—a stonemason had no business being an earl, and a dairyman's daughter was even less suited to the role of countess. But he did not care. Alison was the lass he loved, and she was the one he would marry, title or no.

"I shall return," he whispered, more to himself than to her. "Ye must wait fer me, Alison. Will ye dae that?"

Her arms squeezed his waist in silent reassurance. Around them water poured out of clouds and mist, forming a solid curtain off the eave of the barn. The sound muffled her sigh, drowned his heartbeat until he could almost believe this was an ordinary day, an ordinary embrace with his bonnie love. Not a goodbye.

"Wait fer me, lass," he begged, clutching her tighter. "I shall return. That's a promise I mean tae keep."

⤫⤫⤫

One year later ...

NOTHING HAD CHANGED. NOT THE APPROACH TO Netherdunnie with its ripe, green rolls of land and muddy, shorn sheep. Not the odd sandstone cottage with its sagging roof and three ash trees just before the last bend.

"Not even the bluidy weather," James muttered to himself, tapping a knuckle against the carriage's window frame, listening to the rain compete with the creak and rattle of the vehicle.

"*Bloody* weather." The voice came from beside him. It was English, pure and aristocratic. Amused. "Have a care, Tannenbrook. Your Scot is showing."

James glanced to his friend, Lucien Wyatt, a dark-eyed,

black-haired second son wearing a perpetual half-grin upon his too-handsome face. "We are *in* Scotland, ye daft sod."

"Leave him be, Luc." The quiet reprimand came from Gregory, Lucien's older brother. Thanks to a long nose, Gregory was not nearly so pretty, but his calm, serious nature suited his role as their father's heir. "It is the first time he's clapped eyes on his village in a year."

Lucien chuckled. "I doubt the village is what he envisions when he falls abed each night."

James shoved at Luc's lean shoulder, letting a smile take his lips when his friend winced and rubbed the spot. "That is my future countess you speak of. Mind your tongue."

Though only a year younger than James, Luc was a far sight more devil-may-care, having few responsibilities apart from counting the skirts he managed to lift. He and Gregory were the sons of Lord Atherbourne, whose estate, Thornbridge Park, neighbored his own in Derbyshire.

Neighbors. James wanted to laugh aloud at the thought. Even the names of the two properties compared poorly. Thornbridge Park was a shimmering, golden palace composed of exquisite Palladian symmetry and the finest limestone. Shankwood Hall, on the other hand, was composed of square blocks with no pediments, no columns. Just a series of chimneys poking at the sky like the last, wiry hairs upon old McFadden's head. When James had first glimpsed his crumbling gray sprawl, he'd noted immediately the deterioration: The widening cracks beneath the first floor. Stone walls discolored red by fire on the second floor.

The narrow, spidery windows infrequently dotting the façade gave it little elegance. Indeed, the entire structure might as well have been a prison for all its beauty. The house ran in an unimpressive, ungainly U around an overgrown courtyard. All in all, there was little to recommend it apart from size and a certain sturdiness. It had lasted more than two hundred years, after all.

Hargrave had spent the entire journey to Derbyshire explaining the repairs that must be approved and funded. Ever efficient and helpful, the solicitor had made a list. He had estimated that, with the income from the estate's farms and rents, the repairs would take a mere ten years. Ten. Years.

Upon his arrival at Shankwood, James had wanted nothing more than to ball Hargrave's list into a wad and shove the paper down the solicitor's narrow throat. Then, he'd wanted to leave the way he'd come—leave England and return to Scotland. To Alison.

Instead, he had grudgingly agreed to meet the servants who had stayed on after the fifth earl's death. Most of them were nearly as aged as the hall itself, but they had greeted him as though he were both a long-lost son and their liege lord. It had been a wee bit embarrassing, in truth, but he'd been unable to rebuff their kindness. Afterward, he had reluctantly agreed to tour the village. This had sealed his fate in a way he could not have predicted.

Shankwood Hall sat squarely—and he did mean *squarely*—in the midst of a picturesque village known, oddly enough, as Shankwood. Home to fewer than seventy people, the tiny collection of humble stone cottages and shops had instantly reminded him of Netherdunnie.

He'd first encountered the blacksmith, Jones, whose broad grin and bulging forearms had reminded him of his father. Then, he'd met the Starlings, an ancient, kindly pair of sisters who took in sewing when their fingers did not pain them. "The rain, you know," they'd whispered confidingly as they had poured him a cup of the finest ale he'd ever tasted. Over the following week, he'd met every villager, down to the new babe born to Mr. and Mrs. Fellowes—their fifth child, a boy they had named James in honor of their new lord.

All the natural Scots resistance had drained from him like ale from a cracked tankard. In every face, he had seen his mother, his father, McFadden or Nellie or dozens of others he had known for a lifetime. They were familiar, these people. Perhaps they did not speak like him, but as Hargrave incessantly repeated, they *needed* him.

No one else was permitted to manage their rents or authorize repairs to their roofs or approve the construction of a new bakehouse. Only he, James Kilbrenner, the sixth Earl of Tannenbrook, could do these things. Without him, every servant and villager would eventually be forced to leave their home.

And so, he had stayed. Through the summer, he'd become acquainted with Gregory and Lucien, who were fascinated with his accent and his size, his facility with stonework and his rough manner.

After learning from Hargrave how much of his role as Lord Tannenbrook involved not only governance of his lands but influencing the laws and policies of the entire kingdom, James had realized how poorly prepared a Scottish stonemason was to take a seat in the House of Lords. Fortunately, Gregory and Lucien had been eager to help. They had taken him under their tutelage, sharing their knowledge of proper manners and dress, sharing their tutors and dance instructor and tailor. They had even helped him chip away at his brogue until he could scarcely recognize his own voice.

All the while, through the summer and autumn and long, cold winter, he'd assured himself that he would visit Netherdunnie again. In another month, when the harvest was completed. In a fortnight, when Shankwood's annual well-dressing festival was over. In the spring, when the ice had receded and the roof repairs were done. Each week, he had written letters upon letters—to Mam, to McFadden, even to Nellie.

And, above all, to Alison. His bonnie lass. Lucien was right. He had dreamed of her. Remembered her smell and her eyes and her voice as he lay in the master bedchamber of Shankwood Hall. But after the first month, she had ceased responding to his letters. He'd written to ask Mam about it, to which she had replied, "Focus on your duties there, my son. After a time, you shall return, and you may ask her reasons yourself."

He'd pressed several times more, but she had only advised him to forget the lass, emphasizing that his "preoccupation can come to no good." Nellie was equally unhelpful, but that was hardly a surprise. His sister had never taken to Alison, often implying the "dairyman's daughter" was loose with her favors and did not love him as she pretended.

Now, however, he would finally see her again, hear her rasping voice and smell her milky skin. He would propose marriage—her father was certain to agree, given the title he could offer—and they would be wed before returning to Shankwood.

If she was not too angry with him for staying away so long. Perhaps that was why she'd not answered his letters. Again, he drummed his knuckle against the window frame.

Gregory glanced up from his book to interrupt James's thoughts. "That will not hurry the horses, James," he said quietly.

James sighed. "The coach is too bloody slow. We would have arrived yesterday had we simply taken our mounts."

"Yesterday, indeed," commented Lucien, wryly nodding toward the downpour beyond the window. "Had we not drowned first."

With his usual calm, Gregory closed the book and set it beside him on the seat. "You are both so young."

"You are only three years ahead of me, oh aged one," said Lucien.

Gregory grinned. "A long three years, in your case." His eyes moved back to James. "Regardless, I know this much: Little good has ever resulted from rushing things. Your impatience is unusual. This girl must mean a great deal to you."

James met his older friend's eyes solemnly. "She does."

Gregory nodded as though he understood.

Lucien snorted. "Pure and utter madness to let a female twist you up in such a way."

It was an agonizingly long twenty minutes before the coach arrived at his family's cottage. He had the door open before it stopped. Slammed his boots down into the mud. Rushed through the gate and watched as the red door opened to reveal his mam, dressed all in brown, apart from a white cap, wearing a broad, teary smile.

"Son," she breathed, though he read the word on her lips more than heard it above the rain.

Within a few paces, he had wrapped her up, lifted her off the ground, spun her in a circle. This time, he heard her whisper it. "Jamie. My son."

After a time, the tightness in his chest eased, and he was able to speak. "How I missed ye, Mam."

She welcomed them all inside with fresh ale and much news—McFadden had begun training a new apprentice. Patrick Abernathy had accompanied Nellie to the fair in Coldstream; matters between them were "growin' a mite more earnest," according to Mam's estimation.

James's knuckles were drumming the edge of the kitchen table when his patience broke. "What of Alison, Mam?"

She stopped in the midst of a word, her mouth open in an O. Soft, serious eyes turned dark and grave.

He did not like it.

Her hand covered his.

He liked that even less. "Is she at her father's farm?"

"Nae, Jamie."

He ground his teeth. "Tell me."

"Ye willnae like it, son." She squeezed his hand as though bracing him. "A month or sae after ye left, she married the oldest Campbell lad. Douglas. They live wi' his mother now at the Campbell farm."

He scarcely heard a word beyond "married." She was married. His bonnie lass. To another man.

"It's sorry I am tae be tellin' ye this now, Jamie. But had I said somethin' sooner, ye would hae left England before ye had finished yer work. An' fer what? The deed was done."

He did not remember rising from the table, nor stalking out of the cottage, slamming the red door, and striding back through the rain to the coach. He scarcely recalled barking directions to the Atherbourne coachman and climbing inside.

It was less than a mile to the farm, but for the entire journey, he could only hear his final entreaty to her: "Wait fer me, lass. I shall return." She had not answered. She had not waited. She had chosen to become a farmer's wife rather than his.

He wanted to be sick, his stomach churning, his head floating and fogged.

Within minutes, he was rattling Campbell's door with his fist, noting the green moss upon the wet stones of the old farmhouse. If Douglas Campbell could not bother with cleaning the stones around his door, how could he care for a wife? Answer: He could not. Surely she would have realized that James was a far better choice for husband. Why, then, would she—

The door opened, first a crack, then wide. And there she stood. Alison.

He breathed, the motion of air into his lungs painful. She was thinner than before, her hair coiled at the back of her head, her gown covered by an apron.

"Jamie?" Her voice was the same, currently soft with wonderment. "I–I didna expect tae see ye ... here." Warm brown eyes scoured him from head to toe.

His cravat and silk waistcoat choked the air out of him.

She stepped back, opening the door wider to a dim interior. "Come in frae the rain. I'll fetch us some ale."

Automatically, he removed his hat, shaking the rainwater

from the brim before stepping inside. He'd visited the Campbell farm a handful of times—he and Douglas had played in front of the hearth in this room as boys.

Alison brushed one hand along the side of her head and another along her hip. "No' sae fine as what ye're accustomed tae, I've nae doubt."

"Alison," he said, the word dragged from the dark, burning stew inside his gut. "Why?"

In her eyes, first lowered and then raised to his, he saw resignation and sadness. "I didna belong wi' ye, Jamie. I belong here, on a farm. This wis always my place. Ye need a wife who will no' embarrass ye wi' her rough ways."

"Blethers. Ye had only tae wait."

"I couldna wait."

"Why?"

She swallowed. Her arms fell loose at her sides as though she knew not what to do with them. "There was a bairn, Jamie."

He hadn't imagined anything could hurt more than learning of her betrayal, but this was ... agony. Like being blasted through with molten metal then crushed beneath a two-ton slab of granite. The room shook in his vision. Perhaps it was his head.

"Wh—whose?"

Her lips pressed together. "Yers."

"Where? Where is—"

"Gone. I am sorry, Jamie." She covered her mouth with her hand and squeezed her eyes shut briefly before explaining what had happened. After he had left, she'd missed her monthly courses and, fearing she carried his child, had persuaded Douglas to wed her, pretending the child was Campbell's. "A laddie," she rasped. "I named him John, fer yer faither."

"Where is he?" he growled.

"In the last weeks of carryin', a fever burned through

Netherdunnie. It took hold of me. When he came, he was weak. Too weak." A tear tracked down her cheek. "He died no' three days after he was born."

The granite slab was grinding his bones. Grinding him to dust.

"Where is my son?" He cared nothing for the gritted roar of his demand. She had hidden this from him. He would have returned to Netherdunnie. He would have come back and married her, had she only written to tell him the truth. He would have cared for her properly, made her a countess, for Christ's sake. Taken her away from here. Then, his son—his *son*—would have lived.

"We buried him on the brae, beneath the largest willow. There is a marker there. McFadden's work. I—I planted daisies."

He left without saying goodbye. Left her there, tears upon her cheeks, clinging to the frame of the open door. But that did not matter. He could barely see through the rain, but he remembered the hill, several hundred yards from the farmhouse, topped by a small copse of willow and birch. By the time he reached the tiny gravemarker, he was soaked and cold, the linen of his shirt and cravat a sodden skin leaching all heat from his blood.

McFadden had done well, chiseling gray granite into an elaborate cross. Etching the name of his son—his *son*—into the hard stone.

John. After Jamie's father.

Jamie's knees were in the mud, now. His hand clutched the cross until he feared it might crack. It did not, of course. Granite was dense and tough by nature. It resisted. Endured.

No, it was not the stone that fractured beneath the dripping willow and his great, muckle fist. Instead, it was he that cracked, cleaving forever in two.

Chapter Two

*"Your error lies not in your admiration, Miss Darling, but in
failing to properly disguise it. Obviousness is appalling
strategy. A man may partake of that which is served to him
upon a silken pillow, but only a daft one marries it."*

—THE DOWAGER MARCHIONESS OF WALLINGHAM to Miss Penelope
Darling upon being regaled with extravagant praise for
Lord Mochrie's questionable wit.

∽

March 14, 1818
Bowman's on Bond Street

"HE LIFTED THE GENTLEMAN ... BY HIS CRAVAT?" VIOLA
Darling blinked slowly up at her dearest friend, Charlotte
Lancaster, who stood beside her in Mrs. Bowman's lovely, blue-
draped shop. The difference in their heights could be felt in the

accustomed crook of Viola's nape. She was reminded again that she should not stand so near Charlotte, for she always came away from their conversations nursing a vague pain in her upper spine. However, considering they were presently perusing the same fashion plate—and Viola was not about to wait for an answer—there was little choice in the matter.

"Mmm. With one hand, he dangled Mr. Maynard ten inches above the floor," Charlotte murmured, absently tracing a gloved finger down the lines of the azure velvet riding habit. "Quite a shocking display of strength, really."

Viola blinked again, redirecting her gaze to the sketch and suppressing a relishing shiver. They were discussing an incident that had occurred the previous November, when Charlotte had visited London with her aunt and uncle. After taking a mortifying tumble on the ice in Hyde Park, Charlotte had been dubbed Longshanks Lancaster by a handful of spiteful, wretched, thoroughly disgraceful young men. Later, at a rout hosted by Lady Rutherford for the smattering of beau monde in town during winter, a valiant champion had overheard Mr. Maynard taunting Charlotte and had promptly come to her defense.

Admittedly, Viola had developed a rather sudden and alarming fascination with the story. And with its hero, a mysterious earl whom she'd not occasioned to meet—yet. She intended to rectify the oversight soon, for such *nobility* among the nobility was far more rare than it should be.

Swallowing, Viola said as casually as she could manage, "One hand. How ... brutish of him." And impressive. "What did he do next?"

A single red brow arched. "He forced the lout to apologize and promptly tossed him onto the refreshment table. Broke the thing in half."

Viola's shivers worsened until she feared she was losing her breath. In fact, she had no reply. Such physical power, particularly in the midst of a London ballroom, was simply outlandish. Preposterous. Fascinating.

"Do you suppose I should take this in emerald?" Charlotte murmured. "It will be costly."

Viola cleared her throat and focused on the sketch. Perhaps a distraction was wise for the moment. Her belly was fizzing as though she'd imbibed an entire bottle of champagne. "You are an heiress, Charlotte. Your father could buy you a thousand such habits."

A smile lifted Charlotte's lips, still pale from their jaunt along Bond Street on this chill morning. "If only I could justify such an expense. Surely I could sell nine-hundred and ninety-nine of them and purchase passage to Boston."

Although Charlotte had spent most of her life in England—even her diction was indistinguishable from any other Mayfair miss—she was half-American by parentage and entirely American by sentiment. Charlotte's fondest wish was to return to the land of her birth and enter trade. Charlotte's father, on the other hand, wished to marry his daughter to an English title. The result was five London seasons during which Charlotte had received not a single offer.

Frankly, Viola did not begin to understand what the gentlemen of the ton were thinking. They flocked around her but paid no mind at all to Charlotte, who was one of the loveliest women she had ever encountered—honest and kind and sensible and good-natured. Granted, she was absurdly tall and dotted with freckles. And vermillion was not a particularly fashionable color for a lady's hair. And Charlotte had an unfortunate tendency to trod men's toes or dislodge their hats or elbow their noses. But these were meaningless trifles. One need only glance into her friend's intelligent eyes when they lit with knowing humor to be utterly charmed.

"Why did he not propose marriage to you?" Viola asked, curious about the intriguing gentleman they'd been discussing.

Green-and-gold eyes flared. "My father?"

Viola giggled. "Silly goose. Your gallant. Lord Tannenbrook."

"Oh! Er, doubtless Papa would be pleased by an offer from an earl." Charlotte waved a hand dismissively, nearly batting Viola's nose. "However, James and I are not ... that is, Lord Tannenbrook does not view me in such a way. He is simply the sort of man who would defend a woman's honor."

"A woman with whom he was not previously acquainted and in whom he had no prior interest?" Was her voice growing tart? It was. How strange.

Charlotte shrugged. "Yes, I suppose so. But it was hardly due to a sudden affection. He is honorable, Viola. A genuinely good man. He heard Mr. Maynard's vile taunt and took it as his duty to—"

"Break the refreshment table in half with Mr. Maynard's backside." Now she sounded sharp to her own ears. Viola found herself frowning. She never frowned. What was wrong with her?

Charlotte sighed and rolled her eyes. "I hear your implication, you know, and it is not true. Lord Tannenbrook and I are merely friends who have enjoyed a correspondence. There is more romantic sentiment between me and this riding habit." She waved at the fashion plate.

Forcing her brow smooth, Viola sniffed, uncertain if she should believe her. Surely any woman who had been defended so heroically could not help falling in love with her rescuer, if only a little. Viola had never met Lord Tannenbrook, but based on Charlotte's description, she found the protestations of mere friendship dubious, particularly with Mr. Lancaster pressing Charlotte to marry.

However, Viola had no desire to argue with her dearest friend over romantic sentiments that may or may not exist. "Well, it is a most fetching design," she conceded, glancing again at the sketch. "If you must have it, take it in blue. Green is lovely but predictable."

Smiling, Charlotte nodded. "Your instincts are beyond compare."

"I know."

Charlotte's sigh was long-suffering. "Not this again."

"Do not question the Inkling. It has never led me astray."

"Never?"

"It guided me to this magnificent bonnet." Viola waggled her fingers at the elegant confection currently perched upon her head. Covered in midnight silk, the hat was adorned with silver rosettes and tiny white feathers for leaves. She had discovered it one day whilst accompanying Charlotte to a shabby Oxford Street pawnshop. The bonnet had been covered in dust, but her eye had been drawn as though the item glimmered diamond-bright. Charlotte had scoffed at Viola's impulsive purchase—until it was cleaned and restored to its present glorious state.

Viola continued, "The Inkling helped my father choose our town house, which has since become one of the most fashionable addresses in Mayfair."

"Coincidence."

"And, let us not forget, this instinct at which you scoff insisted that I befriend you."

"That was not the Inkling. That was my perpetual clumsiness meeting your generous nature. We get on splendidly, you and I."

Their friendship had begun the previous season when Charlotte's elbow collided with Viola's ear during a quadrille. Charlotte had muttered a flushed apology. Viola had laughed and linked arms with the tall redhead, spinning them both around in the center of the floor merrily, causing everyone around them to cheer and laugh along. Charlotte's flush had faded, her grin had grown, and they had charmed each other silly. It was one of Viola's favorite memories.

"Of course we get on, Charlotte." Vexing. That was the word for Charlotte's persistent skepticism. *Vexing.* Viola smiled wide to disguise her irritation and enunciated clearly so as to be understood. "Since I was a child, whenever I have followed the Inkling, it has rewarded me immeasurably. Whenever I have ignored it, I have languished in regret. These are *facts.*"

Charlotte gave her a considering glance before softening. "I am sorry, Vi. Insulting you was not my intention."

Viola waved away her apology and laughed away the sting. "Think no more of it. Do you suppose I should purchase a new ball gown? If Penelope is to be believed, Lady Gattingford's fete will be larger than ever this year."

Charlotte glanced toward the curtained area at the back of the shop. "Mrs. Bowman would certainly approve."

Viola sighed. "Alas, Papa would not. He insists my current assortment of gowns is sufficient."

Lowering her voice to a whisper, Charlotte leaned in close. "Even with the discount I negotiated for you?"

Nodding, Viola gave her a small smile.

"Perhaps if Mrs. Bowman created something for me, and purely by chance, we found it was fitted much too short—"

Viola covered her friend's hand and squeezed. "Whatever we Darlings lack in wealth is more than compensated by our pride, dearest."

A dark-haired, elegant woman swept aside the blue curtain with a dramatic wave of her arm and glided toward them, trailing behind her a string of mixed English and Italian commands intended for her two young assistants, who scurried meekly in the modiste's wake. "Ah, Miss Darling," Mrs. Bowman cried in her musically accented version of the English language. "You require another ball dress, no?"

Viola beamed a broad smile at the Italian woman—one of the most gifted mantua-makers in the city—and met her halfway across the floor of the shop to squeeze her hands fondly. "I would purchase one of your splendid confections every day of the season if my father would permit it, Mrs. Bowman. Your talent is unmatched."

Her reply was a sniff and a lift of her lips. "This is true."

The woman turned to snap at her assistants, "The new fashion plates for ball gowns. Fetch them for Miss Darling."

Tilting her head in regret, Viola protested quietly, "Alas, Papa insists I must practice restraint, though it pains me greatly. The indigo silk your husband displayed last week has me dreaming in magnificent shades of blue."

Renata Bowman's English husband was a textile merchant who occasionally featured offerings in Bowman's shop. It was another reason Viola and her friends frequented the place—it spared them a stop at the draper's. Similarly, the milliner several doors down from Bowman's had entered into an agreement with the modiste to display selected bonnets and turbans inside the shop, serving as inspiration to ladies seeking a complete ensemble. Both partnerships had been Charlotte's suggestions, and the measures had put the dressmaker in high demand, indeed.

"Besides," Viola continued, grinning up into the woman's shrewd, dark eyes. "So many ladies clamor for your designs, it would be months before you could possibly complete another order, would it not?"

"*Non essere sciocca.* For you, Miss Darling, always there is time."

Viola thought she heard one of Mrs. Bowman's assistants squawk in protest. The dressmaker fired a rapid blast of Italian at the poor girl before striding away, snapping her fingers impatiently.

Charlotte came to stand beside Viola. "Unfortunately for her assistants, I believe she means that. A good deal of credit for Mrs. Bowman's success may be placed at your feet, Vi."

"Mine? How do you mean?"

"Come now. You have worn her creations exclusively both last season and this. Every young lady in Mayfair now scurries to Mrs. Bowman's door seeking a mere drop of your sorcery." With a wry quirk of her lips, Charlotte angled a glance toward the corner where Mrs. Bowman stood thumbing impatiently through pages of fashion plates, thrusting this one and that into the trembling hands of her harried assistant. "If I am correct, I may be able to increase your discount. Perhaps even negotiate an arrangement involving no funds at all, merely a recommendation of her services to a few more of your acquaintances."

The calculating glint in Charlotte's eye was a familiar sight. It appeared often during Charlotte's visits to the pawnbroker, where she sold her possessions to accrue her "nest egg." Viola occasionally accompanied her on such outings. They had been educational.

"You believe you can persuade her to create my gowns *gratis?*" Viola laughed lightly. "I fear you overestimate my influence."

Green-gold eyes flared in disbelieving silence, searching her face as though bewildered. "Vi, your beauty is ... otherworldly. No diamond of the first water has ever shone brighter. You realize this, do you not?"

As always when anyone commented upon her appearance, a prickle of discomfort itched beneath Viola's skin. "Silly goose. I am as human as anyone. Have you heard me play the harp? Dreadful noise."

"Musical talent is not why gentlemen behave like hounds scenting a beefsteak whenever you enter a room."

Viola wrinkled her nose and smoothed the white embroidered cambric of her skirt. "Fools, all. Why do you suppose I have not accepted any of them? With scarcely more than a single glance, they declare their deathless affection."

"Precisely. They are enchanted. Bewitched."

"Fiddle-faddle. They seek to possess a shiny bauble. To them, I am a novelty. Nothing more."

Charlotte sighed and rolled her eyes. "Believe as you will, but I have seen it. Even my cousin Andrew has fallen under your spell."

Tiring of the subject, Viola replied, "Perhaps if one of my

admirers had hoisted Mr. Maynard aloft with a single hand and tossed him upon a refreshment table defending my honor, I would take their regard more seriously. However, I have not been so fortunate."

Her friend's snort was followed by a shake of her head. "If you are so intrigued by Lord Tannenbrook, I shall introduce you. Once you see us together, all will become clear."

A silvery shiver ran down Viola's spine. "He is in town for the season?"

"Mmm. Arrived two days ago. He may even attend Lady Reedham's gathering this evening. Have we decided if it is a supper or a musicale? Her note was rather vague. I do hope it is a supper. Musicales are ..."

Viola did not hear the rest. The most peculiar sensation had settled in her belly—like a glowing stone surrounded by excitable champagne. Something about this Lord Tannenbrook quickened her breath. Made her want to dance and twirl for no reason at all. "I should meet him," she breathed.

"Well, yes." One red brow arched in a queer look. "I thought we had agreed upon that point."

"Tonight."

"*If* he attends."

"Will you ensure he does?"

"Viola."

"Please. I wish to meet him."

A gentle hand settled upon her arm. Viola peered up into Charlotte's dear, freckled face. It crinkled with concern.

"He is not like the others, Vi. You mustn't harbor fanciful notions—"

"Tell me what he is like. Everything."

Silence. Pink lips pursed and sighed. "He is ... a mountain. A great, solid mountain."

The warmth in her belly expanded until it pulsed against the underside of her flesh. "I must meet him."

Charlotte huffed out a chuckle. "I heard you the first time. Bear in mind, he is not a hat with little white feathers that can be purchased on a whim. He is a man. He will have a say in where this Inkling of yours leads."

The warm stone resisted every word. Every one. She squeezed Charlotte's fingers harder. Insistently. "Please."

A long sigh fell between them. "Very well." Then her friend's smile turned wry. "In any event, it is doubtful you could miss him."

⁂

THE EARL OF TANNENBROOK WAS NOT HANDSOME—HIS NOSE was blunt, his brow heavy, his jaw hard and wide. On the whole, his face resembled granite that had been carved with an axe. He did, however, stand two heads taller and two times wider than any other man in Lady Reedham's drawing room.

Viola's breath had left her the moment she'd glimpsed him, leaning in the oddest way with arms crossed over his chest, one enormous shoulder braced against the window casing, as though he wished not to be noticed. As though such a thing were possible.

He wore the same clothing as all the other gentlemen— black tailcoat, white cravat. His waistcoat looked to be fawn brocade, his breeches white to match his stockings. The garments were finely made, well fitted to his sizable frame, obviously of superior quality.

But in no other way did he resemble any gentleman of her acquaintance. From the size of his gloved fingers to the cleft in the center of a squared chin, he was ... different.

"Ah, I see he has answered my summons," came a voice from behind and above her. "How unexpected."

She turned to greet Charlotte, dragging her eyes away from

the extraordinary man only with the most determined effort. "Introduce us."

Charlotte grinned. "Patience, Vi. I fear you are about to be accosted by my cousin. First, you must attempt to dissuade Andrew of his foolishness. Then we shall—"

Viola gripped Charlotte's elbow and tugged a bit harder than she'd intended, causing Charlotte to stumble. "Now. Please."

Perhaps Charlotte protested, perhaps not. Viola dragged her past the blur of ladies either glaring or smiling, eager men murmuring, "Miss Darling," with varying degrees of hopefulness, and entirely too many pieces of mahogany furniture. She heard nothing, saw nothing except a man who was different from the rest.

"Oh, apologies, Lady Randall," Charlotte muttered as Viola tugged hard to wrench her friend past a particularly cozy pair of matrons. Their disgruntled gasps mattered not a whit.

Viola was close. Then, she was there, sidling past the final obstacle, her steps slowing to a stop as she came within feet of her quarry. The window was dark behind him, candlelight reflecting richly gold in its panes, in his hair—dark blond, thick, and shadowed. His face was turned slightly away, his eyes focused on a door to the right of the fireplace on one end of the Pomona-green room.

My, he is indeed a mountain, she thought breathlessly, neck craning, gaze flared wide to take him fully in.

"Er, Viola. I seem to have dropped my fan somewhere in this crush. I expect you will help me locate it, considering your dratted impatience is the reason—ow! Stop that." The last bit came out as a hiss when Viola's fingers unwittingly dug into the crook of Charlotte's arm.

"Terribly sorry," Viola whispered, loosening her fingers and glancing to where her friend stood beside her. She met green-and-gold eyes and an exasperated smile. Returning that smile sheepishly, she reiterated, "My sincere apologies, Charlotte. Truly."

"You are forgiven. Come. Before you generate a calamity more severe than damaging my arm or knocking Lady Randall's turban askew, allow me to comply with your gentle invitation. Are you ready?"

Viola swallowed. Pressed her lips together. Nodded. Followed Charlotte as she approached the towering, dark-blond mountain. Inside, she was floating in champagne—bubbling and fizzing, warm and giddy.

"Lord Tannenbrook," said Charlotte cheerfully.

The mountain turned, dropping his arms to his sides and straightening away from the window. Although he gave Charlotte a polite nod, and his expression softened around the eyes, there was no welcoming smile, only a look of stoic forbearance. "Miss Lancaster. A pleasure."

Oh, his voice was a rumble. A deep, resonant rumble like distant thunder or rolling rocks. It traveled across her skin in pleasurable shivers.

She wished to see his eyes. She wished to know their color.

"... present James Kilbrenner, the Earl of Tannenbrook. Lord Tannenbrook, this is Miss Viola Darling, one of my dearest friends. Her grandfather is Lord Redlington."

At last, he turned to her. Green. They were deep, dark green, the irises nearly black in the low light. She waited for those eyes to flame and surge upon glimpsing her, as other men's were wont to do.

Instead, they journeyed slowly from her hairline to her chin before she received the same polite bow he'd given Charlotte. "Miss Darling," he said.

Her answering curtsy, lowered lashes, and murmured "Lord Tannenbrook" was intended to give him time—time to display the spark of interest she was accustomed to seeing. Perhaps he required a moment longer than other gentlemen. Surely that explained his odd restraint.

Charlotte filled the ensuing silence with inquiries about Tannenbrook's journey from Derbyshire to London, which he answered with brief, uninformative rumbles. "Damp," he replied. "And long. As one might expect."

He was not precisely curt, although if Charlotte had asked a similar question of Viola, her answer would have been far lengthier and more detailed. For example, she might tell about the innkeeper with an amusing lisp who persisted in offering the "fineth thoop in Thropthire." Or share her memory of dew shimmering like crystals upon budding branches as they embarked on the final morning of their journey to London.

But not Lord Tannenbrook. It appeared he favored fewer words and single syllables.

Perhaps he requires stimulation, she thought. Some people were naturally loquacious, whereas others needed a bit of conversational encouragement. *He must be one of the latter.*

"How true, Lord Tannenbrook," Viola interjected, catching his gaze. "My father and I traveled from Cheshire early for the season and encountered no fewer than five storms. Each one proved too much for either horses or driver, so we were granted the opportunity to partake of innkeepers' hospitality at nearly every village between Warrington and London. Although, I must tell you, 'hospitality' might be a bit of an exaggeration." She laughed lightly.

He did not.

She fluttered her lashes.

A subtle frown etched creases along his heavy brow.

Charlotte cleared her throat. "Travel certainly does test one's mettle, does it not?"

"Indeed," he responded, shifting his eyes back to Charlotte. "Many necessary things do, though they must be borne in spite of it."

Viola considered whether he was making an oblique reference to her. Given his obvious—and bewildering—disinterest, it was certainly possible, albeit rude. Before she could probe further, however, Charlotte's cousin, Andrew Farrington, approached from her right.

Sand-haired and red-cheeked, he bowed to her more deeply than necessary, his eyes dropping for one greedy glance at her bodice. "Miss Darling," he cooed, his tongue lingering long on the syllables. "You are a vision. Each time my eyes fall upon you, I stand in awe of your radiant beauty, thinking you could not possibly be real. And yet, here you stand to prove the fault in my logic."

Granting him a lighthearted chuckle, she replied, "How you flatter me, Mr. Farrington. I fear your words are far prettier than any lady could hope to be." She had employed similar responses to gentlemen of every rank and age whenever they'd uttered fawning blather over the past two seasons. She did not doubt their sincerity. She doubted their depth. Determined to shift his focus before the young man embarrassed himself further, she inquired, "Are you acquainted with Lord Tannenbrook?"

Mr. Farrington's eyes finally left her face and moved to the much larger man. "Indeed. Tannenbrook."

"Farrington." His rumble drew her again to his face. He was still frowning. At her.

Her heart gave a tiny flip, knocking against her breastbone. For a moment, she dared not breathe as those green eyes scoured her features, lingering on her mouth.

That was when Charlotte, in a moment of inspired brilliance, stepped in. "Tannenbrook, I hope you will excuse my cousin and me. He and I must speak with my aunt and uncle, for I see they have arrived."

Mr. Farrington's eyes flared. "Er, but—"

Charlotte grasped her cousin's arm and discreetly tugged him past Viola toward the fireplace. "Come, Andrew," she gritted. "Aunt Fanny is waving to us."

Then, they were gone, weaving back through the crowded drawing room. Leaving Viola blessedly alone with the fascinating lord who made her insides effervesce and her blood run uncomfortably hot.

She swallowed. "Miss Lancaster speaks highly of you, my lord."

"Call me Tannenbrook."

"She described your encounter with Mr. Maynard."

"Did she, now?"

The air felt thick around her, turning her words breathless. "I found her tale most ... captivating."

"Why?"

"You defended her honor in a way most gentlemen would not, a way that put Mr. Maynard and all others who would insult her firmly in their place. I find much to admire in such bold actions."

Enormous shoulders rolled in a shrug. "Nothing to admire. Maynard deserved what he received."

"Do you enjoy dancing, Lord Tannenbrook?"

"No, Miss Darling."

She inched closer, wondering how warm he would be if she pressed herself against him. Surely a body of his size would heat her through until her skin tingled. "Are you certain? Perhaps with the right partner, you would—"

"Where is your chaperone?"

She blinked. Twice.

He glared. Hard.

"Well, I ... I suspect she may be napping."

"That explains much."

"My aunt has an infirmity. These late evenings are trying for her. Often, she must find a quiet corner in which she may rest her eyes unnoticed, the poor dear."

"Leaving you free to proposition men you have only just met."

This time, she blinked at least four times while she came to the stunning realization that his disapproval was genuine. He was outraged. At *her*. "Proposition? Silly goose. I inquired as to whether you enjoy dancing. It is called conversation, Lord Tannenbrook. I trust they have such a phenomenon in Derbyshire."

He moved closer, robbing her of what little breath she had remaining. Now, he loomed like a great granite ledge, his head bowed. Finally, his eyes had ignited. Except that the spark of interest resembled displeasure far too much for Viola's liking. "I have no wish to be rude, Miss Darling."

"A bit late for that," she breathed, her eyes devouring every ridge and slope of his enthralling face.

"But you should know I've no interest in marriage."

"My, you have positively *galloped* ahead of me. Miles and miles. You are in another county altogether."

Eyes of deep, coniferous green gleamed knowingly. "Am I?"

Her lips pursed on a smile. "Perhaps I am merely the curious sort."

"I think you desire that which you perceive to be unattainable."

"Miles and miles," she murmured, largely because she had no better answer. He was not wrong.

"As you are Miss Lancaster's friend, I shall offer this advice: Flirtation for a woman of your beauty is a dangerous game, doubly so when one's chaperone prefers napping to minding her charge."

"You think me beautiful?"

He sighed. Straightened away from her. "I knew I should not attend this evening," he muttered, his gaze drifting up past her head to the other side of the room, his jaw flexing. "No good can come of it."

She disliked seeing his focus wander away. How could she persuade him of their obvious affinity if he did not look at her? "I beg to differ. In the unlikely event that Lady Reedham has managed to keep her third French cook, I expect you shall have an excellent meal. That is one good thing, is it not?"

Ah, yes. That did it. His eyes returned to her, both exasperated and amused. "Aye. A good meal is a good thing."

"There you have it. Of course, if her cook has departed, we may be subject to an evening of dreadful music. You must brace for that eventuality."

"Do you always chatter on this way?"

"Only when I wish to converse with someone who interests me." She tilted her head in mock inquiry. "I could teach you, if you wish."

He snorted. "No. Thank you."

She raised her brows. "Really, conversation, when done well, can be most ... stimulating."

Perhaps she had pushed too hard, for his green eyes narrowed and his massive arms crossed. "Miss Darling."

"Yes?"

"I suggest you find your chaperone and remain at her side, come what may."

"Are you concerned for my virtue, Lord Tannenbrook?"

He leaned forward to murmur close to her ear. "No, lass. For mine."

When he withdrew and strode away, his gargantuan shoulders creating their own path through the throng along one wall, she could only stand like a dizzy goose, breathless and swaying on her feet. He smelled heavenly, like the pines around the lake near her home in Cheshire. And he *was* warm. As warm as a great hearth. Having his breath so near her cheek had sent gooseflesh shimmying over her skin.

She'd never felt the like.

She wanted him. James Kilbrenner, the Earl of Tannenbrook. She wanted him as she'd never wanted another thing. Ever. This was more than the Inkling. This was destiny.

And he would be hers, she decided, still struggling for breath, her gloved hand brushing the side of her neck where she'd felt his words slide over her skin.

One way or another, he would be hers.

Chapter Three

*"Ah, yes. How swiftly 'daring' becomes 'foolhardy' when one
recklessly abandons all good judgment to gain favor
with the object of one's affection."*

—THE DOWAGER MARCHIONESS OF WALLINGHAM to her son,
Charles, upon learning of another disastrous outing involving a
malfunctioning carriage, unruly weather, and a certain widow.

❧

"A LITTLE ADVICE, JAMES," SAID JAMES KILBRENNER'S BEST
friend as an unruly gust of wind attempted to unseat them
from their mounts and topple them onto the gravel-and-tan of
Rotten Row. "Avoid swearing that you will never marry. It
only invites the fates to laugh and plot your comeuppance."

James grunted at Lucien Wyatt, who spoke from
experience. After Lucien's unlikely marriage to the sister of the
man who had shot Gregory in a duel, Lucien was well

acquainted with the perversions of fate. First, he had inherited his brother's title. Then, he had plotted revenge. Then, he had promptly fallen in love with the instrument of his vengeance, Victoria Lacey.

James had remarked often that it was a good thing Victoria was the forgiving sort. Lucien always agreed.

James now cast his friend a sidelong glance, noting the contentment on the too-handsome features, etched there permanently by Victoria's gentle hand. "Marriage has served you well, Luc, I surely cannot deny it."

Lucien raised a brow and navigated past an aged man who had stopped in the middle of the path to retrieve his windblown hat. "But?"

Shifting in his saddle, James sighed. "It is not for me. You know I have my reasons."

Lucien had been present the day James had returned to his mother's cottage after seeing his son's grave. Never again could he endure such pain. And if he avoided marriage, then he would not have to. In James's estimation, the logic could not be simpler.

"You realize your title and the care of Shankwood Hall may only pass to your heir, yes?"

James shot him a glance. "Why do you suppose I am in London for the season?"

"Not to find a wife, clearly."

"No. Because *she* demands that I participate. Wretched old woman."

Lucien's lips twitched. "Remind me again why you are permitting Lady Wallingham to lead you about like a prized ox through the marriage mart?"

This time, James's grunt was one of frustration. "Gates has reached a standstill with his inquiries. Lady Wallingham is the only known link to the grandmother of my heir presumptive. She refuses to contact the woman until I meet her demands."

Indeed, James had only learned that he had an heir

presumptive two years prior, when Hargrave had died. James still mourned his longtime solicitor, who first had been his guardian in all estate matters until he'd reached his majority, then had been his advisor and friend. He missed the man as he would a father.

Yet for years, Hargrave had misled him, insisting no other line of the Kilbrenner family remained to inherit the Tannenbrook title and take charge of Shankwood Hall. James could only guess that, much like Lady Wallingham, Hargrave had wished to force him to accept his duty to marry and procreate—a duty to which he'd been decidedly resistant.

But upon hiring his new solicitor, Mr. Gates, James had learned of a distant cousin from a branch of the family that had settled in America. According to Gates's research, James's great-uncle, Robert Kilbrenner, had married an Englishwoman named Ann-Marie Roxham before leaving Scotland to work as a printer in Philadelphia. Robert and Ann-Marie's grandson, Elijah Kilbrenner, would inherit both title and estate if James failed to marry and beget a legitimate heir.

Providing the man was alive. Reports were conflicting in that regard.

"I assume you have attempted to contact your heir's grandmother, yourself," said Lucien, brushing a wayward seedpod from his shoulder and tipping his hat at a pair of elderly women in a passing landau. The women fluttered and blushed as though they were thirty years younger.

"She refuses to answer anyone except Lady Wallingham. Apparently, they have shared a correspondence since they were girls. Lady Wallingham claims Ann-Marie Kilbrenner is her 'source inside the Colonies,' and she does not wish to press her and risk the connection." James paused while another gust blew a leaf past his nose. "Which is perfect rot, but I cannot find a better option. According to Gates, Ann-Marie's son remained a British loyalist throughout the American rebellion, returning to England after the war. Gates has determined that while the parents appear to have perished in a house fire, it is unclear what became of Elijah Kilbrenner. All traces of the boy disappear around that time."

"Mmm. Uncommon name, Kilbrenner," Lucien observed. "I assume he either changed it or—"

"Or he is dead." James tightened his jaw. "Yes, it has occurred to me. Hargrave may have known, but I've found only vague references to a living heir in his papers. Unless Gates discovers some new revelation, Lady Wallingham is my only conduit to the truth."

Lucien snorted. "You do not wish to be beholden to the dragon. Trust me on this."

"There is nothing for it."

"You could reconsider—"

"No."

"Come now, marriage can be delightful with the right—"

"No."

"—woman. Imagine having one at your disposal, managing your household, seeing to your comfort, legally bound to obey you."

James shook his head. "Victoria obeys you, eh?"

"Victoria is different."

"Mm-hmm."

"She is less a woman and more an angel. Divine creatures do not adhere to earthly rules."

Unbidden, a face appeared in James's mind. Not the gentle, even features of Victoria Wyatt, but a vision of pure ivory skin, black-lashed eyes as blue as twilight, a nose so tiny it was but a whisper, and lips as sweetly curved as flower petals. He had never imagined such beauty existed. Until two weeks ago, when it had sparkled up at him, glimmering with mischief and fascination, glowing like a gem warmed by moonlight.

And, of course, at every gathering he had attended since, the daft woman had pursued him with intractable persistence and a concerning lack of caution.

"Leave off," he grumbled now, perturbed that she had intruded on his thoughts again. She was a flirtatious fribble, a tiny sprite he could crush with one careless hand. Even if he had desired a wife—which he did *not*—she was the last woman he'd choose.

Lucien chuckled. "Very well, no more talk of marriage. For now. Incidentally, what has brought you so readily to the toilsome task of locating your heir? You are in excellent health if your bout at Gentleman Jackson's is any indication."

Silence fell between them for long minutes, the only sounds the clop of hooves upon gravel, the chatter of passersby, and the relentless rush of wind through newly sprung leaves.

Lucien clicked his tongue. "No answer. This is dire, indeed. Is there a murderous plot afoot? Someone has, at long last, tired of your surly ways and weighty brow. Or perhaps has grown resentful of your general intransigence." He sighed theatrically and shook his head. "It was bound to happen. I would guess Gibbons."

James glowered. "My valet?"

"He has the patience of a saint, unquestionably, but every man has limits. Merely stuffing those gargantuan feet of yours into boots each morning would send anyone into fits of madness. Say nothing of tying a cravat 'round that thick neck."

"Don't be ridiculous. Gibbons and I get on quite well."

"Your tailor, then?"

"Nobody is aiming to murder me, ye daft sod."

Lucien's glance was half sardonic amusement, half concern. "Then, what is it?"

He did not wish to say. It would only serve to reopen Lucien's old wounds. But Luc's dark gaze would not leave him, rocking in time with his horse. James squeezed his reins tighter before deliberately loosening his fists. "Gregory."

Lucien's eyes shadowed and flattened. He turned to glance ahead for a moment then gave a single nod.

Gregory had been Lucien's brother and James's friend. More than that, he'd been honorable through and through. James had stood at his side the day of the duel. He had watched the Duke of Blackmore put a ball through a good man's heart from forty paces.

He shifted in his saddle, pushing past the memory to continue explaining the nature of his urgency. "My father died of injuries caused by a fire. Hargrave died of a lung complaint." He blew out a breath and gestured to the path before them. "Bloody hell, I could have died right here last winter."

Lucien grimaced. "It would take more than a scurrilous knife attack by a pair of brigands to kill you. I'd wager their bells are still ringing."

"Perhaps. But my duty is to those who depend upon me. I cannot leave matters unsettled."

Shooting James a considering glance, Lucien opened his mouth to speak, but a commotion from behind them had them twisting in their seats. It was a phaeton, speeding recklessly toward their position. A dark-coated gentleman and a bonneted female sat on the high-perch driving bench, the man struggling to regain control and the woman keening her distress and gripping the man's arm.

Swiftly redirecting his horse nearer the wooden fence bordering the Row, James squinted to get a view of the driver's face. His eyes widened as recognition settled in.

"It's Wallingham." Lucien had fallen in behind James on his own mount. "What the devil?"

The driver was Charles Bainbridge, the Marquess of Wallingham—Lady Wallingham's son. James shared Luc's incredulity. Lord Wallingham was among the foremost horsemen of the aristocracy. His stable was legendary, his skills as a driver nonpareil. In his youth, the man had co-founded one of the most exclusive driving clubs in London. Further, his air of quiet dignity and competence virtually precluded any act of recklessness—of which losing control of one's high-perch phaeton on Rotten Row whilst accompanied by a frightened female constituted a perfect example.

"He lost hold of the reins," James called to Lucien as the carriage careened toward their position. The pair of white horses galloped as though they'd been bit, eyes rolling, reins dragging and whipping as they skipped along the horses' flanks and grappling legs.

Above the escalating clatter of wheels and hooves, warnings from Wallingham, cries of distress from his companion, and exclamations from other riders fleeing the carriage's course, James shouted to Luc, "We must slow them!"

Nudging his own horse forward, he pointed to indicate Luc should take the right side then accelerated to match the pace of the approaching carriage. Soon, the phaeton pulled between them, the white pair heaving and pounding as though the devil himself were waving a torch at their backsides. Eyeing the path ahead and the pace of the horses, calculating that he had perhaps thirty seconds to slow the vehicle before it careened into a sedate barouche, James inched his mount closer, patting the animal's neck to reassure him as they drew within feet of the frightened carriage horses. He levered carefully up in the stirrups, steadying himself with a hand on the pommel, then reached across to the mid-back of the carriage horse, taking pains not to frighten it further. Slowly, he reached out, brushing the rein terret with gloved fingers. Light leather reins flicked and slid through the metal loop. The horse shied, its pace faltering for one heart-stopping moment.

"Bluidy hell," he muttered before edging close once again, repositioning himself until, at last, his fingers slid between hard metal and writhing leather, taking the strings in his fist.

"James! You have it?" shouted Lucien.

"Aye! Slow them easy, beginning now!"

Simultaneously, he and Lucien tugged the reins. James focused on slowing both the phaeton and his own mount, balancing his weight in the saddle to maintain his seat. The pounding pace of all four horses eased gradually to a walk and, finally, a stop. The barouche sat a mere thirty yards away.

"Tannenbrook. Atherbourne," uttered a pale but otherwise remarkably calm Wallingham. "I am in your debt."

Lucien's half-grin was wry, his breathing still fast from the sudden sprint. "We accept payment in horseflesh, Wallingham."

"Done."

Laughing, Lucien shook his head. "A jest, my good man." He nodded toward James. "Tannenbrook here has a penchant for heroics."

Frowning at his best friend, James touched the brim of his hat and nodded to the pair. "It is reward enough to see you and your companion are safe."

Wallingham's companion, an attractive blonde whose bloodless lips currently matched her lavender pelisse, shrugged against the comforting arm wrapped around her slim shoulders. While Wallingham did not release her, he did introduce her. "Gentlemen, may I present Lady Willoughby." James watched Wallingham's gloved hand squeeze her upper arm gently, as though willing her to remain calm. "Our rescuers are Lord Tannenbrook and Lord Atherbourne."

As he moved to return the reins to Wallingham, James noted the man's hat had flown off in the melee, exposing a full head of dark hair dusted with white at the temples. The hair reminded him of Hargrave, but the nose reminded him of Gregory, long and prominent with a slight hook at the end.

"Th-thank you both," Lady Willoughby panted, her eyes darting frantically between them. "You saved our lives." Obviously, the woman was still frightened out of her wits.

"Be at ease, my lady," James replied, keeping his voice low and holding her unblinking gaze with his own. "All is well. The horses merely suffered a fright. They've calmed now."

Her lips pressed together, and her eyes sheened for a moment before she blinked and nodded. Notably, her resistance to Wallingham's soothing gave way, and her shoulders relaxed beneath the marquess's protective arm.

When James and Lucien finally bid the pair good day and continued on their course along Rotten Row, James expected Luc to rib him about his habit of rescuing all and sundry. But Lucien said only, "Locating your heir suddenly seems a rather sensible thing to do."

As they approached the barouche, now halted awkwardly in the center of the Row, James spotted one of its passengers standing in the rear-facing seat, leaning across one of her companions, her gloved hand holding the top of a dark-blue bonnet upon her black curls. The hat appeared to have white feathers on it. And beneath its brim were eyes as blue as twilight.

"Lord Tannenbrook," she called breathlessly. "That was ... astonishing."

Her companion pushed at her hip, which currently pressed the companion's nose. She did not move.

Beside him, Lucien leaned forward with interest. "Who is that? She is quite—"

"Nobody," James snapped.

Lucien raised a single brow. "Well, she is obviously somebody, or you would not be so out of sorts."

"Ignore her."

"Now, that would be ill-bred of me. And of you, should you offer insult to one so lovely and so clearly admiring of your gigantic self."

"Bloody hell." James released a breath of exasperation. "Very well. We will speak to her, but only for a moment."

James could not be certain his gritted message was received, because a grinning Lucien had already turned his mount toward the center of the Row where the carriage was parked. He felt the usual prickle of irritation beneath his skin, tightening and tingling at her presence. Swallowing it down, he followed Luc and approached the newfound bane of his existence.

"Miss Viola," he greeted her, unable to disguise the vein of annoyance in his voice. It must be annoyance. What else could this prickling heat be?

He quickly introduced Lucien to Penelope's mother, the chaperone with a tendency toward napping, before repeating the process with the two Darling cousins. Penelope, who continued attempting to elbow Viola's hip away from her nose, was older, so he introduced her as the first Miss Darling. Referring to the second Miss Darling as Miss Viola forced him to turn his tongue around her given name. For some reason, saying it always sent an odd, pleasurable sensation down his spine as though he were committing an act of intimacy. Annoying, indeed.

"I daresay, I have never witnessed such bravery," the vexing Viola said, her eyes positively glowing, her pale cheeks delicately flushed, her gloved hand moving from the top of her bonnet to lay flat over her bosom.

Drawing his eye. Making him imagine what lay beneath her bodice.

"Anybody would do the same," he replied.

"Oh, but anybody didn't. *You* did. It was extraordinary." As usual, her gaze was fixed upon him, devouring his shoulders and thighs and face. She scarcely acknowledged Lucien's presence. Given that Lucien nearly equaled her aesthetic perfection—albeit in a male form—this was unexpected.

He glanced to gauge his friend's reaction and wanted to groan. Luc's grin was wide and knowing as it ricocheted between James and the vexing Miss Darling.

"An admirable display, indeed, my lords," echoed Penelope, who had finally scooted to the other end of the bench, allowing Viola to plop down in the seat nearest him. Penelope's nasal tones and ungainly features compared poorly with her cousin's. And he had found the girl's wits approximately as sharp as a soup spoon. But she was a good-natured sort who displayed no resentment or jealousy of her beauteous cousin. Penelope leaned forward to address Lucien. "Lord Atherbourne, I had the pleasure of becoming acquainted with Lady Atherbourne before your marriage. Is she in town?"

While Lucien explained that Victoria had stayed behind at Thornbridge with their son, James dodged the twilight gaze of the daft chit who had set her sights relentlessly upon him. She wore blue today. Pale, sky blue approximately the same shade as the inner ring of her eyes. Those eyes were darker around the edges. More the color of her bonnet. They were quite the most beautiful eyes he'd ever seen. But, then, she was quite the most beautiful woman he'd ever seen. Not that it mattered. Despite her persistent and bewildering regard, he had no intention of taking what she offered. None whatsoever.

A quiet snore sounded from the seat opposite Viola and Penelope. The aunt had fallen asleep while her charges conversed with two men. But he did not glance in the aunt's direction. His gaze had snagged upon Viola's lips. Full and curvaceous, the petals were parted ever so slightly, as though they longed for his tongue.

He swallowed. "I fear Lord Atherbourne and I must be on our way."

"We must?"

Ignoring Lucien's dry tone, James tipped his hat to the Misses Darling—and the somnolent Mrs. Darling—and took his leave. Blindly, he directed his horse down Rotten Row, feeling a bit like he'd stared into the sun too long. Fifty feet on, he heard Lucien chuckle. "She is still watching you."

"Matters not. She is nobody to me."

Lucien's infernal grin only grew. "Hmm. An interesting nobody, indeed."

YOU ARE A PERFECT GOOSE, VIOLA CASTIGATED HERSELF AS SHE absently refreshed her tea and stirred in a bit of sugar. *You will see him again this evening. For now, focus upon your embroidery.* But she couldn't. She still hadn't stopped tingling, could scarcely draw breath, hours after witnessing Tannenbrook's daring rescue. The strength of the man, the sheer power in his arms and his thighs. *Oh, his thighs.*

"Mama has fallen asleep again," said Penelope, completing another perfect red stitch in her embroidered floral masterpiece.

Glancing down at her own efforts, Viola grimaced, her fingers tightening on the embroidery hoop. Loose brown loops formed what should have been a pinecone, but instead resembled a pile of muck. She sighed and set the hoop down on the sofa beside her without touching the needle. *Tea.* She was adept at pouring tea, she reminded herself as she picked up her cup and took a comforting sip. *Tea and conversation. And dancing. Do not forget dancing.*

A snuffle emanated from Aunt Marian's end of the sofa.

"Oh!" exclaimed Penelope. "Perhaps she is awake after all."

Viola smiled gently at her earnest cousin. "No, dearest. She is simply breathing. I believe our adventurous jaunt may have overtaxed her delicate constitution." Indeed, as their barouche had arrived at the family's shared town house on North Audley Street, Aunt Marian had managed to shake herself awake. She had even conversed pleasantly for an hour or so before drinking her medicinal tea and slumping into her current state.

Laughing with her distinctive honk, Penelope agreed. "She *is* delicate, I daresay. Do you suppose she will be rested enough to accompany us to the Pennywhistle supper this evening?"

Alarmed at the possibility that they might be prevented from attending a function where *he* would be present, Viola looked to Aunt Marian's sleep-pooched features. "She will accompany us if you and I must lift her into the carriage upon our backs."

"Oh, dear. You are not vexed with Mama, are you?"

"No." Viola calmly sipped her tea. "I am determined. Tannenbrook will be there."

"You fancy him."

Viola nearly rolled her eyes at her cousin's tendency toward stating the obvious, but she managed to suppress the urge. Instead, she settled for a dry tone. "Rather a lot, actually."

"He is not handsome."

Viola disagreed, but she would not argue the point.

"Nor as amusing as my Lord Mochrie."

Amusing. She supposed Penelope would consider the Scottish baron so, although Viola found him a frightful bore. Further, her cousin had not witnessed the subtle spark of humor in Tannenbrook's eye, piercing the green like a shaft of sunlight through a woodland canopy. He found humor in odd things, such as Lord Reedham's obsession with snuff and Lady Jersey's nickname—Silence, in reference to the woman's unceasing chatter. Viola often had to stifle her urge to smile and laugh along whenever she spotted the small quirk of his lips.

"And he is quite ... large."

Heat washed her skin. She sighed quietly and closed her eyes, picturing him as he'd been earlier that day, gripping his horse with his thighs, balancing his great, muscled bulk as he deftly grasped the reins of the speeding vehicle. "Yes," she breathed, her heart even now pounding as the horses' hooves had done. "He is."

Every time she saw him, her fascination grew. Charlotte had cautioned her against it, saying he did not bend easily to another's will, and that Viola was entirely too accustomed to having her own way. That last bit had stung, but Charlotte favored honesty over politeness.

"Well," continued Penelope, focusing on rethreading her embroidery needle with green floss. "One cannot deny he is gallant. As is Lord Atherbourne. Now, *handsome*—oh my, yes. *That* one is positively splendid. Pity he is already married. Still,

Lady Atherbourne is most pleasant, as I recall."

A number of the gentlemen who routinely sought Viola's favor were handsome, too. Viola did not want their sort of handsome. She did not want fawning compliments or elegant brows or thin, spindly shoulders. She wanted Tannenbrook.

"Penelope." Viola plastered a bright grin upon her face as her cousin glanced up. "I believe I shall wear the new gown."

"To the Pennywhistle affair? Oh, but it is only a supper. Surely a ball would be more fitting."

"It is time Lord Tannenbrook comprehends the seriousness of my regard."

Blinking slowly, Penelope lowered her embroidery hoop to her lap. "Er—Viola?"

"I must persuade him that we are ideally matched. And this evening, I shall begin that effort in earnest."

"Oh, I should think—"

Aunt Marian snorted and jerked as a knock sounded upon the paneled drawing room doors. "What—what is all that banging about?" she said, dabbing the usual bit of moisture from the corner of her mouth and pulling herself upright on the sofa.

Owens, their butler-cum-footman-cum-valet, entered the room accompanied by an unwelcome, unannounced guest. "Mrs. Cumberland to see you, miss."

The woman was ungainly. Tall and mannish with a florid complexion and dark eyebrows that did not match her white-streaked, wheat-colored hair. Additionally, she always wore gray and white. Gray pelisse, white gown. Gray spencer, white gown. White turban, gray gown. Very well, that one had been silver. But now, standing here in Viola's drawing room, the woman was once again garbed in gray—a dark-gray riding habit with frog closures across the bosom, to be precise. Viola would wager every shilling in her reticule that Mrs. Cumberland wore a white gown beneath the lightweight wool. And surely she could have selected a hat in a color other than white.

"Miss Viola, I do hope you will forgive my intrusion." The woman's brisk, authoritative demeanor chafed Viola's patience. Nevertheless, Viola rose to greet her, as was proper. Mrs. Cumberland would, after all, be her stepmother one day soon. "Mr. Darling asked that I wait with you." She glanced about the sparsely furnished drawing room, her expression carefully neutral to Viola's eye. "He wished to settle his horse after our ride in the park."

No sooner had the woman spoken his name than he appeared. Her papa. Merry eyes so like her own. A short, slight frame with a small paunch at the middle. Twin tufts of gray hair flanking his spotted-ivory head. To her, he was adorable, a welcome sight in his brown riding coat with the black lapels she had selected for him. He slipped past Owens, grinning and handing the servant his hat before clasping Viola's elbows and bestowing his usual affectionate kisses upon her cheeks. He smelled warm and comforting, like bay rum and her childhood in Cheshire.

"Papa! I did not expect you to return quite so soon." Viola smiled wider and moved her eyes to Mrs. Cumberland. "Or to return with the delightful Mrs. Cumberland. How lovely."

"Yes, yes," he replied, patting the sides of her shoulders and aiming a baffling ray of affection toward the other woman. "We were having a bracing ride, weren't we, until the wind absconded with my hat." He laughed and shook his head. "Ah, led me on a merry chase. How was your turn about Hyde Park?"

Everyone chatted for a bit as Viola poured tea. Mrs. Cumberland sat primly erect in a yellow painted chair. Papa listened to Penelope's tale about the Great Phaeton Rescue. And Aunt Marian nibbled a biscuit in an effort to stay awake.

"Lord Tannenbrook, you say?" Papa's eyes twinkled at Viola. "He is the one you fan—"

"Oh, dear," Viola interrupted, rising and moving to the doors. "It appears we've run out of biscuits. I shall ask Owens to bring more."

If she hoped to escape the conversation with Papa, she was soon disappointed. For, he followed her out into the corridor. "Viola, dearest. I had hoped you might spend a bit more time in conversation with Mrs. Cumberland. You know she and I have had an ... understanding of some duration."

Yes. She knew. She knew that he intended to marry Mrs. Cumberland, and that he had delayed their union for over a year because he wished to see Viola settled in a marriage of her own before he brought the other woman into their household. He'd assumed a match for Viola would be a simple matter, but as she had explained to him, none of the gentlemen she'd met last season had tempted her in the slightest. So she had asked for a second season, one he had hinted they could ill afford. In his usual indulgent fashion, he had granted her wish.

Now, the time had come to repay his generosity. She could see in his eyes, in the avidness of his inquiry, that Papa—an infinitely patient and kind man—was growing anxious. He wanted her safely married so that she would leave his household and he could marry Mrs. Cumberland and they could live together without her in Cheshire.

A queer, sickly sensation twisted her stomach. Perhaps it was the biscuits.

Straightening her spine, she gave him her prettiest smile and grasped his hand, squeezing her reassurance. "Not to worry, Papa. I understand your dilemma perfectly. And I have found a most promising prospect."

"Lord Tannenbrook does appear to be a gentleman of great character."

The knot in her stomach began to loosen. "He is." She felt her lips curving more naturally, just speaking of him. "The finest of men. Brave. Loyal. Selfless."

"Well, now, I would never doubt your Inkling, my dear, but have you considered this Mr. Farrington chap? I understand he is as keen for you as a calf for clover. A future baronet—not an earl, mind you, but not bad. Then, there is Lord Reedham's son. The teeth are a bit unfortunate, but deep pockets compensate for any number of ills, I daresay."

Again, she smiled as though he'd said something silly. In fact, this was not the first time he'd advised looking elsewhere in her husband hunt. For that matter, he was not the first person to suggest cultivating alternatives—Charlotte had done so only days ago. But, as Viola had explained, her hunt was not for a husband in general. If it had been, she could have landed a duke's son on the first outing of her first season. No, her hunt was for a *particular* husband. Tannenbrook. Thus far, her Tannenbrook Hunt, as she'd dubbed it, had met with only minor success—an introduction, a handful of "chance" encounters, such as today's serendipitous meeting. But she had only just begun her pursuit.

"Mark my words, Papa. I shall be Lady Tannenbrook before the leaves begin to fall."

Papa smiled, his eyes soft and fond. "If that is what you want, then I've little doubt. He'd have to be mad to resist you, my beautiful girl."

Chapter Four

"Size is not important. Cleverness. Character. These are the
qualities one must seek in a ... oh, very well. It matters.
Are you happy, now?"

—THE DOWAGER MARCHIONESS OF WALLINGHAM to Lady Berne
after enduring said lady's unseemly laughter during a discussion of
potential matches and desirable attributes.

HE WAS IGNORING HER. SITTING RIGHT THERE, FOUR CHAIRS
away, across the Pennywhistle dining table, he had not looked
at her once. Not once.

"Best plan a trip to Angelo's, Bennett," Lord Reedham's
son, who sat to her left, sneered at the gentleman on her right.
"Your rapier could use some sharpening."

"Rapier? Perhaps *your* sword is deserving of that
description. Mine is more nearly a broadsword, I daresay."

Viola set her spoon precisely next to her small lump of strawberry trifle and gathered her patience.

They had been at it for the entire meal—two hours of incessant sparring and insufferable boasting with her playing the bone between two dogs. She was tempted to dump the silver tureen of béchamel sauce over both their heads.

I did not wear my new gown for this, she thought. No, she had worn layers of delicately embroidered indigo silk for *him*. Her eyes wandered again across the table to Tannenbrook's shadowed crags and flexing jaw. Tonight, he wore gray. Dark gray and white. Across those broad shoulders, somehow, the colors were not objectionable in the slightest. But he refused to look at her, casually taking another bite of fish and nodding at something Mrs. Pennywhistle said. Of course, she'd noticed how he had fled from her in the hour before dinner, escaping the drawing room to who-knew-where until she'd been forced to hide behind Charlotte's tall form to keep him from leaving Pennywhistle House altogether. Thankfully, her quarry had calmed and stayed for the fish and trifle and poorly salted white soup.

"… stalked a stag with a crown at least seven feet in breadth."

"In Yorkshire. A broad tale, indeed."

"The trophy is displayed in my father's library there. Perhaps you will find his descriptions persuasive, as I am certain your hired post-chaise would make Yorkshire a *costly* journey."

The none-too-subtle jab at Mr. Bennett's financial difficulties made Viola long for a return of the sword comparison. "Gentlemen, have you contemplated a bout at Mr. Jackson's boxing saloon? I understand the sport is most refreshing to the spirits."

Reedham's greedy eyes settled upon her lips. "Miss Darling, you say the most amusing things. Females are not permitted at Gentleman Jackson's, of course."

Bennett took a drink of his wine. "Would that they were. I should like for Miss Darling to witness my victory."

The two men continued to ignore her by attempting to astound her with ever more florid descriptions of their superior pugilism skills.

She sighed and sipped her own wine, contemplating how best to proceed without Charlotte, since her best friend had disappeared from the Pennywhistle drawing room a half-hour before dinner. According to Mr. Farrington, Charlotte had been summoned by her father, who was visiting from America. While Viola hoped the meeting proved amiable for Charlotte's sake, she now must substantially revise her plans for the next phase of her Tannenbrook Hunt. Her scheme for this evening required sound timing, a facility with persuasion, and a stomach for mild deception. Charlotte lacked only the latter.

Viola's second choice of partner, on the other hand, lacked all three. She grimaced as said alternative laughed—nay, brayed— at something Lord Mochrie said, the honking sound carrying the length of the gold-toned room. Grateful not to be seated near enough to hear what passed for Mochrie's humor, Viola nevertheless leaned forward to glimpse Penelope's profile. Her cousin was flushed, the tip of her long nose pinkened by wine.

Blast. This plan could prove a disaster.

She examined the men to either side of her. They now sparred behind her head. Next, she looked to Tannenbrook. A warm ache invaded her midsection as she lingered over his shoulders, which must be at least a yard in breadth. *Nothing for it. I must speak with him alone, and I cannot very well visit him at his residence.* "Penelope it is," she muttered beneath her breath.

"Beg your pardon, Miss Darling?" inquired Mr. Bennett.

"I heard your dulcet voice, Miss Darling, but I fear the words did not register in my ears," echoed the Reedham heir.

She gave them each a smile as false as their flattery. "How refreshing it is to taste strawberries this early in the season."

Thereafter, the two men vied to establish which of them possessed a superior understanding of glass houses and fruit cultivation.

For her part, Viola sipped her wine and plotted, gazing upon her future husband with growing relish.

⸻

"TAKE THE THOROUGHBRED FOAL, TANNENBROOK. I INSIST." Lord Wallingham took a swig of his port. "It is the least I can do."

James frowned. "Is Lady Willoughby—"

"Furious with me." The flat line of the older man's mouth curved wryly. "Not for the first time. But she is safe and well, apart from the fright, and I have you to thank."

"No need to thank me. I am gratified all ended well."

"I shall have the foal delivered to your stable."

Raising a brow at the man's presumption, James began to suspect Charles Bainbridge resembled his mother in more than intellect, although his quiet mien certainly gave no indication of it. "If you are determined to offer a reward, I would ask instead a favor."

Wallingham frowned. "Whatever you require."

"Intervene on my behalf with Lady Wallingham."

"Except that."

Now, both of James's brows rose.

"Waste of time. My mother will not heed a word I say. Take the foal, Tannenbrook. Trust me on this." The other man's matter-of-fact delivery spoke far more eloquently than his words.

Sighing, James finished his own port and placed the glass on a nearby tray. "I feared as much. Apologies, Wallingham, but having negotiated with her for months now, I am perplexed as to how a man might change her course."

Wallingham set his glass next to James's and gave a nod of deep resignation. "As are we all. Whatever her course, she believes it is right and just and best. Attempting to persuade her otherwise will only end in abject frustration."

"How do you manage?" James did not intend insult—he was genuinely impressed.

Wallingham shrugged. "Avoidance, primarily."

Just then, Mr. Pennywhistle announced it was time to rejoin the ladies. Wallingham followed James out of the library toward the drawing room, continuing their conversation as they traversed the corridor. "What sort of bind does she have you in?" Wallingham asked.

"She has a contact in America who may be able to help me locate my current heir. The contact will correspond only with her."

"What has she demanded of you?"

James felt the scowl descend upon his face. He nodded to indicate their surroundings—the Pennywhistle drawing room, white-walled and glittering with candlelight. "That I be here, among other things. She wishes me to mingle among the husband-hunting set for the entirety of the season."

"Ah, yes. Has you dancing upon her strings, I expect. My condolences. I fear you may be reaping what I have sown. My mother has made it her life's purpose to force me to remarry and do my procreative duty, as is proper for all titled gentlemen. My resistance has no doubt placed you keenly in her sights."

"That makes no sense."

"Only because you do not think like her. If she can force you to bend to convention—and to her will—then it is a victory for her argument." Wallingham chuckled, the sound surprisingly affectionate. "She has turned meddling into a perfectible craft. Impressive, really, even when one is the target of such ... determination."

The comment made James think of another determined female. One with moonlight skin and midnight hair who simply refused to alter her course. He had seen her earlier, flitting about the drawing room, laughing and charming her flock of dandified admirers. She had not yet approached him, but he suspected he'd only been granted a brief reprieve.

"Here now, Tannenbrook, it is not as bad as all that," Wallingham smiled his sympathy. "Rest assured, my mother won't kill you. You'll simply be miserable for a time. Then, she will fulfill her side of the agreement and deliver what you asked. Endurance. Patience. These will keep you sane."

"Really."

"Well, not sane, precisely." Wallingham's wry wit reminded James of the dowager. It shouldn't have been a surprise, given that she had birthed the man. Eyes with the same sharp intelligence gave him an assessing glance. "I shall inform her that you saved her only son's life. It won't win you surcease from the marriage mart, but she may look more kindly upon you, which will make your misery moderately less pleasurable to her."

James huffed out a laugh. "You are too generous."

During their conversation, James had managed for several brief intervals to forget about the tiny, too-lovely thorn in his side. But the respite lasted only until he spotted the thorn's cousin approaching. The pearls laced through Penelope's curls swung oddly against her cheek, adding a comical element to the young woman's equine features. He nodded stiffly. "Miss Darling."

"Lord Tannenbrook. And Lord Wallingham! My, I do hope you have recovered after—"

"I am well, Miss Darling. Thank you. Won't you excuse me? I see a gentleman I must speak to about a horse."

"Oh, I ... yes. A pleasure." She turned to James and blinked. She was taller than Viola, more square and brown. Red stained her cheeks and the tip of her nose. Too much wine, perhaps? "Lord Tannenbrook, thank heavens I found you."

"If you had not, I might have recommended spectacles."

Slowly, the girl blinked. The perceptive spark he was

accustomed to seeing in the other Miss Darling's gaze was entirely lacking. "Spectacles?" she murmured searchingly.

Probably best to forge on, he decided. "Why are you glad to have found me?"

"You are the tallest man here. And I have a peculiar circumstance for which I must beg your kind assistance." She spoke slowly, pausing and lingering over each word as though she'd memorized the sentences. At the end, she nodded, sending those pearl loops swinging against her cheek.

"What is the circumstance?" He asked only because he wished to know how Penelope might explain a request that had obviously originated from Viola.

"A glove."

He waited.

"Upon a tree limb. A *high* tree limb. In the garden. Outside."

He glanced pointedly at her two gloved hands.

She followed his gaze, waggling her fingers experimentally. Her flush deepened. "Not *my* glove. A—a friend went out to the terrace for a bit of air after dinner. She was donning her gloves when the wind took one of them and landed it upon the limb. The tree overhangs the balustrade ..." She swallowed upon seeing his expression. "Yes, you probably know. Naturally, we attempted to retrieve the glove, but to no avail."

"Miss Darling."

"Yes?"

"What precisely does Miss Viola wish me to do?"

Penelope's mouth formed an O.

It was not her fault. Viola was a gale-force wind when she'd set her mind to something. Now, he decided, it was time to inform her in no uncertain terms that her pursuit had grown tiresome and, further, that she was wasting her time because, most emphatically, he would never marry her.

"She—she wants you to speak with her alone. She is w-waiting beneath the tree. Downstairs. Outside. In the garden."

"Very well," he gritted. "Come. You shall accompany me."

"Oh, but I was told my part would be finished—"

He gently placed her hand upon his arm and waved her forward. "Nonsense. We shall need you there to ensure there are no improprieties."

"My mother—"

He nodded to a chair in the corner. "Is sleeping."

"Oh."

In the end, Penelope conceded. Considering she was unmarried, he ran a risk in choosing her as their chaperone. But despite the girl's dull wit, she would not taint her family's reputation by allowing Viola to generate a scandal, for Lord Mochrie would cry off their match before the moon had set on this night.

They entered the garden from the Pennywhistle parlor on the ground floor. The wind was still gusting as it had earlier, rustling the new leaves of a small ash tree. The trunk rose from a garden bed surrounded by a low stone wall.

He looked at the sky, cursing the dark clouds that always seemed to shroud London. What he wouldn't give to return to Derbyshire, to look up and see stars rather than smoke. Squinting up through the branches, he saw that Viola had, indeed, managed to toss her glove onto a limb. She'd chosen carefully, making it too far from the edge of the upper terrace to reach and too high to retrieve from the ground.

Clever, bloody-minded, conniving, vexing chit.

Penelope's hand fell away from his arm.

He leaned into her with his most intimidating posture. "Stay."

She might have squeaked. He did not care. He needed to locate Viola, and he bloody well could not see anything beyond the first eight feet or so. Slowly, he approached the base of the tree, watching for any signs of a raven-haired sprite. He climbed onto the stone wall, braced one palm against the rough bark, stretched his other arm high, and plucked the scrap of white silk from its verdant prison. Rubbing the thing absently between his finger and thumb, he shook his head.

She really was the most extraordinary creature.

Shoving away from the tree, he dropped down onto the flagstones and took a single step back before facing Penelope. The girl was rubbing her arms and tightening her shawl about her shoulders.

"Where is she?" he called.

Eyes wide, Penelope slowly raised her hand to point directly behind him.

"Looking for me, Lord Tannenbrook?"

He closed his eyes briefly before turning to face her.

She stood on the low wall, putting her eyes nearly level with his.

The impact knocked the breath from him, even in the low light.

"I see you retrieved my glove. Thank you ever so kindly." Her grin lit him like a torch. "My valiant champion."

Without ceremony, he dropped the scrap of silk into her outstretched palm. "What is this about, Miss Darling? I weary of your games."

"I wished to speak with you. Alone." Graceful as a dancer, she stretched out an arm and donned her glove, the silk soughing against skin, tiny fingers fluttering to fit.

The sight of that little wriggle—like a butterfly settling upon a stamen—made his flesh heat and harden. Made him want to insist she remove the glove again. Slowly.

He swallowed. It did not help.

"The fact that you regard my efforts to improve our acquaintance as 'games' demonstrates the need for this conversation." She secured the buttons at her wrist with casual flicks, as though she did not suspect how deeply aroused he already was. "I know you think me a flirtatious ninny."

He frowned. "I did not say that."

She half-grinned, but her eyes failed to tilt at the corners.

Further, her nose did not give that winsome wrinkle. "But you think it," she countered softly.

Remaining silent seemed the only reasonable course, considering he did not know how to respond.

"You must understand the earnestness of my regard, my lord."

"Tannenbrook," he corrected.

"Lord Tannenbrook. Your given name is James, is it not?"

"Aye."

She inched forward until her lips were a mere breath away from his.

Wait. It had not been she who moved. He glanced down at his own muckle feet. Glowered deeper. Swallowed again. Bloody hell.

"I wish to marry you, James."

The sweet whisper brought his head up faster than a cricket bat.

"I have never felt this way. And I wish to be your wife." Small, white teeth tugged at a plump lower lip, half of the most perfect pair he had ever seen. "This is not a game to me."

Someone was grunting. Probably him.

He spanned her waist with his hands.

She squeaked and clutched his chest—or, rather, his cravat.

He lifted her from the wall. Turned. And lowered her feet to the flagstones. It was like lifting a bird, light and delicate and soft.

Except that her fingers were still tangled in the folds of his cravat, and she yanked his face closer to hers upon her descent.

"Miss Darling ..."

"Viola," she corrected. Her scent drifted to his nose—wine and strawberries and the peonies blooming in the churchyard at Shankwood. Sweet on the surface, dark and lush beneath.

Tightening his jaw, he wondered if Mrs. Pennywhistle kept buckets of frigid water nearby. A man could hope, he supposed. "Miss Darling, I mean you no slight."

"Of course not. You are the finest of men."

"Marriage is out of the question."

"Nonsense. After we've become better acquainted, you will feel it, too."

"Feel what?"

"Our affinity."

He gently pried her fingers loose from his cravat and attempted to restore his valet's work. "I have determined never to marry. Anybody. Your efforts, as you describe them, are wholly in vain."

She tilted her head, gazing up at him, her gloved hands shooing his away before briskly straightening the mangled folds. "Why?"

"Because you cannot possibly succeed in your aim and may do a good deal of damage to your reputation before you realize I speak true."

"No," she said, patting the center of his chest. "Why have you determined never to marry?"

His ribs tightened around his lungs. His heart twisted and ached. "I made the decision long ago. Reasons are not important. You must stop this pursuit."

"So, it is not that you despise me or that you think me a foolish fribble."

"No."

"And it is not because you find me hideous to look upon."

His eyes roamed her face—the whisper of a nose, the twilight eyes tilted just so. And her lips. Mustn't forget those. "No."

Those lips split upon a brilliant, breathtaking smile. Twilight glimmered with a thousand stars. A tiny nose wrinkled winsomely. "Then, we are in agreement."

He would respond as soon as he could breathe. It took a moment. Perhaps two. "How so?"

"You will not marry *anybody*. You will marry me. And we shall be gloriously happy."

He blinked. "Madness. Pure madness."

"Is it?" Her sweet tulip of a chin tilted the way it often did when she was challenging him. She rose up on her toes and slid her hands down the sides of his arms. Trailed her fingers past his elbows and settled her arms in the cradle of his. "Then why are you holding me so, James?"

His breath shuddered. He shook his head.

And squeezed her waist with his hands.

His hands.

Her waist.

He'd been stroking the lush curve of her waist, spanning it and circling with his fingers, rubbing and learning her shape beneath layered indigo silk for the better part of five minutes. As though his hands knew something he didn't. Wanted her too much to obey his head.

Again, he swallowed, feeling burned by her. Disoriented. He dropped his hands. Hers fell away, too.

"You must stop this, Viola," he rasped desperately, staggering backward, his boots ringing hollow on the flagstones. "I will never marry you. Accept it, for it is the truth. Turn your affections to another." The words tasted sour in his mouth. Foul.

Eyes now accustomed to the dark, he retreated toward the mews gate at the rear of the garden. "Return to the drawing room," he called as he at last found the strength to turn away from her. "Consent to wed any of the dozens of other gentlemen who pen sonnets in your name. And do not ever attempt such a foolish trap again. We men are a disgraceful lot."

Just before the iron gate closed with a loud clang behind him, he heard her voice carry on a suddenly whistling wind. The words weren't clear, but he would swear she vowed, "Precisely why I shall have you and you alone, James Kilbrenner. No other man will ever do."

Chapter Five

"When one is cleverer than everyone else, one is obliged to serve one's fellow man. It is hardly my fault if others perceive my assistance as 'interfering' or 'gossip.' I cannot control everything, after all."

—The Dowager Marchioness of Wallingham to her son, Charles, in response to his complaint about pernicious rumors of an impending proposal to a certain widow.

***

Being invited to Lady Wallingham's first luncheon of the season was either a high honor or a signal of disapproval. Viola had not yet determined which applied to her, even after four biscuits and two cups of tea.

"She does favor that one," murmured Charlotte, nodding toward the painting above the fireplace, a portrait of a tiny woman with a flat mouth, triangular nose, and arched, disapproving brows. It was one of at least ten portraits of Lady Wallingham's female ancestors lining the canary walls of the dowager's fussy, feminine parlor.

Viola nodded. "The wig disguises her hair color, but even if it did not, we would only be guessing that it is her. I doubt her ladyship was *born* with white hair."

Chuckling lightly, Charlotte sighed and sipped her tea.

Viola examined the signs of strain around her friend's mouth, the paleness of her skin, which made the freckles more prominent. "Have you explained to your father why you do not wish to marry him?"

Charlotte's eyes closed briefly, her lips tightening. "Yes. He is adamant that I marry Rutherford. I have tried everything."

The new Marquess of Rutherford—previously known as Lord Chatham—was, as Charlotte often described him, a walking scandal. Tall and lean, sardonic and sensual, to Viola's eye, he'd appeared both dissipated and dangerous, like a wolf that had been starved then set loose upon the female population. He was widely regarded as a disgrace by the beau monde, barred from all but the most salacious ton gatherings. Consequently, she'd glimpsed him only twice, once coming out of a shop on Bond Street and again four days ago, walking away from the Grosvenor Square house he'd been forced to sell to pay his father's debts.

This was the man Charlotte's father wished her to marry in less than a week.

Viola set her tea on a low, marble-topped table and laid a hand gently on Charlotte's arm. "Come stay with me, dearest, I beg you. In my bedchamber, there is a chaise. I shall sleep there, and you may take the bed. I will bring you trays for your meals and make certain your father never finds you. Penelope will help, too. She was surprisingly effective at the Pennywhistle dinner."

Charlotte patted her hand, giving it a squeeze. "Thank you, Vi. But I have known this day might come eventually. My father's fondest wish is for me to marry a title, and he means to have his way. One solace is that he has set a time limit—one year. Afterward, I will be free to leave for America."

Viola's eyes widened. "A year of marriage. With Benedict Chatham?"

Swallowing visibly, Charlotte gave her a wobbly grin. "Do not worry about me. All will be well, I am certain."

Her heart squeezed painfully. Searching her mind for a bit of reassurance, Viola smiled brightly. "Well, it is not *entirely* wretched. He is astonishingly attractive for one so dissipated. Even with the walking stick. And him being so lean and pale."

Charlotte sipped her tea and elected not to reply.

Now that Viola had found her Tannenbrook, the thought of marrying a man who did not inspire nightly visions of broad shoulders, heavily muscled thighs, and gargantuan hands made her stomach churn. She'd dreamed of him only last night, his eyes burning into hers, his lips pressed to hers, his hand cradling hers as they moved into a graceful dance.

She sighed. *Silly. Tannenbrook does not dance.* Still, the prospect of being forced to marry someone—*anyone*—other than the man who made her shiver and heat inside her skin was untenable. *Poor Charlotte. Poor, poor Charlotte.*

Lady Wallingham's sonorous trumpet of a voice carried across the room. "Miss Viola Darling!"

Viola's spine snapped straighter, and her gaze flew to the birdlike dowager, seated in a gold-trimmed, claret-striped chair to the right of the fireplace. "Yes, my lady?"

"What is this I hear about your flirtation with Lord Tannenbrook?"

Six sets of eyes turned upon her, including those of Lady Gattingford, a tall, stoop-shouldered matron with a tendency to exaggerate; Lady Reedham, a shorter woman with large teeth and an air of superiority; Aunt Marian, who was surprisingly alert after four cups of tea; Penelope, who wore an unfortunate shade of brown Viola had vehemently opposed; Charlotte; and, of course, Lady Wallingham.

"Flirtation, my lady?"

"Now, now. Do not be coy. Explain your fascination. Is it the jaw? Many young ladies favor a square jaw, and his is as solid as castle stone."

Viola looked about the room, hoping one of the other ladies might rescue her. Alas, it was not to be. Clearing her throat delicately, she replied, "Lord Tannenbrook is a man of honor and gallantry."

"Rubbish. It is the jaw." The woman's sharp green eyes narrowed upon her. "I assume you intend this Tannenbrook Hunt of yours to conclude in marriage rather than scandal."

Viola's eyes flared wide, then immediately shifted to narrow upon her cousin, who reddened and lowered her gaze. The silly goose could not keep a secret, after all. Raising her chin, Viola answered, "Should Lord Tannenbrook offer marriage, I shall happily accept. He is the finest of men."

Lady Wallingham's thin lips curled and one white brow arched. "So I understand. A rather strapping one, at that. Puts one in mind more of a laboring sort than an earl, I daresay. A blacksmith. Or a stonemason. Perhaps it's the shoulders."

Viola frowned. "His blood is as noble as yours, my lady. And his character unmatched—"

"Yes, yes. We all understand your fascination with the brute."

"That 'brute' saved your son's life at great risk to his own."

The triangular nose pinched. "If my son had not foolishly allowed himself to become distracted, he would not have lost the reins, and such derring-do would have been unnecessary."

"Perhaps," Viola continued, heedless of the dowager's agitation. "Nevertheless, Lord Tannenbrook did come to Lord Wallingham's aid, and quite heroically, I might add. He deserves our admiration."

"Hmmph. Your beauty may purchase favor among the male portion of society, my dear. But never presume such a random blessing of birth compensates for your overweening cheek." Now the woman's lips were pinched, as well. "It does not."

Viola elected to drink her tea and stop speaking. Fortunately, Lady Wallingham appeared satisfied to move on to other targets. Fortunately for *Viola*, that was.

"Miss Lancaster! I am given to understand your father has negotiated an ill-conceived union between you and that devil, Chatham."

Charlotte remained remarkably calm, taking a sip of tea before answering, "Indeed, my lady."

"This will not end well for you." The dowager sniffed. "Was the incestuous Lord Byron unavailable? He could use the funds. Poetry does not pay well."

Viola nearly spewed tea out of her nose at the outrageous statement.

Charlotte scarcely blinked. "Byron fled to the Continent after souring his marriage to the last heiress who accepted him. At last report, he is penning poetry in Rome. And yes, quite unavailable." She took another calm sip.

"Still a better choice than that scapegrace who calls himself Rutherford."

Smiling, Charlotte set her cup in its saucer. "Perhaps. But Byron is a mere baron. My father will countenance nothing short of an earl."

Viola marveled at Charlotte's bluntness. But then, she was often both astonished and admiring of the other woman's forthright nature.

Lady Wallingham appeared to appreciate the honest response. "I might applaud his high standards if I did not know whom he was gifting with your dowry." She turned her attention to Penelope. "Speaking of which, what sort of recompense are you bringing to this match with Lord Mochrie, my dear?"

While the dowager interrogated a red-faced Penelope, Viola leaned toward Charlotte to murmur, "I half expected her to offer her son's hand in marriage, given her interest in your dowry."

Charlotte grinned. "Lady Wallingham as a mother-in-law. Can you imagine?"

Viola shook her head and giggled.

Across the room, Lady Wallingham loudly declared, "Lady Gattingford has suggested a house party at Grimsgate Castle at the end of the season. Miss Darling!"

Penelope sat straighter. "Yes?"

"Not you. Miss Viola Darling! You shall attend."

Viola scoured her memory for the location of Lady Wallingham's country residence. Somewhere north, perhaps. Dash it all, she could not be certain. She mumbled the question at Charlotte, "Where is Grimsgate?"

"Northumberland."

Frantically, she calculated how much such a journey might cost her father. Just the rent on the house they shared with Penelope and Aunt Marian had strained his coffers. Once again, Viola felt a twinge of guilt over her failure to choose a husband in her first season. *Tannenbrook was not present last spring, or you would even now be wed,* she reminded herself.

Struggling for a polite way to decline, Viola offered a version of the truth. "My lady, you honor me with your kind invitation."

"Yes. I do."

"However, I hesitate to accept ..."

Like clouds gathering to threaten the sun, Lady Wallingham's eyes flashed ominously, her white brows descending.

Viola swallowed and hastily continued, "Only because, should I be so fortunate as to receive an offer of marriage before the season ends, I anticipate I shall be preoccupied—"

"How many offers did you decline in your first season, girl?"

She blinked. "Fourteen, my lady."

"And this season? Bearing in mind it has commenced only this week with my arrival in London, leaving fully two months for more foolish fops to pay your father a visit."

"Seven."

"So, with neither a dowry nor even a courtesy title, you have managed to fritter away twenty-one offers of marriage in slightly more than one season."

Beside her, Charlotte whispered, "Twenty-one? Good heavens, Vi."

Viola straightened her spine and refused to be chastened. "I shall accept only one, my lady. From the *right* gentleman."

"Tannenbrook. Yes, the jaw is quite monumental." The dowager strummed her fingers on the edge of her saucer. "Very well. Tannenbrook shall attend my house party. There, now. You have no reason to decline."

Unless I can persuade him to propose sooner.

Before she had finished the thought, Lady Wallingham flicked a wave in her direction. "He is intractable, girl. You will not land him before June."

"We shall see." Within seconds, she regretted the words.

The dowager smiled. Unpleasantly. "We shall, indeed, my dear."

∽∞∽

JAMES HAD NEVER ENCOUNTERED A MORE STUBBORN, WILLFUL, intractable, *frustrating* woman in all his living days.

"You are acquainted with Miss Viola Darling, are you not?" he asked Charles Bainbridge, who had greeted him upon his arrival at Wallingham's Park Lane house. The place was twice the width of a normal town house and five times as opulent. He glanced around the library, admiring the intricacy of the stonework around the fireplace. Twin corbels resembled fantastical oaks in which each leaf appeared almost to flutter upon the fire's updraft.

"Miss Darling." Charles's dark brows lowered thoughtfully, and the hand currently holding a quill pen paused above the paper on his desk. "Dark hair. A rare beauty, as I recall. Why do you ask?"

Ignoring the odd pulse of anger that sprang from Charles's perfectly reasonable description, James gripped the arms of his chair and forced himself to relax. "What is her connection with your mother?"

A single brow rose. "None that I am aware of."

"Lady Wallingham has decided I am to attend her house party at the end of the season. I received a note to that effect this morning. She mentioned Miss Darling will be in attendance, as well."

"This is significant because ...?"

He did not want to say it, to admit how fervently she pursued him. He wanted her to stop appearing at his side during a waltz as though she expected him to beg for a dance. He wanted her to cease gazing up at him with those starlit eyes. He wanted her ... bloody hell, he wanted her to give him some peace.

James tightened his jaw before answering, "Miss Darling has expressed her desire to marry."

"Don't all ladies participating in the season desire matrimony? That is why they refer to it as the marriage mart, if I am not mistaken."

He gave the other man a grim stare. "Me. She wishes to marry me."

Wallingham's calm nod was not the reaction he was expecting. "I see."

But he didn't. He could not possibly understand the relentless intensity, the pressure of resisting her over and over and over. Turning away from those adoring eyes and plump, petal-shaped lips and sweet, peony-scented curves. It was driving him mad.

"I cannot attend a house party with her present." The words emerged from him like a boulder dragged from the sea—heavy, low, and reluctant. An admission of weakness.

"I see," Wallingham repeated, smoothly finishing his signature and sanding the ink. He blew the grains away. "If it is any consolation, Grimsgate is a vast property. I once hid from my governess by moving from room to room in the castle. She waited three days before admitting to my mother that she had 'lost' me. Naturally, Mother found me within hours, and I never saw the governess again, but you see my point. Vast. Hundreds of rooms, along with a great deal of land. Additionally, Mother's parties rarely last longer than a fortnight, as that is the limit of her patience." A smile curved the man's flat mouth. "Avoidance, Tannenbrook. The key to sanity."

James accepted the paper from Wallingham. The signed note transferred ownership of a prized foal from one of the finest stables in England. To him, James Kilbrenner. An English earl who should have been a Scottish stonemason.

Charles came around the desk and clapped James's shoulder. "Come. Perhaps if you speak with my mother, you two may come to a better accord."

James stood and followed the man out of the library.

Twenty minutes later, he yanked his hat from the starchy butler's hand and stuffed it onto his head before yanking open the front door. If anything, upon meeting with James, Lady Wallingham had grown more determined to sink her everlasting tentacles deeper into his life. "If you resist further, Lord Tannenbrook," she had decreed from a red-and-gold chair in her bright-yellow lair, "I shall insist upon seeing you partner Miss Darling for a waltz at Lady Gattingford's ball. Do not test me, boy."

He had stifled his protest. Then he had taken his leave of her. Now, he descended the steps to Park Lane, waiting for his horse to be brought around by one of her many servants.

"Trouble, Lord Tannenbrook?"

He closed his eyes, hoping he had imagined it—the voice, sweet and crystalline, like a fountain. He heard that voice in his dreams and woke up aching.

"Do say you have a better plan than simply ignoring me. I should hate to think your fortitude is lacking."

He sighed and refused to look at her, keeping his eyes trained on the green of Hyde Park. "What are you doing here?"

The quiet tap of her footfalls came closer, stopping as she drew even with him. "I was invited to attend Lady Wallingham's luncheon. My cousin and aunt elected to go for a stroll about the park afterwards. I elected to stay and speak with Miss Lancaster before taking the carriage home and ridding myself of an abominable headache."

He frowned, hearing the weariness in her voice. The slight slur of someone in pain. It pulled him around to face her. She wore a blue spencer that matched her eyes and a gown of lighter blue muslin embroidered with white dots and vines. Upon her black hair, she wore the same dark-blue bonnet she had worn four days earlier in Hyde Park. *Likely her favorite,* he thought.

"Does your head pain you often?" he murmured, seeing how she winced at the bright light of midday. He repositioned himself to stand between her and the sun.

She sighed, the tiny frown between her brows easing. "Thank you. Not often, but when it does, I must have a lie-down." Her smile was strained. "What brings you to Wallingham House, if I may ask?"

He did not know why he answered. Perhaps because his horse had not yet arrived. Perhaps because she seemed subdued, and he wished to cheer her. Perhaps because he savored the sound of her voice, as gentle as a river caressing its banks. "Lord Wallingham signed a note to transfer ownership of one of his foals and to document its pedigree."

"Could he not have sent the note?"

"I met with Lady Wallingham, as well."

"Oh, dear."

Against his will, he felt a smile tug at his lips. "The dowager does try one's patience."

Despite her pain, she returned his smile with a bright one

of her own and tilted her head inquisitively. "Have you business with Lady Wallingham, as well? Or are you simply a glutton for punishment?"

Again, he hesitated to answer. He should be withdrawing from the lass, not satisfying her curiosity. "She is helping me locate my heir."

Why had he said that? A frown settled over his brow. Why the bloody hell was he even speaking with Viola Darling? He should be working to discourage her interest.

"Relying upon the dowager's help? A glutton for punishment, indeed." She glanced over her shoulder as a familiar barouche headed toward them. "One thing I do admire about Lady Wallingham is her constancy. If she has promised to help, then she will."

"Mmm," he murmured. "Not without exacting a steep price for it."

"Naturally. What is her assistance costing you?"

My sanity, he thought. But he could not say that, for it would reveal too much. "She wishes my presence in London for the season. She claims I have neglected my social obligations for too long."

Viola tilted her head, reading his eyes. "Mmm. This explains why you attend so many ton events when you obviously would prefer to be elsewhere. Perhaps having a tooth extracted or a bone reset."

"Indeed."

She nodded to her coachman as the vehicle pulled up. "Do not despair, James," she said softly, her hand discreetly stroking his forearm. "Let Lady Wallingham tend to her task. Meet her demands as you must." Her lips curled up at one corner. "Remember to breathe. Trust that all will come right in the end."

Inexplicably, he felt tension draining from his neck and shoulders, the sweetness of twilight blue washing away the day's frustrations. The sensation reminded him of falling backward into the river's cool rush after a week of hauling stone. It made him dizzy. Made him want more.

"I must go," she said, giving his arm one last caress.

Automatically, he assisted her into the carriage, holding her gloved hand a bit longer than necessary. Feeling the difference in their sizes, the delicacy of her bones before reluctantly releasing her, he swallowed. "How is your head?"

Her glazed, narrowed eyes and subtle wince answered him.

"Where is your footman?"

"He is driving."

Glowering first at her then at the young servant manning the reins, he ordered, "Hold them steady whilst I raise the hood."

The coachman-cum-footman blinked up at cloudless skies in confusion but obeyed his command.

James swiftly unfolded the hood at the back of the open carriage and locked it into place, giving Viola a refuge from the glare of the sun. "Take her directly home. Do not tarry."

"Aye, m'lord."

Moments before the reins snapped and the barouche pulled away, he heard her sigh his name. Just that. "James."

As he watched the carriage recede down Park Lane, the most peculiar ache stole into his chest. Right in the center, where his heart lived. It was almost as though he ... missed her. His thighs burned to move. His gut ached to follow her and ensure she was laid upon a bed of downy feathers in a darkened room. To be there when she awakened, her smile glowing up at him, free of pain.

What was this strange urge?

Foolishness, he answered himself. *Guilt, perhaps, for rejecting her affections. Everyone suffers pain from time to time. Hers is none of your concern.*

He must tend those matters that *were* his concern—finding his heir, introducing the man to the responsibilities that would pass to the next Earl of Tannenbrook. And seeing to the continued prosperity of those who relied upon him.

These were his tasks. These would be his focus.

No room for a lass so bluidy beautiful she makes you ache, Jamie Kilbrenner. No room whatever. Turn your mind to better things, and soon enough she will forget you.

As a liveried groom arrived leading his horse, he watched the barouche turn off Park Lane and disappear from view. Then he wondered if, in truth, a better thing existed on earth than Miss Viola Darling.

Chapter Six

"I prefer to be the wielder of coercion, Humphrey.
Not the recipient."

—THE DOWAGER MARCHIONESS OF WALLINGHAM to her boon
companion, Humphrey, upon discovering the avidity of said
companion's fondness for squirrels.

～∞～

June 15, 1818
Northumberland

VIOLA'S FIRST GLIMPSE OF GRIMSGATE CASTLE COINCIDED—
not unexpectedly—with the drawing of blood. "Ouch!" she
gasped as her embroidery needle pierced the pad of her
thumb. Plopping the bloody thing in her mouth, she lowered
her hoop to her lap and resumed peering out the window of
their travel coach.

The castle was an enormous presence, perched on a hill above a flat, coastal landscape. Square turrets anchored the four corners of a massive central keep while high stone walls encircled the entire hilltop, running lengthwise to encompass acres to either side. Altogether, the keep and turrets and walls and gatehouse, along with numerous stone outbuildings, resembled a dragon sprawled victoriously upon its throne, preening against a clear Northumberland sky.

"You will have to remove that stitch if you do not wish to leave a tangle on the reverse side."

Viola closed her eyes and gathered her patience before turning away from the window to face the woman who would soon be her stepmother. What Papa found to love in her was yet a mystery. But, she was the woman he intended to marry—provided Viola could land Tannenbrook by the end of the house party. After nearly three months of running headlong into his stalwart resistance, she judged that result to be far from certain.

"Thank you, Mrs. Cumberland. How kind of you to alert me to possible calamity."

Her ruddy face framed by the brim of a gray bonnet, the stout woman nodded and returned to her own sewing—a white shirt she was mending, possibly for Papa.

He had elected to ride with the coachman, leaving Viola, Penelope, Aunt Marian, and Mrs. Cumberland to occupy the enclosed carriage.

For four bloody days.

Viola had spent the first two hours of their journey from London conversing with Penelope, who could talk of nothing except her upcoming nuptials with Lord Mochrie. The conversation had only served to remind Viola of her own appalling failures, so she had borne Penelope's enthusiasm as long as she could before pleading a headache and pretending to nap. After that, she had begun assembling a gift for James, a small token of her affection. It was a handkerchief, a white linen square with a bit of embroidery in one corner.

Of course, such a project would have been quite simple if anyone else had attempted to make it. But she was Viola, Mutilator of Stitchery.

On the first day, she had spent two hours cutting the linen. By the time she had finished, the square was half the size it should have been. Then, she'd spent the next six hours hemming three of the edges. The fourth edge had proven the most problematic and now bulged unevenly along one corner. By the time she was finished, she could not bear the thought of reworking the thing yet another time.

Then had come the embroidery. Because she and James had spent a good deal of time together—the natural result of chasing him everywhere short of his front door—she had managed to learn a fair amount about him. For example, he favored coffee over tea and ale over coffee. Wine he only drank for politeness' sake. Also, he was an earl by blood, but he sometimes exhibited subtle contempt for his fellow aristocrats, particularly the insufferable ones. And, his favorite thing to do whenever he had time enough for leisure was fishing. She had coaxed him to talk about it one evening when the tedium of their third musicale had driven them both to the brink of desperation.

"What sort of fishing?" she had probed, grateful to have garnered a response other than dismissive grunts and transparent evasions.

"Rivers, mainly."

"No, silly. What sort of fish?"

"Does it matter?"

"It does to me."

"Why?"

"Because I wish to know more about you."

"You are daft, woman. Why can you not let me be?"

"Because."

"That is not a reason."

"What reason have you for failing to answer a simple question?"

"Because."

Into the silence had fallen a sour note upon the pianoforte, courtesy of one of the Pennywhistle daughters.

"Very well," he'd grumbled. "Trout. I like to fish for trout."

She'd brightened, seeing the first small glimmer of hope since the day he'd handed her up into a barouche on Park Lane. She still felt warm remembering how he had raised the hood to screen her from the sun's glare, all to give her a tiny bit more comfort.

That was why she loved him. Unequivocally, unreservedly loved him.

But, if his coldness toward her throughout the rest of the season were any indication, he did not return the sentiment. No, he merely tolerated her presence with a flexing jaw and a stony expression the way she tolerated Mrs. Cumberland's embroidery advice. Occasionally, he would relent and converse with her, as he had about fishing, but those moments of connection were all too brief and infrequent. While she winced at his persistent rejections, she craved his company too much to abandon her Tannenbrook Hunt.

Now, as she attempted to stitch the tail of a trout on her uneven square of linen, she felt three months of failure weighing upon her until her shoulders wanted to sag with it, until her throat swelled nearly shut with it. She could delay no longer. Papa deserved to be happy with Mrs. Cumberland. He deserved to see his daughter safely married after paying for a second season he could ill afford, to say nothing of the expense of traveling all the way to Northumberland.

If she could not bring James around to accepting her as his wife before the end of the house party, then she would be forced to marry another. It was the only fair course for Papa.

Every inch of her skin, every ounce of her blood, every thought in her mind rejected the notion of taking another man as her husband. Letting another man kiss her. Touch her. Father her children. No. She could not bear it.

"If you take a bit more care with your needle, you should be able to draw the threads back through without knotting—"

"Mrs. Cumberland," Viola snapped. "Thank you, but I shall manage well enough on my own."

The woman's mouth tightened, and she nodded primly before returning to her own work, smoothly pulling the thread tight on another perfect, invisible stitch.

Aunt Marian awakened with a snort. "Have we arrived yet?"

"The gatehouse is just ahead, Mama," Penelope replied, her voice surprisingly low as she cast Viola an acidic glare. "Thank heavens."

A short while later, as they entered the grand hall, Viola took a deep breath and closed her eyes, savoring the relief of exiting the cramped coach. She stood alone and still in the center of the room. Behind her, Papa inquired after Mrs. Cumberland's comfort, and Penelope honked out a laugh at something her mother said. The butler—a lanky, rust-haired man named Nash who managed to be both haughty and obsequious at once—directed footmen in the unloading of their coach.

Viola stood apart from all of them. In the very center of the room, she opened her eyes and gazed up at wood-paneled walls rising twenty feet into a majestic vaulted ceiling. An enormous fireplace—larger than any she'd ever seen—anchored the right side of the hall while three arched openings at the back apparently led to a gallery of windows or glass doors, judging by the bright light streaming onto the floor.

Distantly, she heard the clacking tick, rapid and scrambling, of paws upon polished stone. Spinning in a full circle, she looked about for the source of the sound.

"Humphrey! Do calm yourself." Lady Wallingham's distinctive voice called moments before a waist-high, droopy-faced hound bounded through the left arch, charging straight for Viola. "Your enthusiasm is most undignified."

Upon seeing the folds and jowls flapping in rhythm with the dog's pendulous ears, Viola's heart skipped a beat. Upon being knocked nearly on her backside by the dog's momentous leap, and receiving copious snuffling kisses with a long, wet tongue, she fell in love.

"Humphrey! That is quite enough."

Viola could not help it. She giggled and hugged his neck, scratched his ears, and kissed his brown head. Dark, soulful, droopy eyes gazed up at her adoringly.

"Like most males, you are making a cake of yourself over Miss Darling. Slobbering upon her will only result in her rightful disgust. Stop it at once."

Laughing in delight, Viola shook her head and gently eased the dog's front paws to the floor. She bent forward and took his sweet face in her hands, touching his forehead with her own. "Later, we shall take a walk together," she whispered. "Would you like that?"

His tail wagged his hips comically as he emitted a deep whine of agreement.

She gave his wrinkled forehead one last kiss and straightened.

Then, her breath left her in a rush of heat. Leaning against the casing of the center arch was the object of her heart's most fervent desires. Impossibly wide shoulders. Thick arms folded across a massive chest. Eyes of deep, coniferous green staring unblinkingly, flashing hungrily. At her.

"James." The airless whisper was pure reflex. She could not help it. When he looked at her that way, she wanted to melt against him, to feel the enormity of his hands upon her again. His name was the only word she knew.

She managed to blink upon hearing Lady Wallingham's voice ring out against wood paneling and polished stone like a trumpet blast. "It seems every male in existence is destined to fall prey to your charms, Miss Darling."

Unable to tear her gaze from Tannenbrook's, Viola felt the curve of her smile dissolve into a kind of sadness. "Not *every* one, my lady."

HE WAS DYING BY SLOW DEGREES. FIRST, HE HAD HEARD HER laugh. The sound had echoed from the grand entrance hall like a musical fountain, promising succor to a man perishing of thirst. He'd been lured to find its source, to see her again after an agonizing ten days without a drop. Then, he had seen her. Black hair shining without her bonnet. Soft curves gowned in rosy-pink muslin. Skin glowing like alabaster.

And her smile. Ah, God. It twisted him up inside like a sheet being wrung violently dry. He needed more. But it was fading the longer she stared back at him, turning the corners of those tempting lips in the wrong direction.

"... have stated before, men are simple creatures, but not necessarily easily managed." Lady Wallingham's pontificating snapped the silvery line that bound him to Viola. He blinked. Breathed. Waited for his heart to slow its pounding.

The butler passed between them, approaching the dowager to discuss disposition of the guests.

James willed himself to leave. He needed to stop staring at her.

Instead it was she who turned away. Her bosom rising on a deep breath, Viola calmly removed her gloves and began examining the room, her eyes curiously devouring the large tapestries hanging on two of the walls.

Inexplicably, he wanted her eyes back on him.

One of her gloves plopped onto the floor. Humphrey scuttled away from Lady Wallingham's side where he'd sat shivering, emitting grunting whines, and gazing longingly at Viola for the past minute or two. James could empathize with the dog's sentiment.

As the dog grasped the small leather glove in his mouth, Viola released a surprised laugh. Then Lady Wallingham barked a command which Humphrey ignored, instead playfully running away with his prize, long ears flopping like great banners as he raced toward the archways and, presumably, a safe place to stow his captured treasure.

Calmly, James moved into the dog's path. Paws skidded to a stop. A canine rear hit the polished limestone floor as James held out a commanding hand. He turned his palm up. A slobbery glove dropped obediently into his grasp. With his other hand, he scratched the hound's ears. "Mustn't be greedy, now," he muttered, wondering if he was warning the dog or himself.

He wiped the glove with his handkerchief then delivered it back to its owner. Her long, lush lashes formed fans against her cheeks as she eyed the returned prize.

"Thank you, my lord."

"Tannenbrook," he corrected, though in truth, he wanted to hear her speak his real name again. James.

The fans lifted. Twilight blue shone up at him like a starry sky. "Tannenbrook." It was a caress, her lips pursing and pouting over the syllables. "How do you find Northumberland?"

He did not know why he answered with his rusty humor. Too much time in Lucien's company, perhaps. "Some use a map. I simply rode northward until I was bound to enter either Scotland or the sea. Fortunately, I stopped before suffering either fate."

She burst into laughter, her eyes lighting as though he'd said something brilliant and shocking or silly and delightful.

He wanted to kiss her. He wanted to make her laugh again.

Mostly, he wanted to kiss her.

"Just when I am certain you have no more surprises in store, you manage to prove me wrong," she said.

She smelled of peonies, sweet and full and rich. He breathed in her scent, storing it up in his lungs.

"I am so very happy to see you again." Her words were a murmur, her cheeks now blushing becomingly, her breathing fast.

He was happier to see her. And he should not be. Could not be.

The truth was as immutable as it had been three months earlier when he'd first set eyes upon her—he could not have Viola Darling. Not unless she could be content as his childless mistress. Impossible. And, somehow, deeply wrong. She deserved to be a wife. Cherished. Loved.

"I beg your pardon, my lord," said the butler. "Miss Darling, if you are so inclined, I will show you to your chamber."

"Ah, yes." She grinned at the servant. "Thank you, Nash." Giving James a glance from beneath her lashes, she murmured, "I look forward to seeing you again, my lord."

He opened his mouth to contradict her, but all he could say was, "Tannenbrook."

She shot him a mischievous glance over her shoulder and followed the butler out of the hall.

Behind him, he felt the presence of another stubborn, willful female. "Even for a Scottish stonemason, you are astonishingly dense."

"Have you sent the letter yet?"

The dowager sniffed. "No."

He glared into her eyes and uttered through a clenched jaw. "Do not speak to me again until you do."

Then, he stalked from the grand hall, traversed the long, windowed gallery, threw open the doors leading to the garden, and slammed them closed at a near run. He must escape from this place. Escape from her. Before he lost his senses and chased Miss Viola Darling straight into a life of scandal.

Chapter Seven

"Have you contemplated bribery? It is not so outrageous a suggestion. Bribery is a time-honored method of securing a match, particularly when seduction fails, as it appears to have done with you."

—The Dowager Marchioness of Wallingham to her son, Charles, upon learning of a certain widow's avoidance of moonlit gardens and attempted kisses.

❧

Cringing inside as her third finger plucked her fifth mistimed note, Viola nevertheless maintained a placid expression. She was, after all, playing the harp—dreadfully—before all of Lady Wallingham's guests. Penelope accompanied her on the pianoforte, keeping perfect time and striking every note correctly, if not elegantly. The music room was as cavernous as all the other rooms at Grimsgate, so Viola's errors echoed against white painted paneling and rich oak floors, a resounding reminder of her poor musicianship.

She tried to focus upon her breathing and posture, the demands of the harp's pedals, and the positioning of her fingers, but her mind stubbornly wandered back to him, to their grand moment of connection in the grand hall. She'd been so certain that it signified a turning point in her Tannenbrook Hunt that she had brazenly commandeered one of Lady Wallingham's gigs to follow him on a visit to Charlotte's new home, Chatwick Hall, which neighbored Grimsgate. There, she had hoped not only to discover how her dearest friend was faring in her marriage to Rutherford, but perhaps to spend more time with James alone—or, at least, more alone than they were permitted at the castle. Instead, he had reverted to the Tannenbrook she'd encountered often during the season—brusque, abrupt, and desperate to escape her company.

When she had stood in Charlotte's kitchen garden and pretended surprise by claiming not to have noticed him standing ten feet away, he had replied in a low rumble, "Of course you didn't. Nor did you follow me. Nor are you the veriest thorn in my side." Then, fury blazing, he had stalked past her to leave, pausing only long enough to growl, "Perhaps the next thing you should *not* do is grant me five minutes of blasted peace."

His words had struck her like being shoved into frigid water, coming as they did a day after he had gazed upon her with near reverence, laying her wayward glove in her hand like a supplicant's offering. Charlotte had advised that Viola give him room to breathe. But she could not. And she could not bear explaining to Charlotte that she was running out of time.

Now, her fingers rushed to catch up with Penelope's pace, but her eyes drifted to where he stood at the back of the room near a window. He kept his arms folded across his chest, leaned those massive shoulders against the paneled wall.

And he watched her.

For him alone, she wished to play well. But she had never quite mastered the art.

Her papa was beaming, of course, seated next to Mrs. Cumberland, who naturally was gowned in gray silk. Viola returned his smile, her own feeling a bit wobbly. Next, she noted Lady Wallingham's glowering wince. And the calm forbearance of her solemn-eyed son, Lord Wallingham. And the rapt expressions of four young gentlemen in the front row who appeared to be rather preoccupied with her gown. She supposed the lilac hue was rather fetching, but she suspected the bodice in particular held their interest. The neckline scooped quite low.

At last, the final chords of the tune they played approached. She strummed them with a flourish and listened as the odd smattering of polite applause contrasted with the bravos of the bodice admirers.

"It was supposed to be three-four," her cousin hissed as they stood for a curtsy. "What tune were you playing?"

Viola sighed. "I was distracted."

"Obviously. You sounded even worse than usual."

As they moved toward the now milling crowd, Viola rose up on her toes to glimpse Tannenbrook, but she was soon surrounded by gentlemen vying to describe her performance as "splendiferous" and "transcendent" and "heavenly" and "angelic." She wanted to roll her eyes, but that would be rude, so instead she smiled and thanked them for their kindness.

A rather odiferous Sir Barnabus Malby sought to lay a kiss upon her bare hand, but she managed to evade him by turning away to don her silk gloves and ask Lord Underwood's younger brother about his favorite composer.

All the while, beneath her skin, she bubbled and burned, ached and yearned. For James.

Earlier that day, she had asked Charlotte about her relationship with Rutherford. She'd asked whether the man had kissed her yet, for, in her correspondence, Charlotte had only described their marriage as a business partnership. And yet, Viola had sensed in her letters a budding admiration—even affection—for the devilish lord.

That morning, Charlotte had confirmed Viola's suspicions with a blushing description of her husband's kiss and an admission that she had lost her heart. A short while later, Viola had understood why—Benedict Chatham was much changed from the man he had been. Physically, he was bigger about the shoulders and neck, his leanness now that of muscularity rather than deterioration, his color that of a man who had taken up *farming,* of all things. One quality that hadn't changed was the look in his extraordinary turquoise eyes—that of a hungry wolf. Only now, he gazed at Charlotte as though he intended to devour his wife freckle by freckle.

It had given Viola a notion. Perhaps it was foolish, but she was growing desperate.

She must persuade Tannenbrook to kiss her.

Even now, the thought made her heart pound like a great drum in her ears, drowning out the voices of the gentlemen arguing over whose music room would better suit Viola's musical "talents."

She went in search of him, making her excuses and stopping briefly to accept Papa's kiss upon her cheek, before crossing the room to where James had stood.

But he was gone.

"I recommend a stroll about the gardens."

She spun to see the dowager behind her, a blue feather bobbing as the lady fanned herself with matching blue lace.

"The fountain in particular is lovely in the moonlight."

"Oh! I—that is, I was only wondering—"

"The gardens, dear girl," Lady Wallingham said, turning away to speak with Lady Gattingford.

Quickly looking about to ensure no one watched her, Viola slid along the edge of the room, then escaped through the doors into a dark hall lit with tapers. She gathered the silk of her skirts and walked as swiftly as she could toward the rear gallery where the doors opened onto the terrace.

This night, the moon was high and full, the light lending the winding hedges and profuse plantings a silvery magic. Here, away from the coal smoke of London, thousands of stars twinkled like diamond dust on a velvety blue sky. She closed her eyes briefly and breathed the air, soft as a Kashmiri shawl against her skin, smelling faintly of new roses and the nearby sea. She took the terrace steps quickly, hoping Lady Wallingham had not misled her.

She found him sitting on the fountain's edge, his hands to either side of his thighs gripping the stone, his head hung forward as though in pain. Her slippers crunched lightly on the gravel. Her heart thrummed in her ears. Her skin tingled with strange heat.

"James," she murmured, drawn helplessly forward.

His head came up. Silver light and black shadows played over the crags of his brow and nose and jaw. But all she could see were his eyes, tormented and lost.

She reached him in seconds, her hands sliding over his jaw. She wished she'd thought to remove her gloves, but she hadn't time. She stroked his lips with her thumb, his flexing jaw with her fingers. It was not enough. She bent to kiss him.

But he grasped her wrists and pushed her away before her mouth touched skin.

"James," she breathed again. "I ..."

His chest worked like a bellows. Suddenly he stood, his overwhelming intrusion forcing her backward, but he still gripped her wrists, holding her fast.

"Why must you do this?" He ground out the words in a harsh rumble. "I cannot marry you, Viola. Tempting me will only invite scandal."

"Kiss me," she pleaded, uncaring that she sounded desperate. She *was* desperate. "Give me this one small thing."

"You do not belong with me." He shook her wrists, moving one of them in front of her eyes so she could not avoid seeing where his huge hand encircled her arm. "Look." His face came closer to hers. "Do you see? I could snap your bones in two with one careless move, you are so fine."

"Oh, James. I have never feared your strength."

"Bluidy hell, lass," he muttered, an unexpected brogue emerging. His swallow was visible in his throat. He let their hands fall together, but he did not let her go. "You don't want me. I am no better than the stones beneath your feet."

"How can you believe that? I've wanted you from the first moment I saw you." She laughed in disbelief. "Before that, even. Charlotte described how you defended her, and I fell madly—"

"No, lass."

"—in love with you."

His eyes squeezed shut.

"It is true. You may choose not to believe me, but it is the truest thing I know. And if only you will kiss me—"

"I cannot kiss you."

"Yes." She nodded and tried to move closer to him, but their hands were in the way. "Please, James. I've laid everything at your feet. My pride?" She laughed. "It is nothing. It was the first thing to go."

"I cannot. Marry. You." The words were rusted and hoarse.

She swallowed, blinking up at him, her bones squeezing her heart until it felt strangled. "I have only until the end of this party." Something warm and wet slid down her cheek. "Then, I must choose. Please. I cannot wait any longer for you to come to your senses."

A ferocious glower took that heavy brow. Eyes already burning with intensity flashed an ominous white and black. "Choose?"

"Yes," she whispered. "A—a husband. My father has no funds for another season. And he has already waited too long to find happiness with Mrs. Cumberland. I must accept an offer before autumn. For his sake."

His breathing roughened. His thumbs stroked the insides of her wrists.

She inched into him. "This is why I have pushed you so. You are ..." She swallowed again. "It is not just that you are the one I want. You are the *only* one I want."

"Certain of that, are you?" His voice had worn down to a thread, his eyes all but burning her flesh. "Have you any idea who I really am, lass?"

"You are the man I love."

"No."

"Then prove me wrong. Kiss me."

He was panting now, his eyes upon her lips. "You've been kissed many times, no doubt."

She shook her head. "Never by you."

He groaned and closed his eyes, loosening his grip upon her wrists.

She took the opportunity to step into him, to draw his huge, wondrous hands to her waist, to raise her mouth toward his. "Kiss me," she whispered again.

His eyes opened above hers. "I am not the man for you."

She said nothing, unable to speak for the beauty of this night, of feeling his heat against her, albeit through layers of silk and linen.

"This means nothing."

Again, she simply waited, loving the way bright silver played with his thick hair, savoring the scent of his skin. Like pines around a lake.

"Let this be the end of it, lass." It sounded like a plea.

Then, his head was lowering. His eyes loved her lips first, stroking over them as though he would commit her to memory.

But that was nothing compared to the first touch of his mouth. The heat of his skin against hers. The soft caress of his lips. The tingle of his bristled chin sliding against her. His nose angled beside hers.

She gasped as the sensations spun and coalesced. She pulled his breath into her. Pine and summer and heat and James. Sliding her hands up his arms to his shoulders, then to his muscled neck, then to his precious jaw, she pulled him closer. Kissed him harder. Wanted inside.

"Mvolah." His incomprehensible word vibrated deliciously against her lips. His hands gripped her waist harder. His head tugged away, creating intolerable distance between their mouths.

"Again," she moaned. "Please."

There was little warning. Only an explosion of heat in his eyes and a low, rumbling groan in his chest. Then his arm was behind her back. And she was leaving the graveled ground. And her breasts were flattened deliciously against his chest. And her face was nearly level with his. And his other hand was gripping her nape, his fingers shaping her jaw from behind.

And his mouth was grinding against hers. And his tongue—his *tongue*—was sliding hot and slick and a little salty inside her mouth. Oh, Charlotte had mentioned that kisses involved tongues, but it still made her squeak in surprise.

His mouth was open against her, his tongue stroking in the most intriguing way, pulsing in and out, exploring her teeth and lips. She experimented by mimicking his motions, and his grip tightened all around her. She squeaked again, but she clawed his hair in both her hands, her knees rising along his hips, frustrated by her skirts.

He was delicious. A tingly, delicious drink. A hot, hard, ferocious, pine-scented man who she would be deliriously happy to kiss for the rest of her life. With tongues. And probably more touching.

Of their own accord, her hips writhed against his waist. She needed him to do ... something. What that was, she did not know, because his kiss was divine. Gentle strokes of sleek, wet tongue mingled with the firm, grinding pressure of his lips. Oh, she wanted to do this forever. But she wanted more. Was there more? There must be.

He hitched her up higher against his chest, causing her breasts to signal a response. Good heavens, she'd had no idea this much pleasure existed. Her nipples were hardened points, deliciously pressured against him as though they'd craved this all along. The strength of his arms and hands was a marvel. The feel and smell and sensations of him like nothing she could have imagined.

Indeed, she had imagined something sweet. Something chaste. Like a painting of a maiden and her gallant suitor.

Instead, she'd been set afire, the longing a deep ache in her belly and chest, the kiss both a release from the heat and its ever-burgeoning source.

And just when she thought it all might go on forever, his arm loosened around her. And she slid downward against him, startled to feel an odd, stone-like bulge against her belly. Then her feet touched the ground. And his warm, strong hand left her neck to stroke her cheek. And his mouth eased its pressure. And his tongue withdrew.

Then his heat was gone.

And then he was gone.

And all her breath had gone, so that the only sound she could make was her mouth shaping his name.

And the only thing she could feel was a breeze that smelled of rich pine and new roses and the endless sea.

Chapter Eight

*"A temporary victory is merely a meandering path to defeat.
And I do not accept defeat."*

—THE DOWAGER MARCHIONESS OF WALLINGHAM to Lady
Gattingford regarding her efforts to persuade the intractable
Lord Tannenbrook of his continued folly.

❧

MISTS ROSE OFF THE RIVER FENN AS JAMES THREW HIS FLY
fifteen yards upstream, just above a promising eddy. He
watched it drift into place, calmly drawing the line through
his fingers in small strokes and letting the slack pool at his
feet. Within seconds, he felt the tug, gave a flick of his wrist,
and lightly set the hook. Then he watched the end of his rod
bow alarmingly and jerk as the trout struggled against its fate.

"Good God, man," murmured Wallingham, sitting ten feet away
beneath a rustling willow tree. "What the devil are you using?"

"Green drake." James employed first his hand then his winch to play the fish, carefully drawing up the remainder of the slack line and following the creature's course.

"Do you suppose this catch will be weightier than your fourth?"

"Must land him first." The tension on his rod indicated the fish might be as much as ten pounds, quite large for a trout.

He did not care. For the first time in his many years of angling, he felt not a drop of excitement, nor a crumb of peace. For this, he blamed Viola Darling.

Minutes later, Charles helped him net what was likely his largest catch of the morning. The ordinarily serious-eyed lord grinned like a lad of thirteen as he held the wriggling thing aloft, as pleased as though he'd caught it himself.

"I say, it must be twenty-five inches. Remarkable." Wallingham moved to stow it with the others in James's borrowed basket. As he crouched over the creel, he glanced over his shoulder to where James stood gathering up his tackle and securing his line. "I should think you'd be pleased, Tannenbrook."

James's frown deepened. "I am," he lied. He could not explain his discontent to Wallingham, even though the man's fifteen-year resistance to remarriage paralleled James's own decision to remain unwed.

In simple terms, Viola had tempted James beyond his sanity. For a brief moment beneath the moon and stars, he had taken the thing he wanted more than breath, more than his own life. And he had not known a peaceful moment since.

How could a man sleep when his body burned hotter than a blacksmith's fire? The answer: He could not. So, instead, he'd set out at dawn, joined by a surprisingly agreeable Wallingham, who'd been preparing to take a ride about Grimsgate's abundant acres.

He wanted to forget. Her lips. Her smell. Her sweet, murmuring cries of need.

"You wish to concede early, then?" Wallingham inquired now, hefting the basket and adjusting his hat.

James blinked, wondering what the older man was asking. Did he know of the kiss? Did he know of James's hellish battle against his own desires?

"Tannenbrook?"

He could not possibly know, for James had told no one. Not even Viola knew his reasons—and, unless he wished her admiration to dissolve into disgust, he would never tell her the truth.

A soft breeze eased past him to ripple the slow water. "I mustn't concede," he murmured. "I would destroy her."

Wallingham appeared deeply perplexed. "Her?"

"Miss Darling."

Wearing a thoughtful expression, the marquess climbed the bank to where James stood. He set the basket on the grass beside his boots. "How much have you slept?"

"Last night?"

"Yes."

"Not at all." James could not be certain why he kept speaking. Perhaps because, in the buttery light of early morning, Charles Bainbridge looked a good deal like Hargrave. And he missed having someone older, wiser to advise him. Perhaps he was a fool.

No 'perhaps' about it, he thought. *You become a bleeding mooncalf every time you think of her. A daft, lustful sod.*

Wallingham nodded, a wry smile forming at one corner of his mouth. "Some females will do that—drive you half mad one moment, enchant you the next. Have you considered altering your stratagem regarding marriage?"

James's hand tightened dangerously on his fly rod, but he stopped himself before it cracked. "Impossible. I do not intend to marry."

"Yes, so you have said." Wallingham clasped his hands behind his back and gave James an assessing glance. "I had a similar notion, myself, only a short time ago. I have since ... reconciled myself to a new course."

Swallowing, James squinted at where the sun began topping the willows along the winding bank. He wished to know what would prompt a man like Wallingham, after resisting the fiercest of opponents for fifteen years, would suddenly change his mind about something so fundamental. "Why?" James grunted, against his better judgment.

Wallingham's smile grew mysterious. "Why else? I am enchanted. Half mad."

"Lady Willoughby."

"Mmm. Indeed." The smile changed again into one of affection. "Now, this is not to say you should follow my path, necessarily, for it has not yet ended happily, as one would hope. But, I will tell you this: Ambivalence is your enemy. If you are firm in your resolve never to marry, then state it clearly—brutally, if you must. Cutting her bond to you can only be a mercy, in that instance. Do not mire yourself in regrets. If, however, you cannot abide the thought of another day without seeing her laugh or hearing her speak your name, then do not hesitate to change course, and do so with all haste." Wallingham dropped his gaze to the toes of his boots then turned to stare out across the water. "We are men, Tannenbrook. By definition, men are creatures of imperfect vision. A decision made at age twenty-four is a decision made by a boy. We are boys no longer."

For James, he'd been seventeen, but he took Wallingham's point. Still, James was not acting out of some momentary pique. He was trying to protect Viola from a union she would come to bitterly regret.

Eyeing the other man's patrician profile, the white flags at his temples, the faint creases at the corners of his eyes, James flashed to a memory of Hargrave, gazing out the window of the library at Shankwood, explaining to a boy of seventeen why taking his seat in Parliament mattered. It felt good to remember him. Comforting.

"I am glad for your company this morning, Wallingham."

He leaned down and picked up the heavily laden basket, giving it a shake to settle the fish more firmly inside. "You appear to be good luck."

Wallingham chuckled and followed James as they made their way back toward the castle. A quarter mile on, they heard barking in the distance. "Blast," muttered Wallingham. "Mother's hound. Must have caught our scent. Deuced creature could track a man from here to London."

As they came over a small rise with waist-high grass, they saw the unlikely pairing of a determined Humphrey all but dragging a tiny sprite in a blue dress and spencer, holding the dog's lead in one hand and the top of her bonnet with the other.

James's heart kicked wildly. His feet halted.

"Humphrey! Slow down, for the love of heaven." She laughed breathlessly, the sound like a fountain beneath a skyful of stars.

Her beauty washed him with a tingling current. Stole the air from inside his chest. Made him remember the sweetness of her mouth, the softness of her breasts.

"Steady on, Tannenbrook," Wallingham said quietly.

It was enough to start him breathing again, but he still could not move. Those magnificent blue eyes flared over his shoulders and up to his mouth. Set him to burning inside his skin.

As the dog's snuffling nose came within inches of his boots, Humphrey wagged his tail and let out a triumphant howl.

Viola laughed again and tugged at the brim of her bonnet. "Good morning, Lord Wallingham. Lord Tannenbrook." She nodded toward James's creel. "I see the fish found your offerings enticing. You must be terribly proficient with your rod."

A thousand responses ran through his mind, all of them inappropriate. Before he could utter a word, however, Wallingham answered, "Tannenbrook had great success. Would that I could say the same."

"Oh, isn't that the way of it?" Her smile was dazzling—and focused upon Wallingham. "My cousin and I were constant companions as children. I recall our rambles about the lake near my father's house in Cheshire. We collected butterflies. I could never understand how she managed to capture five when I had none. As it happened, she later confessed to dabbing her flowers with honey." She rolled her eyes and laughed. "Silly me, I hadn't thought of luring them with a sweet."

Wallingham chuckled lightly and nodded. "I fear my angling methods may require similar diabolical strategies, for I haven't the patience to improve my technique."

Viola continued chatting with Wallingham—and entirely ignoring James—for several minutes. They talked of Cheshire and how she missed the scent of bluebells that bloomed near her home in spring. They laughed about Humphrey's overdeveloped sense of smell and Lady Wallingham's fondness for his pendulous ears. They traded recollections of Lord Gattingford's more egregious choices of waistcoat.

And all the while, James stood in his boots, wondering why she did not look at *him*. Why she did not speak to *him*. Why she'd never told *him* about the lake in Cheshire. Or her fondness for lemonade. Or her contrary dislike of the color yellow, particularly in waistcoats.

Because, you daft sod. You have been beastly to her. Treated her as little more than a pest. How else is she to respond?

But she had kissed him. She had claimed to love him, though that could not be true. She knew nothing of who he was.

A cold, canine nose rubbed the back of his hand where it was clenched into a fist over the top of the creel. With a pitiful whine, Humphrey mouthed the upper edge of the basket where several fin tails splayed, the fish too big to be contained completely inside. James idly nudged the dog away and returned to following the conversation between Viola and the man she apparently found terribly, unspeakably fascinating. So much so that she hadn't stopped bloody speaking to him and smiling at him and laughing at his every quip for ten bloody minutes.

His only warning was a tug. Then Humphrey was charging across the open grass, his prize clutched between droopy jowls, his ears flapping like banners, the lead trailing behind, loosed from Viola's grip.

"Humphrey!" she shouted, clapping her hands as though the damned hound would heed any sound over the scent of victory.

Then, she bunched her skirts in hand and gave chase.

Bloody hell. He didn't care a fig for the fish, but he would not have Viola running about after that stupid hound, who could knock her tiny form flat with one overzealous leap. Dropping his rod and creel in the grass, he barked at Wallingham, "If he comes back this way, take hold of his lead."

Then, James was running. Chasing a girl who was chasing a dog. Like a bloody, besotted fool.

He watched her stop suddenly and veer to the right as Humphrey rounded the trunk of a willow. He took the left, anticipating the dog's reversal. But he didn't anticipate Viola's speed. She reached the trailing lead before he could get to her. And her breathless shout of triumph ended in a yelp as she was yanked forward, her feet stumbling on the exposed tree roots.

He pushed harder, wrapping one arm about her waist and gathering her into him half a second before the bloody, stupid dog nearly cracked the side of her skull into the trunk of the tree. His free hand wrapped around the lead and yanked hard, growling at the dog to stop. It took every ounce of his control not to choke the careless thing. Not to squeeze Viola Darling until her skin merged with his.

But he could not do either one. The dog did not belong to him. And neither did Viola.

He released her tiny waist. Pulled away before she felt how he'd reacted. Then, more calmly than he had any right to, he pried open the dog's jaw and retrieved his mutilated fish.

"T-Tannenbrook. I am so sorry. Your poor fish."

"It doesn't matter. Wallingham!" he shouted.

Wallingham approached through the tall grass.

James handed him the leash. "I trust you can manage him. You may wish to inform your mother that her hound requires further training and should not be handled by young ladies until he can be trusted not to pull them off their feet."

Perhaps his tone was severe. He did not care.

"I shall," Wallingham replied solemnly, his eyes understanding far too much. "Miss Darling, my sincere apologies. Humphrey will not harm you again, I promise." He tugged the lead and started back across the grassy clearing, a chastened Humphrey loping behind, head lowered and ears swinging far less merrily.

"Oh, no," Viola protested. "But, he is still just a pup! He didn't mean any harm. Tannenbrook, don't punish him. Really, Humphrey is a delight. He was simply ... caught up in the moment. He would never purposely hurt me."

James braced one palm against willow bark and leaned down until his face was directly in front of hers. "No. Because he will not have the opportunity."

Her eyes dropped to his lips. And just like that, she was too close. Too damned close.

He straightened, eyeing the fish in his hand and shoving away from the tree to stride back to his creel. Quickly stuffing the half-mangled thing back into the basket, he picked up his rod and turned southwest toward Grimsgate.

"Tannenbrook!" She caught up to him a moment later. "Wait a moment. I—I have something I wish to give you."

He turned to find a scrap of cloth presented on her gloved palm. It had some sort of embroidery on it—purple and green. He could not quite make out what it was meant to be. "What is it?"

"A handkerchief, silly. You can carry it with you when you go fishing." Her tiny nose crinkled adorably. "To wipe your hands. If you like."

"Handling the fish is an expected part of angling."

"Yes, I'm certain it is." Boldly, she moved closer, lifted the edge of his coat away from his shirt, and tucked the square of linen inside his pocket. "There." She patted his chest familiarly, then lowered her lashes and swallowed. "Yours now, Lord Tannenbrook."

Good God, he could scarcely breathe. He wanted her so badly, his thighs and cock were like stone, his heart kicking and writhing with need.

"I—I should get back before I am missed," she said. "Penelope will wonder where I have wandered to."

He wanted to refuse her gift. He wanted to tell her she could not bloody well tempt him this way. But all he could think to do in that moment was watch his beautiful lass turn and flit away from him like a butterfly escaping his grasp.

When she disappeared over the next rise, far enough ahead that he could no longer see her or smell her sweet scent, he staggered forward several steps.

Ambivalence is your enemy, Wallingham had said. *If you are firm in your resolve never to marry, then state it clearly—brutally, if you must. Cutting her bond to you can only be a mercy.*

A mercy.

He closed his eyes, squeezing as though the landscape would change. It would not. He'd known from the age of seventeen that he would never marry. Because to marry meant children. He did not deserve children. Not after he'd killed his son.

So he must be brutal with Viola, he decided, pulling out the white square with the strange purple and green embroidery. He ran a thumb over its surface.

To set her free, he must sever their bond. It would hurt like the fires of hell. But he would do it because it was right. And James Kilbrenner always did the right thing.

Chapter Nine

*"Doling advice is an art akin to swordplay. While experts
dazzle and strike the heart of a matter in but a few strokes,
amateurs swing wildly about, achieving little more
than perforating their own trousers."*

—THE DOWAGER MARCHIONESS OF WALLINGHAM to her son,
Charles, regarding his abysmal attempts to offer romantic counsel
to Lord Tannenbrook.

❧

UPON RETURNING TO GRIMSGATE, VIOLA HAD SPOKEN WITH
Lord Wallingham about Humphrey, begging him to treat the
dog with kindness. She needn't have worried. The dear man
had taken her out to the garden and shown her the proper
technique for walking with Humphrey on a lead.

"You mustn't allow him to pull at you. That is the key,"
he'd explained gently. "A dog will get the wrong end of things

if he believes he is in command." Then, he'd handed Viola the lead and shown her how to walk beside Humphrey, correcting the dog's attempts to pull ahead of her. For an hour more, she had practiced, her arms and shoulders relieved at the alternative to being dragged like a plow behind an ox.

Now, having delivered a happy Humphrey back to Lady Wallingham, Viola was free to embrace Charlotte, who had come to Grimsgate for a visit with the dowager. They were standing in the center of the cavernous drawing room, chatting and laughing over Lady Wallingham's idiosyncrasies when Charlotte smiled down at her and asked about her stay at Grimsgate.

Reading the shadow of concern in her friend's eyes, Viola countered, "Are you asking about my Tannenbrook Hunt?"

One red brow arched. "I am."

She kept her tone light so as not to cause further worry. "He is most resistant. I admire his fortitude, frankly. However, I admit to a small degree of annoyance that he does not find me as irresistible as I find him."

As expected, Charlotte chuckled and, linking arms with Viola, led them both into the grand hall. "Your harp playing did not sway him?" she teased.

"Laugh if you wish, but many gentlemen said they thought me an angel, I played so sweetly."

"I have heard you play, Viola. With the greatest affection, I must tell you, they lied."

After days of tiresome fawning from a dozen gentlemen—not to mention contradictory responses from the one man whose good opinion mattered—Viola felt a kind of release in Charlotte's fond humor. She laughed helplessly, playfully swatting Charlotte's elbow. It felt good to be teased about one of her more obvious shortcomings. "I know that, silly. Though, I do admire your honesty. It is one of the things I love best."

They were facing the south entrance, so they did not see him enter through the arches. Instead, they heard him first.

His deep, rumbling voice sent tremors running through her spine—and he wasn't even speaking to her. "Lady Rutherford."

Charlotte turned abruptly, yanking Viola's arm and spinning her about like Humphrey taking after a squirrel. She apologized to Viola and greeted James.

He entered like a great, towering storm.

Viola said nothing. She was too busy trying to breathe. After one glimpse of him, her head lifted off her shoulders. *My, he is wondrous. A giant, rumbling mountain dressed in brown wool and white linen.* She wanted to kiss him again. Even though he was charging toward her with both speed and purpose, as though intent on throttling her.

But he could not be angry, she reasoned. She hadn't done anything wrong. Had she?

Her heart slammed repeatedly against bone at his thunderous expression, his intimidating posture. Her fingers brushed her throat. "Tannenbrook, I ..."

"I believe this is yours," he snapped, extending a hand toward her.

Her eyes dropped curiously. It was the handkerchief.

He held it between his forefinger and middle finger as though touching the cloth were distasteful.

She had spent hours just thinking about the design, never mind the endless toil of stitching and re-stitching and embroidering and cutting away the dreadful mistakes only to labor over the loops again and again. Perhaps it was not *good* work, precisely, but she had thought of him every second, imagined the linen touching his skin. Imagined his thumb stroking the ugly, overripe trout.

A lump formed in her throat. She willed the tears not to form. Blinked so that they would stay away. "I—I made it for you," she managed.

"How many times must I say it, Miss Darling?" His jaw was a grim, cold cliff, his eyes a dark forest of fury and resolve. "I do not want your favors. Nor your gifts. Nor your hand in marriage." Every word gored her like a blade. With a contemptuous flick, he tossed the white square upon the floor. It fluttered onto the toes of her slippers, brushed by her dew-dampened hem. "Nor you. Cease this nonsense. Now."

He barked those final words, rough and harsh.

And then, he was gone. Like a storm that had come on shore to ravage and tear asunder, he disappeared without a care for the damage. Only the echo of his boots thudding on polished stone gave evidence that he'd been there.

Oh, and her heart, of course. Shattered inside her chest. That was evidence, she supposed, though no one could see.

Her eyes fell to the ugly handkerchief. Slowly, she bent to retrieve it.

Her heart tried to beat, but it couldn't. Her lungs tried to breathe, but they couldn't. Her gasp was as ugly as her embroidery. Her fingers tried to stifle it, but it escaped.

Long, slim arms came around her shoulders. Squeezed. Charlotte. She was still there.

Viola let herself slump against her friend.

"Oh, Viola. Do not cry."

She hadn't realized she was. Then she felt it. Warm streams upon her cheeks. She heard it. Gasping animal sounds.

Charlotte's cool hand stroked her cheek and her hair. Her tall form rocked them gently back and forth.

Embarrassed that she was standing in Lady Wallingham's grand hall being comforted like an infant, Viola sniffed and swiped at her cheek with her fingers. "I—I must go and wash my face. I am certain I look dreadful."

"Tell me what you made for him, Viola."

She supposed it would do no harm to explain. "He enjoys fishing. So I made him a handkerchief with a trout embroidered on the corner."

"A trout? Is that the—er, purple bit?"

"I ran out of silver thread."

"And the green stem is a ... tail?"

"I also ran out of purple."

Charlotte sighed and gave her a squeeze. "Perhaps it is time to consider suspending the Tannenbrook Hunt."

Every ounce of her body and soul filled with lead at the mere thought of giving up.

"Only for a short while, Vi. Just to give you both time to consider … everything."

She shook her head. Charlotte did not understand. There *was* no more time. If Tannenbook refused to marry her before the end of the house party, Viola would have to choose someone else. Someone fawning and dreadful, who treated her like a mindless doll or, worse, like an oversized set of stag antlers. A prize to be displayed at some country house to symbolize his hunting prowess and virility.

And yet, the only man she wanted had just declared in the most brutal of terms that he wanted nothing at all to do with her.

So, rather than arguing with Charlotte's gentle suggestion, she chokingly thanked her for her kind friendship and fled the grand hall for the grand staircase. She rushed down an empty corridor lined with portraits of men who all had Lord Wallingham's long chin. And, at last, she burst through the door of her chamber. Fortunately, Grimsgate had so many bedchambers that every guest was afforded one of his or her own. She did not think she could bear explaining her distress to Penelope, whose happiness over Lord Mochrie's proposal had abraded Viola's nerves like sharp pebbles lodged in her slippers.

Glancing down, she realized she still clutched the ugly handkerchief in her fist. She threw the scrap of cloth with a sudden, furious grunt. It did not travel far, unfolding midflight and drifting to the dark-blue carpet like a butterfly in a downdraft.

He does not want me.

Her hands covered her mouth.

He does not want me.

Her arms moved down to clutch her chest, where the pain throbbed worst.

He does not want me.

She stumbled to the bed and crumbled onto its edge.

Then, she wept like a ninny for far too long, succeeding only in turning her eyes hot and swollen, her nose red and clogged, and her throat sore. Eventually, she tired of her own misery. So she pushed herself upright beneath the dark-blue canopy. Stood and stalked to where the handkerchief had fallen. Used it to wipe her eyes and, just for spite, her nose. Then, she rang for a maid to bring her some cool water.

After an hour or so, her face returned to normal, though her heart remained torn. She sat at the dressing table and worked on repairing her hair, which had gone oddly lopsided.

A light knock sounded. Thinking it was the maid returning, Viola bade her enter. Except that it was not the maid. It was Mrs. Cumberland. Wearing gray and white. Appearing red-faced and tight-lipped, as usual.

Viola had nothing left inside with which to fake a smile. "Now is not the best time, Mrs. Cumberland."

"Your father ..." The square-set woman shifted oddly from one foot to the next. "Your father asked that I come and speak with you."

"Regarding?" Viola stabbed a pin at one of her more unruly curls.

Mrs. Cumberland came further into the room, halting a few feet away. "He wishes for you to understand a bit more about ..."

She waited, lacing the curl back into the coil where it belonged and adding another pin. "Yes?"

"Marriage."

Viola's arms fell into her lap. "I know you and Papa wish to marry. He needn't have sent you to tell me that."

She cleared her throat. "You misunderstand. He wishes for me to speak to you regarding the ... relations ... between a husband and wife." The woman turned redder. "So that you will be prepared for the eventuality should you accept a gentleman's offer. Also, he wishes you to be on your guard should you be ... importuned whilst we are here."

"Oh! Oh, good heavens."

Square shoulders slumped in apparent relief. "You understand. Good."

Viola turned on her seat to face her future stepmother. "Really, this is most unnecessary, Mrs. Cumberland."

The woman searched about for a chair and, finding none, elected to seat herself on a chaise at the foot of the bed. "Soon, I shall marry your father."

Acid churned in Viola's stomach. "I know that."

"I love him. Very much."

"As do I."

Dark eyes that had always appeared inscrutable to Viola softened and sheened unexpectedly. "He is kindness itself. I have never known a better man. Not even Mr. Cumberland, God rest his soul." The woman blinked until the sheen disappeared. "He loves you more than his own life."

Viola felt the blasted thickening in her throat. But she refused to descend into maudlin weeping again. It was simply wretched and solved nothing. "I know that, too."

"Do you?" Now, those dark eyes were probing. "He has delayed his own happiness—"

"To guard against thrusting two women into opposition within the same household. I know." She raised her chin. "You may regard me as spoiled and selfish, Mrs. Cumberland, and you would not be far wrong. Although we have never been a family of means, I have been spoiled by Papa's love." Blasted tears stung her eyes again. She swallowed them down. "Is it selfish to want my husband to love me with equal devotion? Perhaps. For whatever postponement of your happiness I have caused, I do apologize. But you should know I have tried mightily to rectify the situation. Mightily."

Having sat with her hands folded in her lap, listening to Viola's speech, Mrs. Cumberland's inscrutable expression abruptly lifted in an oddly affectionate smile. "I know," she said. "I have seen you with Lord Tannenbrook. So has your father. That is why I am here."

Viola's mouth opened to speak, but nothing emerged. She did not know how to respond. Mrs. Cumberland had always appeared rather remote and difficult to read. It was not that Viola disliked her, precisely. She simply did not understand her.

"I am not your mother."

Well, no. Viola's mother had died three days after giving birth to her. For twenty years, it had only been her and Papa.

"It has never been my intention to replace her."

Viola shook her head. "Of course not. I don't—"

Mrs. Cumberland raised a hand to halt her protest. "Please. Let me ... allow me to finish. My greatest regret is that I was unable to have children. It has left an emptiness in my life that is difficult to explain. I was blessed, however, to have been loved by two extraordinary men." She cleared her throat again and folded her hands in her lap. "Now, this may cause you some discomfort, but as your mother is no longer here to provide instruction, I feel it only right that I should share what knowledge and wisdom I possess which may benefit you in your ... pursuits."

"Really, Mrs. Cumberland. This is most unnecessary."

"Please. I would prefer you call me Georgina. As we shall be discussing matters of an intimate nature, perhaps it will make you more comfortable."

"Oh. Yes. Georgina. But honestly, I—"

Dark eyes met hers with great intensity of purpose. "You need to know these things, Viola. Particularly given all that your papa and I have witnessed between you and Lord Tannenbrook."

She sighed, wondering if she should explain that Tannenbrook had all but thrown her affection in her face mere hours ago, and that a marriage between them appeared unlikely. But that would only serve to extend an already uncomfortable conversation. So, instead, she folded her hands in her lap and replied, "Very well."

Georgina nodded. "Now, then, a man is driven by a number of needs. Primary among these is lust. Because you are beautiful, men naturally will feel this urge whilst in your presence."

Oh, dear God. She was not ready for this conversation. Not with Georgina Cumberland of the inscrutable mien and square shoulders. Not with her father's future wife.

"Your task as a lady of virtue is to resist both his urges and your own until marriage."

"If you are referring to Lord Tannenbrook, I am not certain either his urges or a marriage between us should any longer be of concern."

Georgina stared at her for a moment as though she'd said something absurd. "I'm afraid I don't take your meaning."

Viola sniffed. "He feels nothing for me. Apart from vexation, that is."

The other woman frowned. "Is this a jest?"

Annoyed at the obvious disbelief, Viola reached behind her to retrieve the crumpled handkerchief. Then, she held it up, evidence of her heartbreak. "He tossed this at my feet. Declared in no uncertain terms that he will not marry me."

Georgina breathed her name. From anyone else, Viola would have presumed it signified sympathy, but she'd always had difficulty judging Mrs. Cumberland's reactions.

Viola wadded the thing into a ball and dropped it back onto the dressing table. "So, as you can see, Papa's concerns are unfounded. Tannenbrook does not want me."

"But he does."

Frowning, Viola shook her head. "No. He said as much."

"Then, he lied."

"Tannenbrook would not lie. He is the finest of men."

A small smile played with Georgina's lips. "So you have said." Those square shoulders raised on a deep breath before she continued, "Viola, men exhibit certain signs when they want a woman. First, they have difficulty looking away from her. Men are visual creatures, after all. Further, their preoccupation tends to focus upon particular features."

Viola nodded, rolling her eyes. "Bosoms. Yes. I know."

"Not always. For some men, it could be one's lips or eyes or hips. Even a woman's hands."

Curiosity piqued, Viola waited for her to elaborate. Perhaps this conversation would prove worthwhile, after all.

"Mr. Cumberland was rather fond of my hair, for example. He even liked that my brows were a darker shade, though I have always found the contrast strange." She waved a hand dismissively. "Sometimes men see us differently than we see ourselves."

"What are the other signs?"

"Of attraction? Well, there is the obvious one."

Viola blinked. "Obvious?"

"His hardness."

"I don't understand."

For the third time, Georgina cleared her throat. "The member between a man's legs swells and hardens when he is aroused."

Eyes wide, Viola covered her mouth with her hand. "It does?" she mumbled. "Isn't that dreadfully uncomfortable?"

Again, the small smile appeared. "When it goes unrelieved, it can be, yes. But it is necessary for the creation of children." She described how a husband would place himself inside his wife and, upon releasing his seed, find both pleasure and relief from the hardness of his flesh.

Viola found the description inexpressibly fascinating. No one had ever explained such things to her. Certainly not Papa. Nor Aunt Marian, who had only mentioned once that a husband and wife must "know each other" to beget children.

Then, she had taken a sip of her medicinal tea and promptly nodded off.

"If a husband is gentle and kind, a wife may also find the act pleasurable," Georgina continued. "However, to indulge in such pleasures prior to marriage imparts great risk to you and your reputation."

"Because it could result in a child."

"Partly, yes. For a man, it is natural to press for intimacies. After all, the evidence that he has done so does not swell his belly for all to see. It does not brand him forever as less than virtuous. This is why you must—*must*—take greater care, Viola. If you continue to tempt Lord Tannenbrook—"

"I have told you," she said, her voice echoing her sudden chill. "He does not want me."

"Yes. He does. I would go so far as to say he is experiencing significant distress over it."

"Because he stares at me?" she scoffed. "All men do that."

"Because of the *way* in which he stares at you. Particularly when you are speaking with other men."

Viola sniffed. "And how is that?"

"As though you belong to him."

Her heart stuttered. Flopped about in her chest like a fish on a line. "He ... you believe he ..."

"Your father is gravely concerned that you will press him too hard, Viola, and that your reputation will be forfeit. Frankly, he also worries about possible bloodshed."

"Bloodshed? Don't be ridiculous. Tannenbrook would never hurt me. He would die first."

"Not you. But another gentleman, perhaps one whose glance lingers overlong or who presumes too great a familiarity. A man of Lord Tannenbrook's strength and size could do great damage should his jealousy take hold of him."

Jealousy. Viola bit her lower lip, considering this new information carefully. One only felt jealousy over something one desired for oneself. Ergo, he wanted her. For himself.

Come to think of it, she had felt a perplexing hardness against her belly during their kiss, which would correlate with Georgina's fascinating description. But he emphatically denied both his desire and her love. He denied them their rightful happiness for reasons she could not fathom.

His denial cannot be allowed to stand, she thought. *There must be a way to break his everlasting resistance.*

She narrowed her eyes upon Georgina. "Would you consider jealousy a powerful motivation, then? For a man, I mean."

"In Lord Tannenbrook's case, it is as clear as glass. Tread carefully, Viola. Refrain from flirtation with other men whilst in Tannenbrook's presence. You have a charming way about you. I know it will be difficult, but try to focus more on your female companions. Penelope. Your aunt. Lady Rutherford. Even Lady Wallingham."

"Mmm. You believe if I pay a good deal of attention to other men that Tannenbrook will feel an increase in his level of jealousy?"

"Yes. And the consequences could prove disastrous. He might very well lose command of himself."

Smiling for the first time since her handkerchief had been tossed at her feet, Viola nodded. "Thank you, Georgina. You have been most helpful."

Chapter Ten

"At times such as these, a woman must be thankful for men's susceptibility to lustful impulses. It makes certain intractable tasks infinitely easier."

—THE DOWAGER MARCHIONESS OF WALLINGHAM to Lady Atherbourne upon reading said lady's report of Lord Atherbourne's precipitous return to Derbyshire after a mere fortnight in London.

<hr/>

IT HAD NOT APPEARED TO BOTHER TANNENBROOK WHEN Viola danced a reel with Sir Barnabus Malby whilst the pudgy, bulge-eyed baronet eyed her bodice with the same slavish rigor as Humphrey eyeing a slice of ham. Nor was Tannenbrook perturbed when she permitted Lord Underwood's brother to correct her posture whilst she drew her bow during an afternoon of archery, even though the man's hands had wandered and stroked more than was strictly necessary. For that matter, the thoroughly exasperating Earl of Tannenbrook had not batted an eye when the least objectionable of the fawning gentlemen—Lord Gattingford's son, Lord Hugh—had recited a poem describing her lips as "petals blushing with dew, crying for my kiss." Even Papa had objected to that, quietly telling Lord Hugh to keep his dewy petals to himself.

In fact, in the fortnight since she had decided to pursue Tannenbrook by pursuing other men, she had made little progress. Mostly, he avoided her—and gatherings where he might encounter her. To the best of her knowledge, he spent much of his time riding and fishing. He attended some meals, of course, and made occasional appearances at the back of a room filled with guests. But she suspected Lady Wallingham had forced his hand in those instances.

And now, this evening, she had arrived at her final chance. Lady Wallingham had elected to throw a masquerade ball to celebrate the end of the house party. Standing on the dais at one end of the grand ballroom beneath a giant portrait of one of the Henry Tudors, Viola sighed and squeezed Charlotte's arm.

"Do you see him yet?" she asked, uncaring that her desperation was showing.

Gowned in magnificent sapphire blue and wearing a black domino to frame her green-and-gold eyes, Charlotte glanced down at Viola and smiled. "He will be here. I suspect Lady Wallingham would take great offense if he weren't."

In the crowd, Lord Wallingham and Lord Rutherford—both dashing in black masks to match their dark coats—stood chatting near a potted topiary. Lord Hugh and Sir Barnabus laughed uproariously at something the redheaded Lord Mochrie said, while Penelope honked her appreciation. Lady Wallingham wore a purple plumed turban and a similarly feathered purple mask. The plumes bobbed as she drifted from Lord and Lady Gattingford to an animated pair of matrons.

Dash it all, still no Tannenbrook.

"You look lovely, by the by," Charlotte said. "But, then, I suspect you know that."

Viola sighed, glancing down at her pink silk gown. It was one of Mrs. Bowman's more intricate creations, with layers of color—pale, blushing pink to deep red, all overlain with sheer white. Rouleaux of pink ribbon mimicked vines, which, along with silver embroidery, coalesced into a profusion of rosebuds and leaves along the low, square bodice and dainty sleeves. The addition of artfully placed spangles gave the exquisite gown the look of a dew-misted garden in the rosy glow of dawn.

"How well I look will not matter a whit if he is not here, Charlotte." She hated that she sounded out of sorts, but she had one of the worst headaches she'd experienced in months. Even the candlelit room seemed overbright, and the musicians, though talented, played too loudly. Fortunately, she'd been able to disguise the circles beneath her eyes with a rose-hued mask she had purchased in Alnwick several days earlier. It, too, had spangles. Perhaps the glitter of their reflected light would distract Tannenbrook from the unattractive glaze in her eyes.

Charlotte lowered her head near Viola's ear. "Take heart, Vi. If all else fails, I shall implore Rutherford to apply his cleverness to the problem. He is most adept at"—she waggled her eyebrows—"machinations. Tannenbrook will never see it coming."

Viola attempted a chuckle, but it only made her head hurt. She sighed. "Thank you, but I suspect you have better uses for your husband's 'machinations' than to preoccupy him with my problems."

"Well, he is *supremely* talented." Charlotte nudged Viola's arm. "Are you certain you feel well enough to be here, Vi? You are dreadfully pale."

No. She did not feel well at all. But she must be here. It was her last chance. Tomorrow, the house party would end. And she would either be engaged to Tannenbrook, or ...

Her gaze drifted to Lord Hugh. The man of the dewy petals. He was a decent sort of fellow, she supposed. Light-blond hair, blue eyes. A rather weak jaw, but then, they all had weak jaws compared to Tannenbrook. He appeared more sincere, less lecherous than the rest. Perhaps being his wife would not be too ghastly.

All she had to do was let Lord Hugh put his tongue in her mouth. Let him touch her and lay atop her in their bed. Let him put other parts of himself in her ... oh, dear.

"Charlotte."

"Yes?"

"I think I'm going to vomit."

"Oh, dear."

Viola turned to look up into Charlotte's alarmed, black-framed eyes. "My thoughts precisely."

By the time Viola returned to the ballroom after casting up her accounts and rinsing her mouth with a solution of rosewater, Tannenbrook was standing with his back against a golden wall near the glass doors. His arms were crossed over his chest. His beautiful green eyes were framed by a brown leather mask. Having part of his face disguised only served to emphasize the solid square of his jaw.

She sighed upon seeing those broad shoulders, his dark-blond hair thick and lush in the flickering light. Sighed again upon spotting Lord Hugh and the rest of her fawning admirers milling around the center of the room where others danced.

Though her head pounded and her heart ached, she resigned herself to her task, approaching the throng of gentlemen with a brilliant, contrived smile. They greeted her with their customary fawning.

Not one of them had a voice deep enough. Not one of them could name a fish that traveled from seawater to freshwater during winter. Not one of them made her want to drag him out to the garden so she could explore his mouth again.

But because she must, she laughed at their jests. Danced

with two of them. Bantered wittily with the others.

And all the while, she felt his eyes upon her. Burning.

Struggling to appear carefree, she let her gaze drift lightly in his direction. Charlotte was there, standing beside him. She was saying something. Something he clearly did not wish to hear. Moments later, he thrust away from the wall and stalked through the open glass doors, disappearing into the garden.

She wanted to stomp her slippered feet. What had Charlotte said to make him leave? Dash it all, she *needed* him here.

Instantly, Viola's headache worsened, digging at the back of her eyes, pounding and stabbing inside her temples. The odor wafting from the portly Sir Barnabus Malby was threatening to make her vomit again.

She stood on her toes to see Charlotte's bright-red head following Tannenbrook through the doors. Viola waited, hoping he might return, but he did not. Neither, for that matter, did Charlotte. She swallowed hard, her stomach churning.

Quickly making her excuses to Lord Hugh and Sir Barnabus, she started for the garden. But halfway there, she felt her stomach twist ominously, forcing her to change direction, heading up onto the dais and out of the ballroom. The last thing she needed was to vomit upon Tannenbrook's enormous Hessians.

Dashing along the windowed gallery at one end of the castle, she paused in the cooler, darker space outside the grand hall's arches. Here, there were no people to emit offensive odors. No music to ring inside her aching head. Just a bit of moonlight casting pretty shadows on the paneled walls and polished limestone. She tore her mask away and closed her eyes, taking deep breaths, bracing a hand and then a hip against one of the windowsills. With her free hand, she rubbed at her forehead, wanting to gouge out the pain.

As quiet closed in, and all she could hear was her own breath, the reality of where she stood loomed like a great shadow.

He will not come 'round, she admitted silently. The truth rang cold and empty like an icy fissure. *I have lost him. Forever.*

Her fingers dropped from her forehead to her mouth, covering a strangled sob.

She must accept Lord Hugh. She must marry a man she did not love. Bear that man's children. Be that man's wife.

Her head shook. Her arms trembled.

She did not want this. She wanted James. So much that, had he demanded she fall to her knees and beg before the entire ballroom full of Lady Wallingham's guests, she would do it happily.

A warm, damp breeze caressed her shoulders. A door clicked closed. A massive shadow moved across her feet.

She spun so swiftly, her vision swam. When it steadied, she saw him. Big and solid, eyes gleaming, nose flaring, his only mask the darkness.

"James," she breathed.

He said nothing. Not her name, not good evening. Simply stared at her, his chest laboring as though he'd run to catch her.

"James," she said again. This time, it was a moan. She staggered toward him, all pride gone.

Great, muscled arms caught her against him. A giant hand cupped the back of her head, pressed her cheek over his heart. Her own arms clutched at his waist, her fingers clawing at his wool-covered back.

She did not know how long they stood that way, holding each other in shadows and moonlight, breathing and aching together. She only knew she wanted to absorb him into her bones. To feel his lips upon her skin. To hear his voice rumble her name and his heart pounding like stones cascading over a fall.

Distantly, she heard other, more bothersome sounds intruding. Voices. Coming nearer through the darkness. But she was in James's arms, and she did not want leave their safety—not ever again.

I do not want to leave him. I cannot bear it.

She swallowed, an idea snaking its way into her thoughts. A devious, appallingly immoral idea born of desperation. She would be taking away his choices, turning her Tannenbrook Hunt into a scurrilous trap. It was bound to make him furious. But it would also make him hers.

And in that moment, nothing mattered except this—she must make him hers.

～∞～

HE HAD SEEN HER THROUGH THE GLASS, WHITE AND distressed, her hand moving from her forehead to her mouth, her shoulders hunched as though braced against agony.

And he had not been strong enough. His will, tested by the hottest fires imaginable over the past two weeks, finally had broken beneath her delicate shudder of pain.

She had spoken his name twice. Stumbled into his arms. And now, even though he could hear voices behind him at the other end of the dark gallery, even though he knew bloody well he should release her before they were discovered, he could not move.

The voices drew closer, one of them distinct and recognizable. Lady Wallingham.

Bloody hell. He could not be caught here with Viola clutched against him in the dark. It would be a scandal. Lady Wallingham would make certain of it, for she had done nothing but harangue James for the duration of the house party. When would he come to his senses, she had asked. Miss Darling was the best match he could hope for, better than he deserved, she had insisted. Why was he so blasted dense? Couldn't he see what was evident to everyone, she demanded.

He'd silently agreed with much of it, borne all of it. Borne the torment of watching Viola flirt and laugh and be touched and courted by other men until he'd felt like his flesh was being boiled from his bones. All to protect her. Because Lady Wallingham was right—Viola was better than he deserved. A bright, dazzling fairy sprite who carried light with her into every room she entered.

Slowly, he began to withdraw, moving his hands to Viola's tiny, silken shoulders. He pushed gently, but she would not let go. Her arms banded his waist like a belt. Her dainty hands grasped the tails of his coat and held fast.

"Viola," he whispered. "You must release me. We cannot be discovered here, lass. You will be ruined."

Her head tilted up until he could see her eyes. They shimmered with some strange emotion. Determination mixed with ... remorse? He frowned. Blinked. Realized what she intended an instant before her whispered apology, but too late to prevent her right hand from rising up and around his chest, knotting surprisingly strong fingers around the folds of his cravat, and yanking his head down with all her might.

Then, her soft, luscious mouth was smashed against his, and his senses exploded in a shower of stars. Her left arm looped around his neck. He reared up, but she had such a tight grip, he only succeeded in lifting her twelve inches off the floor. Now, she dangled there, draped upon him like a cat clinging to a tree, mouth plastered over his, arms strangling his neck, hands clutching his hair.

He wrapped her waist with his arm to steady her against him and rapidly considered his options. He could tear her loose, force her away from him, but not without bruising her. Deciding the only recourse was to carry her out of view until she came to her bloody senses, he rolled them both against the paneling until he felt the casement for one of the arched entrances to the grand hall. Without a second to spare, he slipped through the opening and flattened her back against the darker wall.

"... refrain from scolding me about Humphrey's instruction. I should think having kept *you* alive for forty years qualifies me as sufficiently competent to manage a hound." Lady Wallingham's distinctive, trumpeting voice echoed off wood and glass along the gallery.

Viola stiffened against him, her lips freezing as she heard it, too. Suddenly, she yanked her mouth away. Drew a breath. And let out a long, sensual moan.

Bloody hell. He slammed his mouth back upon hers.

She moaned louder, the sound vibrating through his lips and chin.

Everlasting, bloody hell. The chit was mad. He broke the kiss. Another mistake.

"Oh, Tannenbrook," she groaned, her voice ringing sweetly and—most of all—loudly to the twenty-foot ceiling above. "Should your hand really be touching me *there?*"

That was it. He was going to throttle her.

Within moments, Lady Wallingham's purple plume had rounded the corner of the third arch, followed by the taller figure of her son. "I say, Lord Tannenbrook," the dowager intoned. "For a man who professes to loathe the very notion of matrimony, one supposes you would opt for trysts of the less *public* variety."

"Oh! Lady Wallingham! And Lord Wallingham!" Viola chirped, now squirming to be released from his grip.

His muscles tightened reflexively. He had no intention of letting her go.

"How embarrassing to be discovered so unexpectedly." Viola dug her fingertips into the nape of his neck. "So *scandalously.*"

James lowered his head until his mouth brushed her ear and murmured, "You will pay for this, lass."

Charles stepped forward into a shaft of moonlight and spoke in his customary quiet, dignified manner. "Miss Darling, rest assured my mother and I shall do our utmost to prevent this ... indiscretion from leading to a scandal—"

Viola's sharp "no!" overlapped with Lady Wallingham's "we most certainly will not!"

Meeting James's gaze with sympathy, Charles nodded to where Viola still dangled between his body and the wall. "Perhaps you should set the lady down, Tannenbrook."

Reluctantly, James complied, turning them both to face Wallingham. He kept one hand upon her, however, spanning the side of her waist and the small of her back with his fingers. "I shall take her to Coldstream tomorrow morning," he muttered, his jaw tight, his gut tighter. "We will marry in Scotland and return here to say our farewells before departing for Derbyshire."

"A capital plan, I daresay," opined Lady Wallingham. "And about time. Now, would you care to explain this abrupt change of sentiments to Miss Darling's father, or shall I have the pleasure?"

"Mother," Charles muttered. "Give the man a moment."

"I don't know why I should. I have given him months to see reason. Ample time *and* opportunity, in my estimation."

Charles sighed. "Tannenbrook, are you certain about this? There are a number of gentlemen in the ballroom who will happily accept Miss Darling as their bride, scandal or no. I happen to know Lord Hugh—"

"Should I not have a say in whom I marry, Lord Wallingham?" Viola said indignantly, her back stiffening against his hand.

"Indeed you should," replied the dowager with a sniff. "Really, Charles. True love suffers no replacements."

"Weren't you the one who said true love is a fanciful tale designed to comfort children and simpletons?"

"Must you always take me literally, boy? One would suppose you have no capacity for nuance."

James scarcely heard a word of their bickering. He only heard blood pounding in his ears, the clamor of his life being forcibly altered. Restructured to suit Viola Darling and her relentless, unceasing will.

He had underestimated her. After everything she had done in an effort to persuade him, he had not imagined she would stoop to laying such a trap. Flirting, yes. Tempting, most certainly. Demanding, even. But not this.

He supposed he could take Wallingham's suggestion. Let her go to Lord Hugh.

Never. The answer was immediate. And it came from the blackest part of his soul. The one that had longed to crush Lord Hugh's throat for daring to speak about Viola's lips. *She made this choice,* the voice crowed. *Now she must pay the consequences. She is mine, and no other will ever touch her.*

"Viola and I shall be wed tomorrow," he barked, interrupting Lady Wallingham's castigation of all sons who failed to heed the wisdom of their mothers. "I will speak with Mr. Darling this evening. Wallingham, I would appreciate the use of your library."

"Of course," the marquess replied.

Tentatively, Viola cleared her throat.

James continued, "Lady Wallingham, as your manipulations have at last achieved your desired result, I trust you will write my relation in America with all due haste."

The woman sniffed. "I shall take your request under advisement."

He lowered both his head and his voice. "No. You will comply."

"Bah! Very well. I suppose you have met the terms of our bargain sufficiently. I shall post the letter."

"Er, Tannenbrook," said Viola weakly, tugging at his coat.

"What is it?" he snapped.

"I—I don't feel well at all." She slumped against him, her hand coming up to cover her mouth.

The deep, thrumming fury he felt toward her receded long enough for alarm to take him in its grip. Without another thought, he bent and hoisted her in his arms. She weighed nothing. He looked at her face for the first time since declaring he would marry her. She was grayish white, her lips pale, her eyes glazed with pain.

"Your head?" he murmured, cradling her close.

She nodded and closed her eyes, clasping his neck with her arms. "I fear I might vomit upon you."

He sighed. "It would not be your worst sin of the evening." He looked to Charles. "I will take her upstairs to her chamber. Fetch her maid. And her cousin, Penelope."

"No," Viola whispered, her head tucked against his neck. "Georgina. Mrs. Cumberland. Please."

James nodded to Charles. "Inform her father I shall meet him in the library in twenty minutes."

"Twenty?" snorted Lady Wallingham. "You disappoint me greatly, Tannenbrook. I always regarded you as the burly, robust sort. Stamina is a virtue, you know."

Charles coughed and cupped the dowager's elbow. "Mother, we should return to the ballroom. Your guests will wonder where you've gone."

James did not wait to hear the old woman's retort. He carried Viola out to the moonlit gallery, up the grand staircase, and, following her directions to her bedchamber, laid her gently upon her blue-canopied bed. Her arms fell from his neck, limp and listless. Her eyes drifted shut. The only light in the room was the soft glow of the moon through the window. It painted her exquisite features silvery blue.

With his thumb, he stroked one of her silky brows. "Do you have laudanum?"

"No," she murmured. "It worsens the nausea and doesn't relieve the pain very much. Sometimes tea helps. But, mostly, I must sleep." Her words were slightly slurred, as though she'd had too much wine.

He swallowed hard against the lump in his chest. Tomorrow, she would become his wife. His responsibility. His to care for and protect. His to touch and kiss and stroke and pleasure.

Mine, that dark voice from earlier repeated, filling his veins with euphoric heat at the thought, quickening his breath. *She is mine.*

He'd resisted for so long, he hadn't prepared for the onslaught. For her to neatly dispense with his self-imposed barriers, tearing apart the only thing standing between her and his need for her. Perhaps he was a fool. Or a primitive brute.

It really should bother him more, exposing the savagery of how he felt about her. The possessiveness. The ferocious triumph.

But it didn't. Not half as much as the thought of some other man taking what belonged to him.

"I am sorry, James," she slurred softly before sliding into slumber.

He leaned down and pressed a kiss to her forehead, breathing in her peony scent. Then, he breathed out words he should not feel, let alone say. But she was asleep, so she would never know. "I am not, lass. In truth, I am not sorry at all."

Chapter Eleven

*"True to form, my strategies have proven a resounding success.
And do you know why, Charles? Because I am right.
I am always right."*

—THE DOWAGER MARCHIONESS OF WALLINGHAM to her son,
Charles, during a debate about the perils of resisting the inevitable.

❦

THUNDER CONCUSSED THE AIR AROUND THE COACH.
Blackening clouds loomed and flashed white. Not a drop of
rain had yet fallen, but as Viola stared out the window of Lady
Wallingham's opulent carriage, a shiver shook her flesh.
Perhaps it was the wind, howling its fury in true
Northumberland fashion.

She glanced to her left where another thunderous presence
resided. After her actions the previous evening, James had
spoken no more than ten words to her. She did not blame him,

of course. Forcing a man of honor into a marriage he had steadfastly opposed was the lowest thing she had ever done.

Sighing, she turned back to watch lightning sizzle and arc along the eastern horizon. The storm had roiled onshore unexpectedly after a clear, humid night. Viola suspected her headache had been caused in part by the anticipated shift in weather, as that was a pattern she had noticed over the years. Fortunately, the pain was little more than a memory this morning.

Despite his obvious—and justifiable—fury with her, James had been all that was gentle and protective, carrying her to her bed, stroking her brow with the softest touch. That capacity for kindness was one of the reasons she loved him so.

Georgina also had been kind, placing a cool, damp cloth on her forehead and helping her undress so she could sleep more comfortably. But then, Viola had come to expect such kindness from her future stepmother. Over the past two weeks, she had sought out the other woman's counsel on a number of occasions. Twice to inquire about strategies for handling men, and seven times to improve her admittedly inferior embroidery techniques. On the latter subject, Georgina had proven an invaluable resource. In fact, once Viola abandoned her pride and confessed how mightily she had struggled to conquer the deficiency, Georgina had responded with warmth and graciousness, sharing her knowledge without a hint of resentment for Viola's prior peevishness.

"You may wish to trace your design with a pencil first," she had advised in their first lesson. "It is surprisingly helpful to know where you are going before you begin." In their second lesson, she had demonstrated the importance of taking one's time. "Follow my motions as you complete your loop. You see? A bit of patience in the moment will save you endless toil later." Her instruction had brought them closer, revealing much about why Papa loved her. Georgina gave without asking anything in return. Viola hadn't known many women like her, and she often wondered if this was what it would have been like to have a mother.

Only that morning, before Viola had climbed into Lady Wallingham's carriage for their journey to Scotland, Georgina had hugged her tightly, whispering, "Are you certain you do not wish us to come along?"

Viola had squeezed those square shoulders in return and given her and Papa a watery smile. "Thank you, dearest Georgina. But I suspect the weather will make the ride less than pleasant. We will return swiftly. And I shall be Lady Tannenbrook." She'd tried to sound cheerful, but her voice had strangled on the last few words.

Georgina had discreetly pressed a handkerchief into her hand. "He is a good man, Viola. Trust him to care for you."

Now, as thunder boomed outside the carriage, and deadly silence reigned within, Viola braced a hand on the brown, tufted leather of the seat and scooted closer to the window, giving him what little distance she could in the small space.

"Don't bother," he rumbled, increasing his number of words to twelve.

She blinked, startled to hear his deep voice after two hours. "Bother to what?"

A dark-green glower turned on her from his great height. Even seated, the man was a giant. "Escape."

"I—I do not wish to escape. I was merely—"

"We are nearly to Coldstream. This trap you've sprung is as permanent for you as it is for me. You'd best swallow down the truth now, for I'll not have you balking and making a scene."

She frowned, thoroughly confused. "Me? I have no intention—"

Suddenly, his face was inches from hers. "If you run, lass, I will catch you. Do you ken?"

Lightning cracked deafeningly close. The carriage jerked as

the horses spooked. Outside, she could hear the wind and the shouts of the coachman. Her head swiveled to see a new copse of trees writhing in protest.

"Viola."

"Hmm?" Through the window, she scanned the eerily dark, rolling landscape, her nerves churning.

"I would advise removing your hand."

Her head jerked around. She had gripped his thick leg firmly a few inches above his knee. "Oh! I am sorry," she said, giving his rock-hard thigh a little pat of apology.

He deposited her hand back in her own lap. "Not yet," he rasped. "Soon, though."

She wasn't certain what he meant, and he did not appear amenable to explaining, so she sniffed and turned again to watch as they rounded a bend in the road. Within minutes, the River Tweed came into view, its waters restless and murky beneath ominous skies.

"The tollhouse is on the north end of the bridge."

Her stomach rolled. "We ..." She swallowed. "We are there, then. Here, I mean."

"Aye."

The carriage started over the bridge, its low, tan stone walls rolling past her window at a rather alarming pace. It seemed only a blink before they were pulling up outside a cottage made of the same sand-colored stone, tucked merrily on the Scottish side of the Tweed where the bridge ended and the road veered left toward the village of Coldstream.

The carriage rocked to a halt. Her heart pounded strangely.

James's massive arm reached across her and pushed open her door. The wind whipped at it, pulling it wide with a clack. "We should go inside now."

She nodded, the motion jerky.

Outside, Lady Wallingham's footman squinted at her, holding his old-fashioned hat on his head with one hand and offering her the other. "Miss?" he inquired.

She accepted his help climbing down from the carriage. Before she could catch her breath, however, James was there, rounding the back of the coach and snatching her hand from the footman's grasp.

"Come," he growled, tugging her forward. Perhaps it was the weather, but his mood had gone from surly to positively foul.

"Tannenbrook," she protested, feeling like she was being pulled by Humphrey again.

His hand pressed the small of her back, pushing her faster toward the door of the toll house. He yanked the door open and ushered her inside. Several windows permitted the meager daylight to brighten the dark wood interior. Otherwise, the small room on the left side of the cottage was lit only with a single lamp. That light rested beside a cross placed upon the mantel of a large stone fireplace. At the rear of the room, a white-whiskered gentleman in a blue coat and blindingly white waistcoat rose from his desk and approached them with a smile. "Ah, I see we have a fine young pair wi' marriage on their minds. Ye've come tae the right place."

After looking long at James's dark-green coat and finely crafted boots, he introduced himself as Mr. MacAfee, a tailor and "parson" based in Coldstream who performed weddings for "a wee, middlin' fee. No' worth mentionin'."

"How much?" James demanded.

Again, that assessing glance at James's garments. "Three guineas."

Viola's eyes flared at the price. The place was aptly named a toll house, though according to Lady Wallingham, it had not served in that capacity for some years. But James did not protest, merely withdrawing the coins from a small leather pouch and dropping them in the whiskered man's palm with a tinkling clink.

The man's eyes gleamed then narrowed on Viola. "Now, then, many a bride's special day has been brightened wi' the addition of a few bonnie flowers, and fer a wee bit more—"

James encircled Viola's waist with his arm, using his height to loom over the much shorter man. "We wish to be married, Mr. MacAfee. Nothing else."

MacAfee swallowed nervously as his eyes bounced between James's intimidating height and Viola's face. "Aye. Well, then. Let us be aboot our business."

Their "business" was completed in a matter of minutes. First, MacAfee recorded their names and home parishes in his register. Then, he called two women into the room from the other end of the cottage—his wife and daughter, as it happened—to act as witnesses. Lastly, he waved them over to the fireplace where the gold cross rested upon the wood mantel next to the lit lamp. Viola noted the gold paint had begun to peel and crack, exposing the wood beneath.

And that was where James spoke his vows to her, promising to have her and hold her for better and worse, in sickness and health, until death. Then, he declared her his wife.

"Now, then fer the wee bonnie lass. Miss Violet Denton, repeat after me, if ye please."

"Viola Darling," she murmured absently, unable to tear her gaze away from James. His eyes shone with a strange, fierce light.

"Oh, yes, indeed. Right ye are, Miss Denton."

"Darling," James snapped.

"Now, dinna be tae hard on yer bonnie lass, m'lord. It's no' unusual fer a bride tae be a wee bit nervous."

James lowered his voice to a menacing rumble. "Her last name is Darling, not Denton."

Finally, MacAfee appeared to understand, leading her in speaking the vows in his funny Scottish brogue. And she repeated the words that bound her to James Kilbrenner, promising to be his forever, declaring him to be her husband before three perfect strangers.

It was the plainest of ceremonies, performed by an

avaricious tailor before a gold-painted cross in a dim cottage on the banks of the Tweed. Her papa was not present to give her away. Neither Penelope nor Charlotte attended as her maids. Aunt Marian and Uncle Edward did not sit in her parish church's pew, witnessing the blessing of the Reverend Mr. Insley as she promised her life to the man she adored. She was not even in England, for the love of heaven.

You have brought this upon yourself, she thought, fighting the sting of tears by pressing her lips together and wandering to the window to stare out at the storm as James signed the tailor's register. *You cannot now cry foul because your nuptials more closely resemble a transaction at one of Charlotte's pawn shops than a wedding.*

A single, fat drop smeared its way down the glass. It was soon joined by dozens more. She glanced up toward the clouds, which looked to be releasing their deluge all at once, and all upon this one small spot on the border of Scotland.

Absently, she twisted her mother's simple gold ring with its one lone sapphire around and around on her finger. The cool band was the only outward sign that anything had changed. She still wore the same silver pelisse and pink gown she'd worn when she'd been Miss Darling. Yet, now, she was Viola Kilbrenner, Countess of Tannenbrook. Just like that.

A great shadow loomed behind her, blocking the reflection of the lamplight in the glass. "We must go, Viola." His rumble sent sweet, heated shivers along her neck and scalp.

"Back to Grimsgate?"

"No. The roads will be a stew before we're halfway there. That's if the horses don't bolt."

"Coldstream, then. Is there an inn?"

"Aye, but MacAfee says it is full. The village is hosting a fair or some such."

She turned to face him. He was so close, she found herself speaking to his cravat. "Then, where shall we go?"

His jaw flexed while his eyes gazed out at the rain, now

blowing in swirling sheets. "A village about ten miles north. I know of an inn there."

"What if they, too, haven't any room?"

"We will find shelter there, you may be certain."

"How do you know?"

Without looking at her, he heaved a sigh and ran a hand through his hair. "Because it is where I was born."

∽∾

THE COACH ROCKED ON ANOTHER GUST OF WIND. SHE DID not envy the coachman and footman their task of driving in the storm, but she was thankful to be safe and dry.

And married. Mustn't forget that.

She cast a sidelong glance at her husband—he of the granite jaw and precipitous brow.

Husband. How extraordinary.

Despite the inglorious circumstances of their wedding, Viola was beginning to feel the satisfaction—the warm, glistening, secretive pleasure—of concluding her Tannenbrook Hunt victoriously. At long last, the big, surly brute was hers.

Of course, there appeared to be much she did not know about her new husband.

Her teeth worried at her lip, and she twisted her mother's ring about her finger.

For example, she'd never asked where James had spent his childhood. That was largely because she could scarcely elicit a response to questions such as "how do you find Northumberland?" and "why do you never dance?" Discovering answers which required more than a single sentence, or which invited further inquiry, had been akin to unknotting a disastrous tangle from her embroidery. In short, it required patience she did not possess.

However, as she was currently headed to her new husband's birthplace, perhaps it was time to delve further into his past.

She cleared her throat. "So, you are a Scot."

His deep hum must have been meant as assent.

"Why did you never say?"

"My name is Kilbrenner. Was this not a clue?"

She sniffed. "Your title is English. Your seat is in Derbyshire. Besides which, you do not *sound* Scottish."

He shot her a skeptical glance.

"Very well, the frequent use of 'aye' and 'lass' might have given some indication."

One corner of his mouth quirked. "Aye, lass. That it might."

Oh, dear. He'd rumbled those words with a rolling, delicious brogue that played down her spine like a harpist plucking a perfect chord. Combined with the gleam of teasing humor in his eyes, it rendered her weak and warm. Why this should be so, when Lord Mochrie's brogue merely sounded distorted and, at times, annoyingly incomprehensible to her ears, she could not say. But this was James. From the beginning, he had been the exception to every rule.

She finally caught her breath. "I assume others know of your background."

"A few."

"Why did you never tell me?"

Those massive shoulders shrugged. "No reason to discuss it."

"Because you sought to rid yourself of me."

He didn't answer, merely turning his head to the squalling storm.

But she was not finished. "Well, I should like to know more about you."

"Why?"

"You are my husband."

Again, no answer. And his gaze remained fixed on the drenching rain.

She frowned. "James."

Those shoulders rolled.

"Look at me."

His head shook. "You are bloody well the most persistent female I have ever encountered, do you know that?"

"Yes, well. It has served me admirably."

He snorted in disbelief, but his eyes did return to her. At least now she could see his expression, even if it was one of perplexed annoyance. "You engineered your own ruination, for the love of God. Not more than an hour ago, you stood in a toll house to hand yourself over to me, a man of whom you know so little, his origins came as a stunning revelation."

"Not stunning, precisely. And I know you quite well in all the ways that matter. You are the finest of men. Why do you suppose I pursued you with such vigor?"

"Because you are daft and maddeningly stubborn?"

She stifled a laugh. He was still outraged, after all these months, at her determination to have him as her own. One would think he would accustom himself to the notion of a woman doing whatever was necessary to secure her heart's desire. "Stubborn, perhaps." She let a grin play about her lips, noting how his eyes followed and lingered there. "Have I ever told you about my Inkling?"

His frown deepened. But he did not look away from her mouth.

Her tongue moistened her lips automatically.

He swallowed. "No."

"The Inkling is simple, really. It is a feeling of ... rightness." She splayed her hand over her belly, just below her ribs. "Here. I feel it here. Whenever I see something I must have. It has never led me astray. I felt it with you. More powerfully than ever before."

His hands fisted where they rested beside his thighs.

"I just *knew*, James. I knew you belonged to me. And that I belonged to you. From the first moment I saw your splendid face."

"My face is not splendid."

"It is to me."

"You have deceived yourself, lass. Fallen prey to the desire for something beyond your reach. You know nothing of the man I truly am."

"I know this is right." Her hand settled over his fist, stroking his knuckles with her thumb. "I am sorry for what I did, but I saw no other way. You refused to see reason."

With a jerk, he withdrew his hand. "I refused to bend to your will. And you answered by denying me a choice that was rightfully mine." As though snow had fallen upon a mountain, ice glinted in his eyes, stiffened his muscles visibly.

She nodded and dropped her gaze to her hand, lying open and alone upon the tufted seat.

"Shall I tell you of the man you married, Viola?" His voice was a lash, sharp and cold. "I am a blacksmith's son from a tiny village in Scotland. Before an accident of birth granted me a bloody English title from an ancestor long dead, I was a stonemason. Not a lord. Not a landowner. Not even a merchant." He took her chin between his thumb and fingers, forcing her eyes up to his. "Take a guid luik at yer husband, my wee bonnie lass. Fer this be the man ye will lie doon wi' a' the days of yer life."

She blinked up at him, enchanted from scalp to slippers. "Oh." Her voice was a panting moan. "Say it again, James. Slowly this time, if you please."

Abruptly, his fingers left her. "Bloody hell, lass."

"No, no. The other part."

"You are completely mad. Do you realize what sort of man I am?"

She longed for him to touch her again, but he obviously did not possess similar fervor. He was too focused on giving her a disgust of him. For what reason, she could not fathom. Gathering her wits about her and stifling the near-painful heat that had invaded her midsection, she squeezed her thighs together and resettled herself against the cushioned seat. "I suspect you are about to tell me."

He ignored her response, lifting one massive hand for her inspection. His fingers were long and thick, the bones and knuckles large and visibly powerful. "These hands should not be permitted to touch your sleeve, much less your skin. Had I no title, and you entered a room where I happened to be laboring over a bit of stone, you would pay me no more mind than you might Lady Wallingham's footman. Justly so."

"Don't be a silly goose. You *are* the Earl of Tannenbrook. Whether you feel deserving of your title or not is immaterial. The man I love is James Kilbrenner. Stonemason or lord. Englishman or Scot." She tugged at his lapel. "Fine tailoring or no."

"You cannot love me, because you know nothing of me."

She clicked her tongue and released a sigh. "Why is it so difficult to accept that I admire you? Most men would be glad of such ardent affection, I daresay."

He stiffened. Withdrew. The snow returned to the mountain in a sudden blast. "You did not marry most men. You married me. Do not ever forget it, Viola."

"Well, as that is most unlikely to occur, I can safely give you my solemn promise: I shall not forget that I married you."

He continued as though she hadn't spoken. "Once we reach Netherdunnie, you will see."

She tilted her head and raised her brows, smiling as though he'd issued an invitation. "Lovely. I look forward to seeing your home."

His expression darkened. He turned to the window. Propped his chin on his fist. "You will see," he repeated, his words low and quiet. "Very soon, you will understand how deeply you have erred, lass. And no amount of regret will save you."

Chapter Twelve

"Mortifying? Bah! I only mentioned that you named your favorite blanket Billy. Is it my fault Lady Willoughby assumed I was referencing a recent appellation rather than a childhood one?"

—THE DOWAGER MARCHIONESS OF WALLINGHAM to her son, Charles, in regard to a recent conversation with a certain widow.

❦

"ONLY LUIK AT THEM!" THE SMALL PAIR OF BOY'S BREECHES dangled merrily from his sister's fingers. "Sae tiny. Can ye imagine Jamie—big, strong Jamie—fitting intae this wee little garment?"

"Oh, a handsome lad, he was," his mam interjected fondly, heaping humiliation upon mortification.

Viola laughed in delight and fluttered her fingers toward the buff breeches. "May I?" she asked politely.

"Certainly," Nellie cried, handing her the small scrap and picking another out of the trunk his aggravating sister had insisted on bringing with her. How else to mortify her brother sufficiently if not by combing through his boyhood possessions, displaying them with great fanfare for his new wife?

Upon entering the village, Viola had not reacted as he'd expected. Not at all. Those twilight eyes had devoured the poor, brown-and-gray cottages of Netherdunnie as though fascinated by hovels and mud.

And when they'd arrived at Mam's cottage with its freshly painted door and familiar garden of delphiniums, he'd been momentarily unable to speak for the wave of longing and remembrance. Viola had hugged his elbow and patted his arm with dainty, soothing motions. Eventually, he'd recovered enough to knock on the door. Mam had cried his name and wrapped him in a hug. He'd managed to introduce Viola as his wife, but otherwise struggled to speak, his emotions choking him. Instead, it had been Viola who had greeted his mother with a smile of such warmth and sincerity, he'd only been able to stare.

"Mrs. Kilbrenner, it is the greatest honor of my life to meet the woman who brought James into this world," Viola had said. "He is the finest of men, and you are to be credited for his superlative character."

His mother had embraced her tightly, wept a bit about the joy of having a "new daughter," and sent her maid out to fetch Nellie. Since then, the feminine conspiracy to embarrass him had only grown more expansive. The three women had gathered around to sip tea and giggle and trade stories as though they'd been doing it for decades. Now, he stood with his shoulders propped against the wall in his mother's parlor, arms crossed over his chest, wondering whether to protest their antics. Likely it would only make matters worse.

"Mrs. Abernathy, is that a pair of James's shoes?"

"Aye, indeed. Dae call me Nellie, dear," Nellie said. "We are sisters now, are we no'?"

Viola's gaze melted into a gloss of gooey, feminine sentiment. "I have always wanted a sister."

Nellie nodded emphatically, grinning wide. "Weel, now ye have one. And a mam, too."

Mam spoke up, as well. "And ye maun think of me as such, dear. Ye may call me Mam, as Nellie's guidman Patrick does. Or, if it be more tae yer likin', call me Bess."

He worried for a moment that his wife would descend into a bout of weeping. Fortunately, she was made of sterner stuff. Sniffing, Viola nodded and thanked them, then gathered herself while sipping her tea. "I find it hard to imagine James as a small boy. Did he love fishing, even then?"

He sighed and rolled his eyes as his mother and sister gabbled on about him while his wife cooed and gasped and laughed. This was excruciating. He'd half a mind to join the footman and coachman out in the stables.

"How stunning it must have been when you learned of his title," Viola was now saying, her eyes wide, her mother's ring flashing blue and gold in the gray light from the windows.

He'd been handed the ring by her father the previous night and told to "remember she is a precious daughter, as well as your wife, Tannenbrook. Care for her accordingly." James had accepted Walter Darling's challenge and tucked Viola's ring into his waistcoat pocket, promising to protect her with his life. The vow had appeared to set Mr. Darling's mind at ease, as the shorter, balder man had nodded, sniffed, and shaken James's outstretched hand.

"We were fair conflummixt, nae doot aboot it," Nellie answered Viola's query. "But none more sae than Jamie. He had his whole life planned, did ye no', Jamie? Doon tae the last, wee detail. Inheritin' an English title wisna part of it."

Viola's gaze turned to him, curiosity shining. "What were your plans?"

He glowered at his sister, who raised a brow and took a drink of tea as if to say, "This is your punishment for staying away so long, Jamie Kilbrenner. Savor the experience."

Clearing his throat, he searched his mind for an answer that would suffice. "Stonemasonry."

Head tilting, Viola's eyes narrowed upon him suspiciously. "For a detailed plan, I daresay it has striking simplicity."

"I am a simple man."

"Hmmph. Well, perhaps that is what sets you apart from other gentlemen."

Nellie intruded again with her unwanted perspective. "Nae. He's a great, muckle giant. That's the difference."

For some reason, Viola's eyes lowered to his thighs. Then, she blushed, a pretty, rose pink. Then, she hid her face by sipping her tea.

His smile grew. It was about time someone other than he was made to feel out of sorts.

"Ye're stayin' fer supper, Jamie," Mam said.

He opened his mouth to answer, but she held up a calm hand.

"It wisna a request."

Feeling like a chastened boy, he nodded. "Aye, Mam."

Thankfully, Nellie departed a short time later to cook for her own husband and children. She hugged him farewell, whispering in his ear, "Come back sooner next time, Jamie, ye big, dense daftie."

Supper was his mother's lamb cottage pie, as deliciously salty and robust as he remembered. He watched Viola eat with dainty little bites, closing her eyes and marveling aloud that Mam was able to find such a talented cook. Of course, when Mam informed her she had made it herself, Viola pretended surprise then marveled further at his mother's many talents, particularly the ones involving pastry.

He watched his new wife's face, the candlelight playing over her perfection lovingly. The tiny nose. The long, black, fanning lashes. Those delicately curved lips. Then, he let his eyes explore lower. The lush, rounded breasts. The skin above her gown's pink, beribboned scoop.

He sucked in a breath. He wanted so dearly to touch that skin. If he could, he would lay her atop this very table and devour her. Lap her up like cream. Let her pour over him until she screamed his name.

"Jamie!"

Jolting at his mother's sharp, two-syllabled douse of cold water. "Aye, Mam."

"If ye intend tae take rooms at the inn, ye'd best be off while the light yet lingers."

He nodded, swallowing and using his napkin to wipe his mouth. In truth, he was delaying while his body cooled.

For the love of God, man. At your own mother's table.

"Oh, are we not staying here, James?" Viola pleaded. "I was so looking forward to a longer visit with Mam."

He could not tell whether she was sincere or merely flattering his mother again. Her eyes were pleading most prettily. "The cottage does not have enough rooms to house the coachman and footman," he lied. It was bad enough fantasizing about Viola at his mother's table. Making love to her under his mother's roof, with his mother sleeping one wall away, was horrifying to contemplate.

And he *would* make love to Viola. Tonight. There would be no waiting.

"Right ye are, Jamie," said Mam, shooting him a wry, knowing grin as she stood and helped the maid begin clearing the table. "The inn will serve ye weel this night. Come mornin', bring yer bonnie lass here fer a guid breakfast afore ye gae."

Viola followed suit, assisting the maid in carrying the forks and glasses into the kitchen for washing. He watched her leave the room, his eyes lingering on her hips.

To avoid further embarrassing himself, he stood to help, as well, and returned Mam's smile with one of genuine gratitude. "Thank ye."

She nodded, her eyes filled with understanding. He was reminded of the day Hargrave had come for him. Mam had known even then what it meant. For him. For her.

Setting his dishes on the table, he came around to embrace her. "Thank ye," he said again, holding her against him, feeling her thinner, slighter frame. "I am sorry, Mam. Sorry I stayed away."

"Ye're my son, Jamie. And I do miss ye. But I ken ye hae yer reasons."

"I should have returned sooner."

She pulled away, patting his shoulders affectionately and swiping her cheek with her thumb. "Ye mauna fret aboot it. Gae now. Take yer wee bonnie bride tae the inn. She's a delight, Jamie. I'm moost proud of ye."

He dropped his gaze and nodded, unwilling to explain further about how this marriage had not been of his choosing. There was little sense disturbing Mam's obvious happiness. The deed was done. The circumstances of their union mattered not at all.

As he and Viola entered the inn a half-hour later, James thought again about how little any of it mattered—his resistance to the match. Viola's scheming. Lady Wallingham's intervention. Nothing mattered but that they were married. She was his wife. And this night, at Netherdunnie's lone inn, he would make her his in truth.

∽◦◦∾

JAMES HAD BEEN ACTING STRANGELY EVER SINCE THEY'D arrived in Netherdunnie. During the carriage ride from Coldstream, he'd been combative and surly by turns. Then, when she had eagerly commented upon how charming she found his home village, he'd gone silent. Later, at his mother's cottage, when she'd been getting on famously with the warm, welcoming Mrs. Kilbrenner and Mrs. Abernathy—or, Mam and Nellie, as they'd asked to be called—he'd behaved as a sullen youth, standing with his arms crossed and answering in single syllables. One would think him resentful of being discussed in glowing and affectionate terms. But that would be silly. Perhaps it had been something he ate.

As they were shown to their room by the rotund innkeeper, a nervous flutter sprang forth inside her stomach. The inn was humble but clean, the room appointed with a sturdy, wood-framed bedstead half the width of the one she'd slept in at Grimsgate. It was covered with plain, brown woolen blankets. A small dressing table in one corner held a chipped white basin and pitcher and a low-lit oil lamp. Outside the paned window, thunder echoed, but it was gentler and longer than before, as though the storm had reached the end of its strength.

She felt him close behind her. Heard him breathing. The creak of the wooden planks beneath his boots.

A knock at the door made her jump.

She felt him turn to answer, heard him murmuring with the innkeeper about the horses. She wandered further into the room, removing her bonnet. She'd worn the blue one with the white feathers. Smiling, she ran her fingers lightly over the silk. Then, she placed the hat on the bed and began unbuttoning the frog closures of her lightweight, silver silk pelisse. It was the finest one she owned, redolent with tucks and pleats and shimmering white embroidery. And beneath, she had worn her ball dress from the evening before, because it, too, was the finest one she owned. On this day, she had wanted to look beautiful for him.

She shrugged away the pelisse, letting it slide from her shoulders in the low glow of the lamp. She removed her gloves and moved to the dressing table. Poured a bit of water and dampened a cloth. Wiped away some of the day's dust and rain from her face and neck. The light caught on her mother's ring. Now hers.

She examined the thing in the crossfire of flashing lightning and steady, warm lamp. It was one of the few items she had of her mother's. She'd never known the woman. And now, it represented her union with James.

The door clicked closed. Boots creaked across the floor then stopped.

She reached up to begin unpinning her hair. One by one, she laid the pins on the dressing table. One by one, her curls came down.

"Bloody hell," he breathed.

She glanced at him over her shoulder. Eyes of deep green were riveted to the place where her hair met her backside. A valise thudded to the floor at his feet.

Her mouth curled in a helpless grin. "See something you like, my lord?" she teased.

"Bloody hell," he repeated, running a hand through his own hair. The motion stretched the fine, dark-green wool of his coat over his abdomen. Emphasized the sheer magnitude of his shoulders and arms and hands and thighs.

Stole her breath clean away.

She turned, bracing her hands and backside against the edge of the dressing table. For a moment, she simply let herself look at him. James. The square jaw and firm lips and heavy brow. Eyes the color of a forest near dusk. He melted her. Made her ache and go soft. Made the heat rise beneath her skin.

"Do you need help removing your coat, James?" she inquired, her voice a raspy purr.

His chest rose and fell at a rapid pace, his nose flaring with every breath. Then, his jaw flexed. And he began pacing. Back and forth. Across the small room. In two or three strides, he reached one wall, only to pivot and, in another two or three, reached the opposite wall. Then, he repeated the process.

"James?"

He did not answer.

"Well, I shall require your assistance with my gown, at least. We left Grimsgate so quickly, I neglected to bring a maid. Dreadful nuisance, but"—she sighed with false regret—"one bears what one must."

He stopped near the window, looking out at distant flashes and gentling rain. "I know what you're about."

She raised a brow. "Do you?"

"Yes." The word sounded like gravel being ground beneath his boot. "You may cease your seduction, Viola. There is no need for it. I bloody well plan to bed you."

Uncertain what he was nattering on about, she gripped the edge of the wooden table harder and tried to tear her gaze away from his thighs. They were thick and heavily muscled beneath the fabric of his pantaloons. Tucked alongside his left thigh was an additional bulge. This, she presumed, was the male member Georgina had described, although the size was both longer and thicker than had been reported, likely because everything about James was bigger than other men. Most compelling. "Mmm. That is relieving to hear."

"It is just that I must ... determine how best to approach the precise ... mechanics of it all."

Alarmed by his stuttering confession, her eyes shot up to his face. His red-flushed face. "Oh, dear," she murmured, blinking rapidly. "This is rather unusual, is it not?"

He sighed and nodded.

"*Both* of us being untried, I mean," she continued, her teeth nibbling at her lower lip, her hands strangling the poor, cheap dressing table as genuine worry began to set in. "Well, I do know a little. Mrs. Cumberland has been surprisingly helpful in that regard. I suppose if you and I both apply what knowledge we possess, and we do those things which bring us both pleasure, then we cannot go too far wrong, can we?"

"Viola."

"Perhaps we should begin by removing our clothes."

"Viola, I am not—"

"Or, rather, do you think we should start with kissing? I adore kissing. At least, I did the first time you kissed me. Come to think of it, you seemed quite skilled in that area, as I recall."

"I am not untried."

"Yes, I am certain we should commence kissing immediately. Removing our garments will feel much less silly after—"

"Viola!"

Startled away from her rapidly progressing plan of action, her eyes flew to his. "Oh! Yes?"

"I am not a virgin, lass." He appeared to be struggling against mirth, as he was wearing both a frown and a suspiciously firmed mouth.

She swallowed. "You aren't?"

"No."

Now, she was the one reddening. "Well, what else was I to imagine?"

"Perhaps that our relative sizes might prove a challenge."

"I don't know why it should matter."

"Because I have no wish to hurt you."

"You would never hurt me."

"I would never mean to, lass. But these hands"—he held them up—"could bruise you too easily. Not to mention, there are other parts of me that might prove difficult for your wee body to manage."

"Don't be foolish."

"The first time a woman lies with a man, she suffers pain, even without such a ... disparity."

She folded her arms across her bosom, thoroughly annoyed with his obvious hesitation. The man had avoided her grasp long enough. "You shall not evade your husbandly duty with this silly nonsense, James Kilbrenner." She turned her back to him and gathered her hair over one shoulder. "Now, unfasten my gown, if you please. I cannot reach all the buttons."

Several seconds of silence ticked by before she felt his fingers plucking lightly, deftly at the embroidered silk covering the center of her back. The resulting tingles spread all the way around to her breasts, where her nipples tightened and strained against their confinement. She lowered the bodice of her gown and slid the straps of her chemise down her arms, bunching the fabric around her waist.

"Good," she said, her voice breathless. "Now, my corset, if you please."

Again, those fingers he so feared might hurt her tripped like a whisper through the delicate laces of her corset. The thing loosened, causing her bosoms to spill forth. She caught the fabric against her with one arm.

"Much better. Now, shall I assist you with your—oh!" The last word was a moan. She could not help it. His big, strong, capable hands had suddenly shifted, sliding beneath her loosened corset and coming around to cup her breasts. She leaned back into his big body, her neck arching with the spectacular pleasure of it, her skin tingling and sparking with it. Then, it got better. His mouth nibbled at her exposed neck. His hands began moving. Stroking. Pleasing her nipples with sweet little circles of his palms. The heat of his breath mingled with the rasp of his jaw against her skin. "James," she pleaded. "Oh, that is really just lovely."

His tongue played over a spot between her shoulder and neck. As he lifted his head, the spot cooled deliciously. "We're only beginning, lass." His fingers squeezed her nipples with a firm pressure that made her gasp and sent her hips writhing back against him. "Perhaps now you'd like to help me with my coat."

Chapter Thirteen

*"A man's most arresting talents may not be obvious,
but a discerning woman seeks them diligently.
And a clever one puts them to proper use."*

—THE DOWAGER MARCHIONESS OF WALLINGHAM to Lady
Rutherford upon said lady's remarkable description of
Lord Rutherford's newly acquired skills.

LYING NAKED ON THE BED AND RAPIDLY DEVELOPING A CHILL,
Viola propped herself up on her elbows and loudly sighed her
impatience. "What in blazes are you searching for?"

James, now garbed in only his white linen shirt and buff
pantaloons, dug through the contents of his valise. "It was
here. I am certain of it."

"Can this not wait?"

His eyes came up. Lingered over the length of her. Went

hot and molten and hungry. His throat rippled on a swallow. "No. It cannot." Frantically, he returned to his task, dumping fistfuls of items—clothing, what looked to be supplies for shaving his whiskers, a small book—onto the floor. Soon, divine relief came over his face. He closed his eyes briefly as though saying a prayer of thanks.

Curious, she frowned at the small, flat wooden box in his hand. "What is it?"

Without answering, he stood and moved to the dressing table. She heard the rustle of paper and a bit of splashing. Beginning to feel conspicuous lying there without any covering, she grasped the edge of the wool blanket and drew it over her body. It was rough and scratchy against her skin, but at least she would not catch a chill. She turned onto her side to face her husband, letting her eyes linger over his broad shoulders and muscular buttocks.

Already, warmth was returning to her flesh. Perhaps it was the blanket.

He reached back to grasp a handful of his shirt, just below his neck, and drew the shirt over his head, exposing a gloriously naked, divinely sculpted male back to her avid gaze. Inexplicably, her heart began pounding, seizing at the sight of so many muscles bulging and flexing beneath his skin. Heat took her in its hold, flushing and throbbing and needing.

He turned around to face her. And it grew worse.

"Oh, James," she groaned, biting her lip and sliding her legs against the sheet beneath the blanket. He was beautiful. So big and heavily muscled, she could scarcely take in the sight of him. A fascinating mat of hair covered his upper chest, diminishing in the space between his ribs, becoming a mere dusting around his navel. The hair was darker than that on his head, swirling a bit around flat nipples. "You are ... you are wondrous."

Those massive, wondrous shoulders shrugged. "I am a brute."

She raised her eyes to his.

He glowered fiercely.

She smiled slowly.

He wetted his lips and ran a hand through his hair. "Viola, you must help me."

She sat up in the bed, clutching the blanket, eager to comply. "Anything."

"Ah, God." His head dropped back and he stared at the ceiling, the muscles of his belly tightening and rippling in the most astonishing, sensual fashion. "Ye must ... stop, lass."

"Stop what?"

"Tempting me."

"But, I want you."

"God be merciful," he muttered, dropping his head to stare at his toes.

She clutched the blanket harder and watched as the singular bulge behind the veil of his pantaloons appeared to swell and lengthen, pressing outward against the fabric. "Furthermore," she continued, "I see no reason we should delay any longer."

"There is a bluidy guid reason."

Again, his brogue tripped along her spine as though he'd trailed his fingertips against her skin. She wanted to kiss his wondrous mouth. She wanted to feel his tongue slide along hers. She wanted all his heat and size and strength pressing against her without a single barrier between them.

"Ye're sae beautiful—" He groaned deeply, his chest heaving, his muscles hardening. Long seconds ticked by while he appeared to struggle inside himself. "Even the thought of touching you arouses me, lass. I must have control if I am to avoid causing you unnecessary pain."

"Oh." She nibbled her lip and rubbed the wool between her fingertips. "Does this mean we cannot kiss? I do so love your kisses."

Her heart sank as he turned away again, attending to a mysterious task involving whatever he had pulled from his valise. She dropped her gaze to her fingers, which worried at the brown folds of wool in her lap. She had rather hoped he'd found her kiss as stirring as she'd found his, but it appeared her skills were as lacking in that amorous art as they were in embroidery or music.

"I am a novice in this endeavor, James," she said quietly to the blanket. "I shall strive to do whatever pleases you. But perhaps soon you will permit me to practice kissing a bit, as I should very much like to mmph—"

His mouth capturing hers was a stunning pleasure. Firm lips caressed her own. An encompassing hand cupped the back of her head, holding her still, pressing her forward. She moaned and released the blanket to cradle his precious face between her hands. She stroked his prominent brow with her thumb and opened her mouth for his insistent tongue.

The mattress shook and depressed beside her as he sat on its edge, facing her. His arm snaked around her waist and tugged her into his body, flattening her breasts into a hot, furred chest. He tasted of salt and smelled of pine. She moaned a hum at the myriad sensations.

Then, she was being lifted, her breath leaving in a whoosh, his strength a marvel. The hand that had held her head dropped to her thigh and bent her leg along his hip. She gasped helplessly as something large, hot, and foreign abruptly pressed and slid against her most intimate flesh. Her head spun. Or perhaps it was the room.

No, it was James, turning them together and sitting on the bed with his back to the headboard, his legs sprawled behind her, his hands now positioning her astride his thighs. As though he were a horse and she a brazen rider. Most brazen, indeed.

Moaning again around his hot, slick tongue, she let her hands slide from his cheeks to his jaw, then down to bracket his thick, muscular neck. She did not know what else to do. Everything was too much. There were too many wondrous parts to touch and stroke. Too many sensations begging to be noticed, each one a revolutionary pleasure.

His hands now cupped her cheeks, his fingers long enough to interlace at the back of her head. She was utterly surrounded, caressed and contained inside his strength and heat.

He pulled away from their kiss long enough to whisper, "I could spend eternity kissing you, lass." He kissed her again to prove his point. "If I did not feel such urgency to move on to other things."

"Such as touching?" she asked hopefully, running her fingers down over his collarbone, feeling the crisp hair of his chest on her palms. "I have wanted to touch you for so long."

A slow grin curled his mouth and lit his eyes as his hands moved around to stroke her back and play with her hair. "Have you, now?"

She nodded and smiled. "There is so much of you, I do not know where to begin."

Those green eyes heated into a blaze. His grin faded. "Perhaps next time. I do not know how much more I can bear."

Unable to help herself, she let her fingers roam down to his nipples, wondering at the differences between his chest and her bosom. That was when she caught a glimpse of the hardness that had been prodding and sliding between them as they had kissed. It was longer even than she had suspected, fully erect against his belly. And it was covered in some sort of sheath, secured two inches short of the root with a blue silk ribbon, of all things.

Her eyes shot up to his. "Am I to unwrap it?"

Groaning laughter rumbled deep in his chest, making her blush and smile at once. He drew her in for another kiss. "No. It is called a French letter. Men wear them to prevent a babe."

Confused, she shook her head. "But, we are married now. Surely ..."

His hands slid to her breasts, ensuring all rational thought disappeared. "Let me touch you now, lass." His thumbs circled her nipples, generating small, licking flames of pleasure that burst from the tight centers outward over her skin. "Do you like that?"

Her fingers dug into his shoulders. She bit her lip and nodded, grinding her hips against his thighs.

He plucked and stroked, cradling and plumping her breasts with his palms. "There now. I have ye. I can feel how wet ye are."

She groaned. Closed her eyes. Tried to control her breathing but only succeeded in making herself dizzy. Between her spread thighs, the muscles deep inside seized and pulsed with want. She felt empty. Achy. She needed him.

"James," she panted. "When do you put yourself inside me?"

"When ye're ready."

"Oh, good. I feel quite ready. You may proceed."

"No' yet." Those diabolical hands continued their torture of her nipples, which now produced raw and fiery bolts with every stroke and tug of his fingers.

"Yes," she growled, digging her fingernails into rock-hard biceps, grinding her hips against his thighs. "Now."

His hands dropped to circle her waist. He lifted her as effortlessly as he would a jug of ale, and laid her back upon the wool blanket, his big body moving over the top of hers. Then, he was propped on straightened arms, his knees between her widespread thighs, his flagrant, giftwrapped male hardness jutting upward in the space between their bodies.

"Not. Yet." His own growl was a deep, resonant rumble.

She let her senses feast on him—the muscles flexing in his shoulders and arms, the ferocious heat in his eyes, the flush upon his skin. "I need you, James," she panted.

Without another word, he lowered himself, crouching between her legs. Then, his mouth was upon her breasts. Her nipples were suckled into an inferno. She dug her heels into the blanket. Dug her fingers through thick, cool strands of hair, satisfied for the moment with the opportunity to touch any part of him she could reach.

Strong, capable hands stroked her thighs, gently kneading. Thick, long fingers brushed against her, right at the center, causing her belly to leap, her heart to pound furiously.

"Be easy, lass," he breathed against her breast, the air cooling the beaded tip after the warmth of his mouth. He kissed her belly, one hand splaying wide over her ribs while the other played among the needy, wet folds at her core. And, suddenly, his mouth was there, too. Kissing her. *There.* Loving her with his tongue. Stretching her with a single blunt fingertip.

She cried his name.

His finger slid deeper. His tongue firmed and found a golden jewel of pleasure.

She sobbed his name.

His finger stretched her further, stinging just a bit.

She writhed and arched and prayed for the everlasting torment of pleasure to go on forever and yet somehow end.

"Please," she begged. "I feel so ... so tight inside."

"That ye are."

"I need you to do something. I am dying."

His shoulders heaved. His body rose again above hers. His hands scooped her up and brought her once again to straddle him. "Now, then. Ye must take me inside ye, lass."

She nodded emphatically, hugging his neck with all her might, breathing in his evergreen scent, working her hips so her folds slid firmly against the hardness that remained between their bodies.

"Nae, no' that way, my bonnie lass. Rise up on yer knees."

She nodded again, but he had to direct her with his hands at her waist, positioning her so that her core hovered above his manhood. He raised her higher with one arm while taking himself in his other hand.

Then she felt it. The blunt, sheathed tip. It was probing

inside where his finger had been. Her eyes flared as she began to realize how very—oh, dear. How very big he was.

She swallowed and winced. "Th-this is what you meant by"—she grunted as the earlier sting she'd felt was dwarfed by a stabbing, burning pain—"by disparity, I take it."

His face was rigid, his eyes ferocious, the muscles along his jaw so tight, she feared he'd crack his teeth. "Only take ... as much as ye can," he rumbled, panting the words.

"I want to take all of you." She leaned closer to kiss his jaw, feeling the prickly tingles of his whiskers against her lips. "Every bit."

"Ah, God."

With a seemingly involuntary jerk of his hips, she received half her wish.

Suddenly. And with no small amount of discomfort.

His long, tortured groan accompanied the closing of his grip on her hips.

She held his neck tighter. Tried to breathe through the shocking invasion. Her breasts loved his chest. Her lips loved his chin. Her heart loved him from the soles of his giant feet to the last strand of dark-blond hair on his head.

But this was genuinely uncomfortable. Her thighs flexed, wanting to close against the invader. Her core did not seem to know whether to drive him out or draw him deeper. Was there a deeper? She did not know.

Placing her lips next to his ear, she whispered, "Take what you need, James."

His head shook. His arms trembled. "I canna," he grunted, the agony in his voice twisting her heart.

"Yes, you can. I am well. Go on, my love. It is all right."

The growling groan which tore through him in that moment was her reward. His arms wrapped fully around her, his hands pressing at her neck and lower back. Then, his hips surged upward, and the fullness inside her grew. Then withdrew. Then returned. Then receded. Then began pounding back inside. And out. And inside. And out again. Over and over, he pushed himself deep into her core, his muscles shivering as he controlled her body's motions, his voice rumbling against her breasts, sounding in her ear.

Although her earlier pleasure did not return, other pleasures did. His voice and his scent and his touch. The feel of his fingertips digging helplessly into her flesh. The heat and roughness of his chest rubbing against her. The light of transcendent ecstasy in his eyes, like the sun shining through verdant leaves. She absorbed these pleasures, storing them up inside her senses as he stiffened beneath her, thrusting one last time and shouting her name over and over.

Viola. Yes, *she* had given him this. And he was hers.

She stroked his face, running her fingertip over the cleft in his square chin, the firm lines of his lips, the bridge of his blunt nose.

He took her face in his hands and kissed her fiercely, panting against her mouth, leaning his forehead against hers. "My God, lass. Are ye ... how bad is it?"

She stroked his cheek with the backs of her fingers. Kissed his lips tenderly. "I am fine."

The tension in his face darkened, turning thunderous. "Nae. Ye bluidy well are no'."

A shiver ran up her spine at his words, his expression. Her nipples beaded again. Without her permission, her sheath squeezed around him where they were still joined.

Holding her tight to him, he swung his legs over the side of the bed and stood, pivoted, and laid her with the gentlest of care onto the bed. Then, he kissed her. And withdrew.

He flinched at her squeak, as though the momentary pain had been his. But he said nothing, instead scooping up her legs and repositioning her in the bed, drawing the sheet and blankets over her naked body. "I'll be but a moment, lass. Don't move from this spot."

She nodded, lying back against the pillows. As she watched

his naked backside in the low, golden light of the lamp, she sighed. He really was a magnificent man. A bit more hairy than she'd imagined, particularly on the chest, but that had turned out to be quite beneficial, in her estimation.

Shifting her legs experimentally, she winced as she felt the residual stinging, burning ache where he'd penetrated. No matter. She was most content. He'd shouted her name four times. Four. She draped the backs of her fingers lazily against her mouth, hiding a satisfied smile. She'd given him great pleasure.

The splashing sounds from the dressing table ceased, and her husband came toward her with a cloth in his hand. And a naked, not-entirely-quiescent male member bobbing rather oddly from a nest of hair between his great, oaken thighs. She blinked at the strange appearance of it. Veined. With a rounded, flared sort of head. The stalk appeared flushed, darker than his other flesh, at least for the moment. Her understanding was that the thing altered its appearance greatly depending on the man's particular condition. For example, according to Georgina, a man who had been submerged in cold water might have a "shrunken" appearance which, she assured Viola, should not be taken as indicative of either virility or size under other conditions.

Really, Georgina had been most informative. She must thank her again when they returned to Grimsgate.

"Viola," he rasped, seating himself beside her on the bed. "You must let me care for you, now."

She reached out to run her fingertips over his thigh. "Why not simply lie down with me?"

He gently removed her hand, silent for a long moment. "I hurt you. I did not want to, but that is what occurred."

"Silly goose. Virgins feel pain. It is of no importance."

Without another word, he drew back the blanket and sheet, exposing her nakedness to his eyes. And his hand. "Your pain will always be of the highest importance to me," he said, his voice roughened by an emotion she did not understand. Then, with surprising tenderness, he used the dampened cloth to soothe and clean her, stroking her gently with subtle, circular motions of his thumb and fingers.

Soon, she was once again heating inside, aching low in her belly, feeling out of breath and needing to move against him. Her hand gripped his wrist, her hips writhing against the mattress as pleasure spiraled and swirled like an eddy in a stream. She moaned and arched, loving the relentless pressure of his fingers, the pulsing sweetness of the sensations he drew from her. He lowered his head to her breast, taking her nipple in his mouth. Then, he suckled. So strongly, so sweetly that the pleasure expanded in a sharp, escalating burst. She gasped. She moaned his name. The burst flew outward, spinning and arcing inside her veins, seizing inside her core, echoing out in ripple after ripple, wave after wave of indescribable ecstasy.

As the waves gentled and receded, she found her husband lying down beside her, drawing the blankets up over them both. She cradled his head in the curve of her neck, felt his powerful arms circle her waist and draw her tightly into his body. And she fell into sleep holding the only man she'd ever wanted—the only man she'd ever loved—as closely as her own heart.

Chapter Fourteen

"Be cautious about indulgences, Humphrey. One never knows when that which is presently pleasurable will spoil and cause a perfect mess. One only knows that it will."

—THE DOWAGER MARCHIONESS OF WALLINGHAM to her boon companion, Humphrey, in response to his implied preference for kidney pie after a good ramble.

❦

SHE DID NOT *APPEAR* TO HAVE BEEN TORN IN TWO, AT LEAST TO James's eye. Indeed, she threw back her head and laughed at the antics of Nellie's two boys, Patrick and John, as they chased one another around Mam's front garden.

"Mind the flowers!" Nellie called, leaning down to murmur something to Viola, who chuckled and nodded.

"She's a guid one, Jamie." Mam said, coming to stand beside him where he had one shoulder braced against the cottage's stone exterior. She sipped her favorite morning tea—one of the first luxuries he'd begun purchasing for her sixteen years ago—and smiled out at her grandchildren. "She loves ye."

He chose not to reply. Viola *believed* herself in love with him. One day soon, he'd no doubt, she would come to her senses.

It was true he'd wrongly presumed she would reconsider once she saw where he'd come from, once she knew how far beneath her he was. Then, he'd thought she would lose that shine in her eyes when he made love to her, further demonstrating how absurd were the disparities between them, how his big, rough body should be nowhere near her dainty perfection.

She'd proven either more resilient or more obstinate than he'd anticipated, for her smile was as breathtaking as ever. She'd even let him bring her to release again earlier that morning. With his mouth. Although it had been torturous not to take a release of his own, he had deemed it just punishment after the pain he'd caused her last night.

This morning, however she was radiant, her black hair shimmering beneath a bright yellow sun, her silver pelisse making her skin appear even creamier and more blushing than usual. Or, perhaps he'd chafed her with his whiskers, he considered with a frown. He looked closely, letting his gaze wander over her face and throat. No, she simply had a bit of bloom to her cheeks, he decided. Perhaps he should awaken her the same way every morning, with his head between her luscious white thighs. It might prove beneficial for them both.

"Dinna know that I've ever seen another lass sae bonnie," said Mam.

"You haven't," he replied. "There is nobody more beautiful than Viola."

He felt his mother brush a lock of his hair away from his temple, the way she'd done when he was a lad. He turned to see her gazing up at him with a peculiar expression.

She squeezed his shoulder and blinked away the look before he could decipher it.

He leaned down to kiss her cheek, and she reached up to pat his.

She smiled. "It's been sae long, I thought the bairns wouldna recognize ye."

"Aye." He glanced out at the boys, who had sprouted up like barley in May. "Four years since you brought them to Shankwood for a visit."

She waved a hand dismissively. "Ask old McFadden, and he's certain tae say it might as weel be four minutes."

He chuckled. "How fares McFadden? Has his grandson finally persuaded him to stay away from the workshop?"

"Hmmph. No' likely. He should hae done ages ago, but every time we suppose he's done fer guid, there be another villager dyin'." She shook her head. "He's convinced his markers are the only ones that'll dae."

His gaze dropped, and he nodded.

Nellie spoke up, apparently having overheard their conversation. "The last one wis fer old Mrs. Franklin. An' ere that, it wis puir Douglas Campbell, God rest his soul."

A shock ran through his body, like lightning striking the top of his hair and singeing him down to his boots. "Douglas Campbell is dead?"

Mam tried to behave as though nothing untoward had occurred. She calmly sipped her tea before replying. "Indeed he is. Took ill two years ago."

"Why did you not tell me, Mam?"

Again, she gazed up at him with that puzzling, indefinable expression. It seemed a mixture of sadness and love and affection and resignation and perhaps three or four other elements he could not decipher. "Ye know verra weel, Jamie."

He tightened his jaw and found his eyes following the motion of Viola's hand as she gestured and laughed. "You should have told me," he gritted. "Is she still at the farm?"

"Aye."

"Has she—"

"Nae. She's no' married again."

Alison was a widow. The day after he'd married Viola, he learned Alison was a widow and had been for two years. He did not know why the revelation should matter, why he should feel as though Gentleman Jackson himself had landed a blow at his navel. Except that he had stayed away this long to avoid seeing her. Speaking with her. Remembering what he had lost.

Again, Viola swam into his vision, her features animated as she described something to his younger nephew, John. Suddenly, James felt as though his chest were being crushed.

"I must go, Mam. I must speak with her."

Mam looked as though she might argue, but instead, she merely nodded, a sad smile upon her lips. "Dae as ye maun, son."

Without another word, he headed out of his mother's garden, tearing his eyes from his wife's small frown of confusion, and striding along the muddy lanes of Netherdunnie to see Alison. As though it had not been fifteen years since he had last traveled the same road.

∞

"WH-WHERE IS HE GOING?" VIOLA ASKED NELLIE AS THEY watched James's broad back disappearing down the muddy path to the muddier road.

Nellie frowned. "Couldna say. Mam! Where is Jamie headin'?"

James's mother approached, stopping briefly to kiss the head of Nellie's youngest boy. "Dae ye recall mentioning the wee matter of Douglas Campbell?" she asked her daughter.

Nellie's eyes widened. Her hand covered her mouth.

"Aye," Mam said, as though that answered Viola's question quite well.

"I do beg your pardon, Mam, but I'm afraid I don't understand," Viola said. "Was Mr. Campbell a friend of James?"

Mam took her hand and led her into the cottage, inviting her to sit on the lovely green velvet sofa in the parlor, then sat next to her, placing her teacup on a small table. "Now, I dinna want ye tae fret, lass. Jamie hasna visited Netherdunnie in many years. He wis surprised tae hear of the passin' of a man he knew as a lad."

A tiny frown pulled at Viola's brow as she gazed into eyes so very much like James's, solemn, deep, and rich. They revealed concern, flickering amidst the shadows of some hidden knowledge. Tensing against a vague chill, Viola pressed her mother-in-law. "Where did he go, Mam?"

Those eyes fell away. Turned to glance out the window. Obviously, his mother did not wish to tell her what was happening or why. It sent a wave of apprehension through her, pulling her breath up short.

She looked to Nellie, who stood in the open doorway chewing her lip. "Nellie? Please tell me."

Even Nellie—the boisterous, outspoken Nellie—hesitated for long moments before responding. "He shall return in a trice. Ye mauna worry."

All the warmth and assuredness she had felt earlier, the resonant glow she'd experienced upon awakening with James, dressing with James, laughing with James about how many pins were required to secure her hair, standing with James in his mother's garden while his big hand rested upon the small of her back. All of it drained away, replaced by a cold, drying wind.

There were few reasons his family would not wish her to know where he'd gone, and none of them boded well. She swallowed and tilted her chin. "Please, Nellie," she said. "I should like to know where my husband has gone."

Nellie clicked her tongue and sighed. "He's gaen tae the Campbell farm tae see Douglas Campbell's widow."

"Widow?" Her voice sounded thin to her ears.

"Aye."

Mam glared at her daughter. "Ye just had tae flap yer jaws, didna ye?"

Nellie folded her arms across her chest in an all-too-familiar posture. "She's his guidwife. She deserves tae know the truth."

Viola was not certain she wished to know the truth. Presently, in fact, she was experiencing an abundance of dread.

"Weel, now," said Mam tartly. "Gae on, then. Tell it, if ye're sae wise."

Nellie's plain features softened into a look of sympathy. "My brither is a guid man, Viola. Ye maun ken that much, aye?"

Viola swallowed hard again, cursing the dratted lump that had formed in her throat. "Yes. He is the finest of men." It came out as a whisper.

"Aye, that he is. Sae I dinna want ye frettin' that he would bring shame upon ye, or anythin' of that nature."

Oh, God. Matters were growing worse by the second.

"Anyhou, he an' Mrs. Campbell—afore she were Mrs. Campbell, mind ye—were a wee bit tangled oop together."

"They intended tae marry," Mam clarified, still frowning at Nellie. "Ere Jamie gained his title."

Nellie nodded. "He had a grand plan tae take over McFadden's workshop, marry Alison, and dwell in Netherdunnie for the remainder of his days. Plans changed once the title passed tae him. Fer a time, he wis in England, tendin' his lordly matters. When he returned, Alison had wed Douglas Campbell."

Dropping her eyes to her hands, Viola wondered if one could suffocate while sitting upon green velvet in a cottage parlor. "Alison," she murmured. "Is that her name?"

"Aye. A milkmaid. Her faither worked the dairy—"

"It doesna matter," Mam said sharply before continuing in a softer tone. "They were both sae young, Viola. It were nothin' but youth's fancy. Calf-love. Ye ken?"

Viola nodded. Indeed, she did understand. Alison had been James's first love. Perhaps he loved her still. "How—how long has he stayed away, Mam?"

Nellie answered flatly, "Fifteen years. We visited England a time or two, of course. He's much tae occupy him, bein' an English lord."

Focusing on containing the cold expanding like icy crystals through her body, Viola carefully brushed at the folds of her pelisse. "I should like to speak with my husband," she said quietly.

"Aye, of course. Nae doot he'll return—"

"No, I mean I would like to know where the Campbell farm is. I would like to find my husband and speak to him. Now."

Both Mam and Nellie stared at her.

"If you please."

Mam took a deep breath and shared a meaningful glance with Nellie. "Weel-a-weel. Nellie shall take ye."

Nellie's brows shot up. "I shall?"

"Aye. An' be quick aboot it. Jamie said they maun depart fer England soon if they are tae arrive at the castle afore dark."

Reluctantly, but with her customary briskness, Nellie led Viola through the lanes of the small village, making a transparent attempt to delay and distract her by sharing fond recollections about this shop and that cottage, this slovenly neighbor and that cantankerous fool. She pointed out the workshop where "auld McFadden trained oop Jamie in masonry." Like many structures in Netherdunnie, it was a humble, rectangular building made of light-brown stone. This one was tucked away behind a bakehouse, just off the path to the broad, open green at the south end of the village.

"We could gae inside, if ye like," Nellie offered helpfully.

"No. Thank you. Perhaps another time."

Nellie sighed, abandoning her cheerful prattle. "Ye're the one he married, Viola. Dinna forget that."

She nodded, though her heart sank deeper into ice with every word. Nellie did not understand. James had only married Viola because he was an honorable man, and she had left him no other choice. She was not the wife he'd wanted. She was the wife he'd been forced to accept.

"Weel, I tell ye this. I never thought her worthy of him."

Viola glanced at the other woman, whose dark-blond hair reminded her of James. Who had accepted and welcomed her new sister-in-law with open gladness and not a hint of reserve. "Why?" Viola asked, even as she wondered if the answer would prove to be false comfort.

Nellie gave a wry smile. "She luiked at him the same way she luiked at other lads. Nothin' particular aboot it. Just ... ordinary lust."

Blinking at the frank language, Viola struggled to reply. But her curiosity was piqued, so she sallied onward. "And you took exception to this?"

"Aye, that I did. Jamie binna the common sort. Ye could see it from when he wis a wee lad. Started workin' when our faither died. Said no' a word aboot it. Just went tae McFadden an' said, 'Here I be.'" She chuckled. "Nae whiskers yet. Puny wee thing. But a sense of duity and honor as solid as the earth. He's a guid man, Viola. Guid an' strong." She patted her hand over her heart. "In here, ye ken."

Viola nodded and battled a choking emotion she could not afford to release. "He is extraordinary."

"An' that be the difference. *Ye* luik upon him like he's the moon an' stars an' all the sweet words Rabbie Burns ever wrote. Ye love him. A body can see it, plain as auld McFadden's knuckles."

They walked a while in silence, the sound of the wind pushing lingering clouds back out to sea, the recent rain and fresh mud and quenched grass scenting the air green and brown and white. But she could not see the charm of Netherdunnie, as she had yesterday. She could only feel the ever-growing dread that had begun the moment she'd watched James stalk past his mother's front gate without a word or even a glance for her, his wife.

Viola tried to reassure herself that he would not betray her, that there was nothing to fret about. Even Mam had implied that James's infatuation with Alison was more the product of youth than heartfelt devotion. But she could not quite dislodge the thought that he had wanted to marry Alison. *Planned* to marry Alison. And he had tried mightily to avoid marrying Viola.

"It's just over this rise," said Nellie, gesturing ahead to where the road topped a roll in the land, splitting a low stone wall. "We shall retrieve my daft brother an' ye shall see there be nothin' tae worry ye."

In minutes, they were treading the pathway to the long, narrow stone farmhouse. The front door was painted white and flanked by pretty red flowers. Nellie knocked. They waited. Viola's heart pounded furiously, wondering what this woman would look like. Wondering what James would say when he saw that Viola had followed him.

Nellie knocked again, and again there was no response. She shrugged. "Luiks as though naebody—"

The door opened. An old, bent crone wearing a filthy mobcap gazed at them with milky eyes. "That ye, Nellie Abernathy?"

"Aye, Mrs. Campbell. How's aw wi' ye?"

"Storms cause ma boons tae curl oop an' stab ma flesh. Apart frae that, I canna compleen."

Viola prayed that this haggardly woman with the incomprehensible speech was James's boyhood love and that he'd taken one look at the wizened old face and sagging, misshapen gown and run in the opposite direction. Alas, she was reasonably certain that could not be true. It would simply be too fortuitous.

After a baffling exchange of Scottish politesse, Nellie asked if the woman had seen James.

"Oh, aye. He's oop on the brae."

Viola frowned, thoroughly frustrated to realize she had no idea what the woman had said. Apparently, Mam and Nellie softened their brogue for her benefit.

Nellie had no trouble, however, and nodded, thanking Mrs. Campbell before turning to Viola. "He is on a hill, just the other side of the hoose. It is a special place tae the Campbell clan." She turned and led the way down a path that wound around the farmhouse, past a row of apple trees, and through a patch of kitchen garden.

The wind came up, buffeting Viola and plastering her skirts to her legs. As they began to climb, she lowered her head and picked her way along the path behind Nellie, trying to decide what she would say when she finally saw him. Wondering if he would tell her she had worried herself over nothing. Wondering if the closeness she'd felt on their wedding night had been real or if she'd merely wanted him too much to see the truth.

She raised her eyes when she saw Nellie's muddy boots and sprigged skirt, halted and swaying several yards away. Tilting her head so she could see past the brim of her bonnet, Viola followed Nellie's gaze. At the crest of the hill, beneath a copse of old willows, stood James, his head bent, his arm braced against the trunk of the tree. And a woman stood beside him—tall and lean with glossy brown hair, wearing a dark gray gown.

The wind blasted through Viola's pelisse. But she did not feel it.

She could not feel anything. Her flesh had gone numb.

Distantly, she heard Nellie say something. Her name, likely.

But she could only hear the drumbeat of blood in her ears. The echo of every time he had said he did not want her.

Because until this moment, she'd not believed him.

Until this moment, when she watched another woman—the woman he *did* want—reaching up and pulling his head down for a kiss.

Now, Viola knew. He'd never deceived her. No, she had done that entirely to herself.

"... Viola, dearie. It canna be ..."

She shook her head. And turned. And stumbled to her knees.

Now, she was covered in mud. It smeared silver silk and white embroidery. She tried to stand, but her boots slipped on the slick ground.

Hands lifted her. Arms came around her shoulders.

"... home, lass. Everythin' will be weel. I shall bash his fool, muckle heid fer this ..."

If she'd still possessed a voice, Viola would have told Nellie that James did not deserve her anger. Viola had brought this upon herself. With great persistence and indomitable will, she had chased James Kilbrenner, a man who had not wanted to be caught. She had trapped him into marriage. Hounded him straight off a precipice.

And if she now lay at the bottom of a ravine, flailing and gasping among the shattered ruins of her own heart, she had only herself to blame.

Chapter Fifteen

"Mistake! Spilling tea upon a lady's slippers is a mistake.
Setting the draperies on fire is a mistake. Dallying in the stable
with not one but two footmen is a mistake. This is an outrage."

—THE DOWAGER MARCHIONESS OF WALLINGHAM to Lady
Gattingford regarding the abrupt dismissal of another lady's maid
for an act too outrageous to mention.

∽

JAMES FELT SO HOLLOWED OUT HE WAS SURPRISED THE WIND
didn't whistle through his bones. He'd spent an hour in
Alison's company. She had changed somewhat—her grief had
made her quieter, more solemn—but he'd noted her laugh was
still the same, her humor warm and comfortable, her voice
only a shade deeper than it had been when she was a lass. She'd
looked well, her skin unlined, her hair still shining and
smooth.

And he'd felt nothing. Not a twinge of longing or regret. Not a tug of attraction or a single thread of heat. In truth, he'd struggled to remember what had so enchanted his sixteen-year-old self. Alison was a good-natured woman. She smiled often and possessed an earthy simplicity that held a certain appeal, he supposed.

But she did not carry an entire skyful of stars in her eyes. She did not set him afire just by breathing his name. In point of fact, she was too tall, too angular, too plain. He did not wish to be uncharitable, but there it was.

She had, however, been kind enough to allow him to see his son's grave. And she had stood with him. Wept with him. Told him he wasn't to blame, that many children had died from the same fever, and there was nothing he could have done. He disagreed, but he hadn't argued the point. Later, she'd even attempted to kiss him and offer him "comfort," but after a moment of surprise at her boldness, he'd set her away and informed her he would seek comfort with his wife. She'd looked at him with sadness, nodded, and wished him well.

Now, he wanted only to see Viola. To kiss Viola. To feel Viola's hands upon him and hear her say his name.

As he opened the gate to his mother's cottage, the blue-painted door opened. Nellie stood in its gap, arms crossed, face tighter than he'd ever seen. He froze. "What is it? Mam? Is she—?"

"Ye, Jamie Kilbrenner, are daft! And a *man*. A daft, dense man, an' ye deserve every bit of what's comin' yer way." His sister then charged past him, smacking his shoulder with bruising force and shouting, "Fix it, blast ye!" as she slammed the gate closed behind her.

Rubbing his arm and reeling at the mercurial nature of women, he walked inside the cottage. Mam was seated in her parlor, knitting. He removed his hat and set it on a small table beside the door, then glanced around the room. All was quiet except for the faint clack of his mother's needles.

"Mam, is Viola—"

"She is at the inn."

He flinched at the coldness of Mam's tone. She still had not looked up from her knitting. "What is—why would she go—"

"She intends tae hire a carriage. I told her the inn may have one or two."

Running a hand through his hair, he stared at the woman who had birthed him, wondering if some foreign substance had been slipped into her tea. "Why in blazes would you tell her that? And why would she wish to hire a bloody carriage when we have a perfectly functional coach waiting to carry us to England?"

Mam sniffed. "Because she asked. As tae the second question, I assume she takes exception tae spending a day inside a coach with ye, son."

He moved to sit beside her, and when she did not look up or stop knitting, he laid a hand over her wrist. "Mam, tell me what's happening. I was gone an hour. I return and my wife has decided she cannot bear to be in my presence."

Finally, Mam turned her eyes to him. They were filled with a mother's pain, a mother's disappointment. "Where were ye during that hour, Jamie?"

His heart thudded. Twisted. "I went to see Alison Campbell. You know that."

"An' what dae ye suppose yer wife thought when ye left her here withoot a word of explanation?"

He frowned. "You told her, then. About Alison."

"Aye. Because she deserved to know."

He ran a hand over his jaw. Now, he understood why Nellie had been angry. Viola had apparently overreacted to discovering that he had gone to see a woman he'd once loved. Nellie had never liked Alison, and she adored Viola. His sister was both fiercely loyal and a mite volatile. Likely she had painted a rather ugly picture for his wife. "I shall explain matters to Viola when I see her. You needn't worry. This is simply a misunderstanding."

Mam's eyes turned stormy. "It was a misunderstandin' that made ye kiss that dairymaid in front of yer wife, eh?"

Good God. He felt the blood drain away from his skin. She had seen? Viola had seen Alison kiss him?

"Honestly, Jamie. I thought better of ye. Alison Campbell is pleasant enough, I suppose, but yer wife is bonnie as a sunrise. An' gracious an' kindly, too. She could charm the fish from the sea. What were ye thinkin'?"

"I must go, Mam. I must find her."

"Indeed, ye maun. Ye may wish tae beg her forgiveness, as weel."

He stood and strode to the door, stuffing his hat on his head.

"An' son?"

"Aye, Mam."

Her eyes swam. "Dinna give up. Marriage binna always easy, but love is worthy of battle."

He charged from the cottage, loping at an unseemly pace. As he passed, he shouted to the coachman waiting in Mam's small stable to ready the carriage and meet him at the inn. Long strides carried him swiftly down the road to the south end of the village. By the time he entered the inn's dark interior, his heart was pounding wildly.

He needed to see her. He needed to explain. Everything would come right if she would only listen to him.

"We dinna accept bonnets fer payment, m'lady. Nae matter how bonnie they be."

He recognized the voice of the innkeeper, a rotund man who wheezed with an odd, rusty squeak at the end of every sentence. Turning into the inn's common room, he saw her. Viola. And he could breathe again.

Her back was to him, her silver pelisse peculiarly bright in the dingy space. She was thrusting her bonnet into the fat man's chest. The blue bonnet with the little white feathers. Her favorite, if he did not miss his guess.

"It is worth twice what you would charge for a post-chaise," she said. "All I ask is that you—"

James swiped the bonnet from her fingers and spoke to the rotund, wheezing man who appeared to be losing his patience. "Thank you, Mr. Ferguson. We'll have no need for a carriage, after all."

The man straightened his waistcoat and nodded. "Weel-a-weel, m'lord."

Viola had gone strangely still the moment James had spoken.

Gently, he took her arm and steered her out of the common room, through the entrance, and out to the inn's courtyard. When he turned her to face him, he saw where mud had stained her pelisse in large, smeared patches. Her skin was ghostly. She refused to meet his eyes.

He sighed, feeling his gut tighten and burn. "Viola, what are you about, lass? Hmm? We have a coach." He waved the bonnet in her line of sight. "You should not be trading this. You should be wearing it."

She took the bonnet from his hands, running her fingers along the brim. Otherwise, she did not respond.

"What you saw ... it wasn't ... I pushed her away, Viola. That was her kissing me, not the other way 'round."

She winced as though he'd trod upon her tiny feet.

"Say something, lass."

For a while, he thought she might never speak to him again. Never look at him again. Then, she did. And he wanted to howl.

With muted tones and admirable composure, she said, "If you will kindly pay for a post-chaise, I shall return to Northumberland on my own. Once there, I shall travel to Cheshire with my father, and he and I will find a way to free you from this marriage. An annulment may not be possible. A divorce will cause a scandal for a time, but you will undoubtedly survive it."

All thoughts of explaining and apologizing fled from him like so much smoke. He could not tolerate this ... this travesty.

The light—that enchanting, Viola starlight—had gone out of her eyes. She talked of divorce as though it were possible, even reasonable. Deep inside, where he stored the dark pleasure of binding her to him forever, he caught fire.

She would not travel to Cheshire. She would not subject herself to such a scandal. And she bloody well would not leave him. He would never let her escape that easily.

Seeing the coach pull up from the corner of his eye, he moved toward her and inclined his head nearer to hers.

She stiffened and held her bonnet tightly over her midsection.

"Here is what will happen instead, lass." He kept his voice low, but even he could hear the ominous rumble of fury that ran beneath it. "Ye will climb into this coach with me, and together, we will return tae Grimsgate. Then, we will gather our possessions, yer maid and my valet, and we will travel on tae Derbyshire, where ye will live as my wife an' the mistress of Shankwood Hall." He hovered closer, his mouth near her ear. "There will be nae more talk of annulment or divorce or even a wee separation." He noted with satisfaction that her breathing had quickened. Good. Perhaps she was sensing how bloody furious he was. "Ye wanted this marriage, Viola. Ye wanted me. Ye bluidy well ran me tae ground sae ye could have yer way. An' now ye've caught me, ye canna simply loose the trap ye've set. It's sprung. Ye're as caught as I. Ye'd best resign yerself tae it, fer I dinna intend tae let ye go."

The coach waited behind her. He waited for her to protest or express outrage. She did neither. Instead, she turned, nodded to the footman who held the door for her, and climbed inside with regal calm.

Watching her, his fury should have abated. She had acquiesced to his wishes. His breathing should be quieting. He should be calm. But he was not.

Acid churned in his gut and in his veins. He wanted to touch her, to lift her hand to his cheek and force her to gaze at him with something other than dull grief. He'd anticipated that she would regret forcing this marriage upon them both, that she would come to realize how ill suited they were. But he'd expected her to balk upon discovering his humble origins or the reality of lying with a man of his size. Not this. Not going colorless and stricken as though he'd broken the light inside her.

Remorse, cold and sour, turned his fury to ash. A rough breeze buffeted him, carrying with it the scent of sunlight warming the damp Scottish mud.

She will come 'round, he reassured himself, feeling desperation squeeze his ribs and lungs. *She is overwrought at realizing the consequences of her pursuit. She'll settle into a better understanding when you bring her to Shankwood. She is a born countess.*

Yes, that would do it. She would see that she was his wife. That she belonged to him and he to her. Surely, she would recover her good sense, and this rubbish about divorce would be but a memory.

"My lord?" the footman said, gesturing toward the interior of the coach.

Consciously relaxing his fists and jaw, James nodded and removed his hat before climbing inside to sit beside his wife. She was tucked into the opposite corner, her bonnet beside her on the seat, her arms folded across her middle, her face turned away from him.

The coach rocked as he settled upon the seat. The door closed with a click.

"Viola," he ventured, his voice cracking. "I am sorry, lass."

Her eyes closed. Her lips pressed together, a small crinkle of pain forming between her dark brows. She swallowed. "It is I who am sorry, James." Her voice was a thread, dull and thin.

The carriage jerked into motion, rocking them both.

"Won't you look at me?" he coaxed, uncaring that it sounded like a plea for mercy.

Her sigh turned into a small shudder. "I fear my head is paining me. I should like to sleep for a while."

Not wanting to cause her another moment of hurt, he gave in, holding his silence. And after a time, her head indeed fell against the tufted wall, her sweet breasts rising and falling with an even rhythm. She slept through their stop at Coldstream, where he purchased some bread and ham and a bit of ale, packing it in a small basket for his wife, should she grow hungry later. When he returned to the coach, she was still asleep, her neck crooked in such a way that he anticipated she would find greater pain upon awakening.

Setting his basket upon the opposite seat, he slowly, gently crouched next to his wife's sleeping form. The mud upon her lovely silk pelisse had dried to a dusty stain. *She must have fallen,* he thought. His chest ached for some reason. He rubbed absently at the spot where the top button of his waistcoat met his cravat. *I need to hold her,* he decided. That thought eased the pain in his chest a bit.

Taking the greatest of care not to disturb her, he slipped his arms beneath her knees and behind her back. Then, in one smooth motion, he sat upon the seat, settling her tiny, precious weight upon his lap.

She sighed sweetly, her head coming to rest in the hollow between his neck and shoulder, her bottom settling upon his thighs. He cradled her against him, letting his hands stroke her fine-boned back and shoulders and arms. Letting his fingers trace the skin along her jawline, hover over her rose-petal lips. She breathed against him, dampening and heating his finger. Her hand came up to tuck itself over the spot where he'd felt that peculiar knot of pain earlier. Her touch unraveled it. Her sweet, soft breaths and the motion of the coach lulled his senses, soothed him until he, too, grew drowsy. Cuddling her closer, he wrapped his wee bonnie wife in his arms and fell asleep to the music of wind blowing and wheels turning and his own heart steadying its panicked beat at last.

Chapter Sixteen

"Pray, do regale me again with your relentless prattle.
I do so enjoy waking to the sound of nonsense accompanied
by the distinct scent of imminent dismissal."

—THE DOWAGER MARCHIONESS OF WALLINGHAM to a recently
acquired lady's maid, the seventh in as many months.

∞

"THIS STAIN WILL COME RIGHT OUT, NOT TO WORRY, MY
lady." The cheerful, chatty girl holding up Viola's silver pelisse
could not have been older than twenty, which made her
approximately half the age of the next youngest servant at
Shankwood Hall. "Just a bit of mud. Had a similar mishap
with my mother's best apron this last spring." She rolled her
eyes and chuckled. "Oh, she was properly vexed, she was. But I
told her true: Mud washes clean away, sure enough. Just takes
patience and scrubbin'. Mostly scrubbin'."

Viola granted the girl a faint smile and continued unpacking her possessions from the trunk lying open on the floor of her new dressing room. As she placed her brush and combs and a small, enameled box of hair pins on the mahogany dressing table, she noticed a white scrap of cloth in the trunk's near corner. It had been tucked beneath the pin box. She bent and took it between her fingers, running her thumb over purple and green embroidery.

"Oh, my lady. You should let me do the unpacking. You must be weary from your travels. All the way from Northumberland! My, what a jaunt. Three days, is it not?"

"Two and a half. We had excellent horses and pleasant weather." The journey had been a torment. Twice she and James had shared a bed, though all they'd done was sleep. Waking up with his arms around her, feeling his heat and hardness against her, his breath upon her cheek, she'd wanted to weep with longing. But, then, that sensation was not precisely new. It seemed she would forever be cursed to want him and be denied the pleasure of having him as her own.

"You have the most beautiful gowns, my lady. This one—oh! How splendid. Look at the spangles. Like little drops of dew."

Viola glanced up from the ugly handkerchief in her hand and saw the girl—Amy, if she recalled correctly—holding the ball dress Viola had worn for the masquerade. And for her wedding. To think only a few days had passed since then. It felt like a century.

After she and James had left Scotland, her world had become a gray haze of turmoil and want. First, she'd awakened in his arms—indeed, cuddled in his lap—as the coach had pulled past the gatehouse at Grimsgate. He'd held her so tenderly, she'd raised her mouth to his, needing to feel his lips upon hers. Then, she had remembered.

She did not deserve to kiss him. She was the woman who had trapped him into marriage, denied him happiness with his real love, the now-widowed, frightfully tall Alison.

So, instead, she had held herself still and waited for the footman to open the door, and for James to loosen his hold, before climbing from the coach.

Thereafter, she'd gone to find Papa, who had hugged her three times, beaming his delight at seeing her mother's ring on her finger. "Why so pale, my sweet girl?" he'd whispered during the third hug. Then, she'd seen him cast a grim eye over her shoulder at James.

Wanting no strife between her father and husband, she'd given him her best false smile and kissed his cheek. "Merely a headache, Papa. James held me as I slept all the way from Scotland. He is taking such good care of me. You mustn't worry."

This had appeared to settle Papa's concerns well enough, but the look in Georgina's eyes, along with a single, silent, overlong hug, told Viola perhaps she had not been as convincing as she might have wished.

For his part, James had loomed like a shadow, trailing her everywhere she went, even following her to her bedchamber where she'd begun to pack, as though he feared she might disappear or collapse into a weepy, hysterical heap and humiliate them both. She'd done neither, of course. She owed him a great debt. He had married her to save her from certain scandal. She would not sully that gift by making a public spectacle, no matter how her heart ached. No matter how many times she relived the moment when the towering Alison had pulled his mouth to hers.

And that happened every time she blinked, every time she breathed.

Unable to bear the thought of being alone with James for three days while they traveled to his home in Derbyshire, she'd begged Papa, Georgina, Penelope, and Aunt Marian to travel with them to Shankwood Hall, as its location in Derbyshire was but a day's ride from their home in Cheshire. For this effort, she'd mustered every performer's trick, every ounce of artifice she'd ever possessed to present the most cheerful of faces to her family. Papa had scoffed and shot James a skeptical look, expressing doubt about a newly married couple having the bride's father along for their honeymoon. It had been Georgina who had saved her, holding Viola steady with a dark, sympathetic gaze and observing that the journey might pass more quickly for them all with a bit of company.

Eventually, her family had agreed. Viola had been thankful for their buffering presence, since James had taken to touching her at every dratted opportunity. He placed a hand on her back while helping her into and out of the carriage. He wrapped an arm about her waist while they stood waiting inside coaching inns for their food or their rooms. And his fingers trailed maddeningly up and down her arm when they sat beside each other, whether in the carriage or in the midst of an inn's crowded taproom. Further, he would not stop staring at her with those haunted, solemn green eyes of his. Every time she cast a furtive glance his way, she found his gaze upon her, sometimes heated, sometimes pensive, always intent.

Avoiding him had proven impossible. At least during the day, she'd had the excuse of dragging Georgina into her carriage to teach her more about embroidery, or riding with Penelope to help refine her cousin's wedding plans, or conversing with Papa over a cup of ale and a bowl of bland stew.

But at night, there was no escape. In the room she shared with James the first night, she had scrambled to finish her toilette quickly and crawl beneath the blankets so she could pretend to sleep before he entered. She'd managed it, but only by a whisker, turning out the lamp just as the door opened. After a bit of splashing, he'd sat on the edge of the bed for a long while. She'd felt his fingers sift through her hair. Then, she'd felt the mattress dip as he'd climbed in beside her, gathering her into his arms. It had felt like being cuddled by a great bear, warm and protected, and she had soon fallen into a deep slumber.

The second night, she had not been quite as fortunate. He'd entered just as she peeled back a yellow coverlet desperately in need of a good washing. She'd spun to face him, her heart pounding so loudly, she'd been certain he would hear it. As it turned out, he had wanted to talk. And above all things, she did not wish to talk.

"We must discuss how we are to go on, Viola," he'd rumbled, sitting on the bed to remove his boots. "You cannot avoid me forever."

She'd pleaded exhaustion, but he would have none of it. He'd come around the bed, his shoulders a yard wide, his eyes tired and red. "We are married," he'd stated flatly. "I realize I have hurt you, and I am sorry for it. Sorrier than you can dream. But you mustn't consign us forever to this misery. You are my wife. I shall sleep beside you, and you beside me. That is as it should be."

After his declaration, she had hugged herself and nodded, half expecting him to demand a repeat of their wedding night. Part of her wanted that more than her next breath, while another part despaired of taking his body and his lust inside her again, only to be torn apart when she remembered that his heart loved another. She did not know if she could survive it.

But he had not demanded anything more of her, merely stripping down to his pantaloons and once again climbing into the bed beside her, dousing the lamp, and pulling her into the curve of his big, hard body. That night, she'd slept not at all, lying awake for hours listening to his heartbeat and his breathing and the faint, funny snore at the top of each breath. She'd soaked in his heat, struggling not to weep at the pleasure of his nearness. Her chest had ached, her eyes had stung, and she'd waited for sleep to claim her, but it never had.

Today, they had arrived at Shankwood, and presently, her newly assigned lady's maid, Amy, was cooing over a pair of slippers she'd purchased two seasons ago. Viola had never had a dedicated lady's maid before. She and Papa had always been too poor for such extravagances. "Keep them," she said to the girl, nodding to the slippers.

Amy's eyes rounded. "Oh, no, my lady, I could never—"

"I insist. To love something with all your heart and then to make it your own is one of life's great joys." She looked down at the handkerchief pressed between her hands, ran her thumb again over what should have been a trout but looked more like an overripe grape.

"Thank you ever so kindly, Lady Tannenbrook," the girl said breathlessly, clutching the shoes to her bosom and hurrying about her work with a new vigor.

Viola's attention returned to the handkerchief. She recalled every laborious stitch. Every thread that had needed to be cut away and repaired. Her skills had improved since then, thankfully. With Georgina's kind instruction, she now contemplated new projects with anticipation rather than dread. Perhaps that was what she needed. A new project. Something to occupy her mind and prevent her dwelling in this wretched pool of sadness.

"Amy."

"Yes, my lady?"

"Is there a shop in the village that sells embroidery floss?"

"Oh, yes, indeed. The Starling Sisters Scone Shop and Haberdashery. You can buy all sorts of bits and bobs there. The scones are lovely, too."

"I should like to go there."

Amy froze while hanging a puce silk gown inside a large wardrobe. "Now, my lady?"

Viola opened the enameled pin box and tucked the ugly handkerchief inside, closing the lid gently. "Yes," she said, rising to gather her bonnet from the low divan along the opposite wall. "Now is the perfect time to do a bit of shopping."

IT WAS A BLOODY GOOD THING HIS SOLICITOR AND ESTATE manager were competent, James thought as he perused the same page of accounts for the sixth time and still had trouble focusing long enough to absorb the figures. Gates and Strudwicke sat across the desk from him. They were discussing the need to replace roofs on three cottages in the village. Or, at least, he thought so. He'd been sitting in his study with the two men for over two hours, but his mind was decidedly elsewhere. Preoccupied. Obsessed.

"Well, that should take care of two of the cottages, at any rate. The third may safely wait until next year if we do a bit of patching, as you suggest, Mr. Strudwicke." Gates removed his spectacles to polish them with a handkerchief, then plopped them back upon his straight, refined nose and turned to James. "Shall we discuss the matter of your heir, my lord?"

His heir. Yes. Of course. Except that he hadn't given his heir a moment's thought since ... well since marrying Viola. In truth, he hadn't thought about much of anything other than his enchanting, maddening, seductive, elusive lass in four months.

"Right," Gates continued, clearing his throat. "Now that your lordship has married, how would you like to proceed in our search for Elijah Kilbrenner?"

James frowned. "Proceed?"

Gates glanced to Strudwicke, who raised his wispy brows then dropped his gaze studiously to the papers in his hand. "Yes. Shall I continue the inquiries into your presumptive heir, now that there exists the potential for an—ahem—heir apparent?"

His head felt light, as though he'd had too little sleep or too much of Wallingham's French cognac. He'd intended never to have children. And he'd resisted taking a wife because a wife would expect children, and all of society would expect her to have children, and if she did not, all of society would blame her for the failure. He'd seen it happen before, and the women always appeared bloody tragic to his eye.

After he'd married Viola, his decision to never have another bairn, never subject another child to his mistakes, had begun to feel a bit less right and a bit more cowardly. He'd even begun to ponder Wallingham's observation that decisions formulated by one's younger self were those of a boy, not a man. In his case, a boy shattered by betrayal and soul-rattling grief.

But then, Viola had made a habit of forcing him to question himself. From the beginning, the indomitable Miss Darling had refused to accept anything other than his unconditional surrender. And he'd wanted her with every inch of his flesh, every thought in his mind, every drop of his blood. He'd wanted her until he thought he'd go mad, wanted that which he should never be permitted. He still did.

He wanted to sink himself inside her tight, wet sheath again, feel her hands stroke his face again. He wanted to watch her flit and twirl about his home, enchanting everyone who saw her. He wanted to see her light up like a midsummer sky whenever she saw him enter a room.

Ah God, he missed her. It had only been a few days, but he felt like he'd caught some sort of wasting illness. To imagine denying his sweet, bonnie lass the chance to be a mother felt wrong. So bloody wrong.

And yet, seeing Alison's grief again, seeing his son's grave again, had firmed the ground in which his original vow—the one he'd made all those years ago—was planted. Reminded him of why he'd made it. How he had failed his son. Failed his son's mother, who had paid her own dear price, never bearing another child.

"My lord?" It was Gates, waiting for his answer.

He could not fail Viola. He could not break his vow to his son. "Continue with the inquiries, Mr. Gates."

After a brief silence, Gates nodded as though James had said something wise that Gates hadn't considered. "Quite sensible, my lord. One certainly never knows what fortune may bring. I have a brother who has an entire houseful of girls." The solicitor chuckled. "Eight of them in all. After the seventh, I believe he gave up hope for a son."

Girls. A ribbon of sensation ran down his spine. He blinked, helpless to prevent the vision that danced through his mind. Daughters. His heart squeezed painfully. Wee little lassies with black hair and eyes full of stars, lighting up every dark corner of his soul without even trying. Just like their mother.

He fought against them, but he could hear their laughter, little tinkling fountains of delight. Saw them spinning and shining and squealing as he scooped them up in his arms. They took hold of him so tightly, he couldn't breathe.

Then, he imagined that light disappearing. Those tiny bodies lying limp and still and gray. He imagined Viola broken by their loss. He could not bear it. Even now, after the wound she had suffered upon seeing him with Alison, his chest ached constantly at her silence, her avoidance of his touch and his gaze.

Gates was nattering on now about some other matter. James didn't know what.

His entire being was focused upon Viola. He must repair the damage he'd done. He must persuade her to take him back into her bed, back into her body. And he would. Because that was his purpose—to ensure Viola's happiness. Perhaps he could not give her children, but he could restore the light inside her that held him in thrall. He must do so as soon as possible. Right now, in fact.

"... so, if Lady Wallingham sent the letter three or four days ago, then by my calculations, we should receive a reply no later than—"

James shot from his chair and rounded the desk.

"Er, my lord? I take it our meeting is concluded?"

"Aye," he replied over his shoulder. "I must speak to my wife."

He yanked the door open and charged into the corridor. He took the west stairs, which were narrow but quicker, and hurtled himself toward Viola's bedchamber, bursting through the paneled oak door with thrumming urgency.

A loud, feminine yelp greeted him. "Oh! It's you, m'lord. Gave me a fright like to stop my old, weak heart, you did." The aged housekeeper, Mrs. Duckett, stooped to retrieve the linens she'd dropped when he entered.

He hurried forward to gather them up and presented her with the stack before she'd touched even one. "Where is Lady Tannenbrook, Mrs. Duckett?"

The old woman's thin, wrinkled lips pursed, her eyes squinting as though she were trying to see a boat far offshore. "In the village, I believe. Yes, I do remember Amy saying something about taking her to the Starling Sisters shop. She wanted floss. And scones. That last bit may have been Amy, truth be known, m'lord. Girl has a fondness for scones."

"When do they plan to return?"

"Of that I cannot be certain." Again, the squint. "They were unpacking her ladyship's belongings only a short time ago."

He bit down on his disappointment. He wanted to see her. Speak to her. He'd been flooded with the need, and now he must wait. Bloody intolerable.

Rubbing the back of his neck with one hand, he glanced around the bedchamber. It was a plain room. A solid oak bedstead with a simple green coverlet. Two chairs near the stone fireplace, both covered with the same green twill. Everything about the room, from the oak paneled walls to the faded carpets covering the plank floor, was wholly wrong for Viola. Too dark and weighty and dull.

Frowning, he wandered through the adjoining door to her

similarly furnished dressing room. Her trunks lined one wall, some having already been emptied, some left open and pluming with gowns in every conceivable shade of blue and purple and pink and silver and white. These were the colors Viola should have, he decided. Not green. Not brown.

Upon the dressing table—a straight, sturdy oak piece better suited to a monk's cell—were arranged a polished silver-handled brush and several ivory combs. There was also a small, hinged box painted with enamel to resemble stained glass. He drifted closer, first running his fingers over her brush, rubbing the long black strands of her hair caught in its bristles. Next, he lifted one of the ivory combs. It had an inlaid design along one side, the swirls so fine, he almost missed them. Viola wouldn't have, though. She would have appreciated the craftsmanship, savored the secret intricacy of it. Finally, he came to the box. With a single finger, he lifted the lid.

And saw his own blindness staring back at him. It was white. Poorly stitched. It had an oddly shaped, purple-and-green fish on one corner.

One day when Humphrey had dragged her about the countryside, and summer had shone upon her flushed cheeks, she had given this to him, tucked it inside his coat pocket, alongside his heart. He now realized that was precisely where it had belonged.

Because this was Viola's heart. And he had tossed it at her feet like so much rubbish.

He must find her. He must beg her forgiveness. He must make her understand how much he wanted her for his wife. Above all, he must do it now, because he could not bear another agonizing moment without her.

Chapter Seventeen

"Your tale is preposterous. Any man who exhibits such appalling judgment once, let alone repeatedly, would surely have perished prior to reaching his majority."

—THE DOWAGER MARCHIONESS OF WALLINGHAM to Lady Gattingford in response to said lady's questionable assertion that Lord Gattingford's waistcoats were lauded by both Beau Brummell and Lord Alvanley on four separate occasions.

❧

HE FOUND HER LAUGHING WITH THE YOUNGEST STARLING sister, who was eighty if she was a day, outside the Starling shop. Her maid was wiping away crumbs from a recently consumed scone, and Viola's eyes were dancing as she listened to the ancient woman explain why she'd never married. James had heard the story before. It involved a pirate, two sailors, and a thwarted attempt to gain passage to Jamaica. *Everyone* in the village had heard Miss Tabitha Starling tell the tale dozens of times, adding a new embellishment with every iteration.

That was why it was so bloody perplexing to find a group of young men gathered around his wife, all laughing along as though they'd never heard a word of it.

Stopping a few feet away from the circle of male admirers, James crossed his arms and glared. Viola had changed her gown, he noted. She now wore white, embroidered muslin topped with a dark-blue spencer and her favorite bonnet. The light breeze caused her skirts to plaster against her legs and backside, outlining her curves in loving detail.

Viola laughed again at the outrageous explanation for why Miss Starling's first love was thrown overboard by her second love. "It cannot be true!" Viola protested. "Captain Farnsworth was wearing your petticoats?"

"Well, he certainly had nothing else to wear, did he? Ah, we were mad for each other, my lady. Alas, pirates are not the forgiving sort."

"Whatever became of him?"

"After that shark took his foot, he was never the same."

"His foot?"

"Well, his toe, really. I told him he should be thankful the fish fancied petticoats, or matters might have ended in far more gruesome a manner."

Viola giggled helplessly. The men surrounding her burst into uproarious laughter, the sound like so many hounds howling and slobbering after meat scraps.

He closed the distance to his wife in five long strides. She glanced up as his shadow moved across her face. A light blush bloomed in her cheeks, but her smile faded. "Lord Tannenbrook," she said, her distant politeness an affront. "Miss Starling was sharing the most amusing recollection."

"Aye," he said, the word grinding from his mouth as he leveled a warning glare at every man standing less than ten feet from her. "I have heard it many times. As have all these men. Which makes me curious as to their sudden desire to hear it again."

"Oh," she answered, looking around at the men, her brows arched in apparent surprise. "Perhaps they enjoy a diverting tale cleverly told."

"Perhaps they should be about their work."

The men all tipped their hats and muttered, "M'lord," before scuttling away like chastened dogs. He followed their progress, his gut slowly releasing its burning tightness. His eyes came back to Viola.

She glared up at him with visible displeasure.

A gnarled, ancient hand patted his elbow. "It has been an age since last these eyes have set upon you, Lord Tannenbrook," said Miss Starling. "Why don't you sit down and have a scone or two? I made a batch just as you like this morning. A touch of lemon. That's the secret."

"Thank you, Miss Starling, but I am not hungry at present." He was not hungry for scones, to be precise. All he wanted was to lift Viola in his arms and carry her back to his bedchamber, where he could speak to her without a bloody dog pack hovering nearby, salivating over her lips and her legs.

Rather than looking at him, however, his wife smiled sweetly at the old woman. "We shall take a dozen, Miss Starling. And a jar of your gooseberry jam, as well. I have never tasted better in all my days."

"You are too kind, my lady."

As the woman ducked into the shop, Viola dug through the silk reticule dangling from her wrist. It was embroidered with what looked to be some sort of rodent. A hedgehog, perhaps.

"What are you doing?" he grumbled.

"Compensating Miss Starling for her wares. And your rudeness." Her tone was more tart than the gooseberries in Miss Starling's jam.

"I need to speak with you, lass."

Her chin went up and her eyes went everywhere except to

him. "I'm afraid I haven't time. Miss Starling did not have the floss I required, so she recommended I visit her sister's cottage. Amy has kindly agreed to take me there."

"I will walk with you."

"Don't be silly. I wouldn't wish to trouble you."

"It's no trouble."

Her lips were stiff, the lines of her throat tight with strain. "Do as you like."

"I shall."

"But it is entirely unnecessary. The villagers have been most welcoming."

"Aye. The men, in particular, I'd wager." He muttered the comment just as Miss Starling shuffled forth with a brown basket, so he wasn't certain whether Viola heard him. After dropping a few coins into the old woman's hand, she took the basket and held it out to him. He shot her a questioning glance.

She sniffed. "So long as you intend to accompany us, you might as well be of use."

Frowning, he accepted the burden. "Is that not what the maid is for?"

"No," she said, turning and waving Amy forward along the lane leading to the other end of the village. "That is what you are for. If you prefer not to help, then I suggest you return to Shankwood Hall. You are a busy man, after all."

Hours later, the sun sat low upon the rolling hills to the west, casting the gray stone village in a rich golden hue. And James carried four more packages. He'd trailed after his wife as she meandered from cottage to shop to village green, gathering purchases, gifts, and admirers of every sort. The purchases were casually offered to him to carry. The gifts she either carried herself—including a bouquet of wilted daisies given her by a wide-eyed, tow-headed lad—or handed them to Amy.

And the admirers. Oh, the admirers. He'd been suppressing a guttural growl for the better part of the afternoon. Every male from age fifteen to fifty had stopped to stare at her, speak with her, tuck his hat over his heart and all but drop to kiss her dainty feet. He'd done the best he could to dissuade them with hard stares of his own, but that proved largely ineffective, since they did not take their bloody eyes off of her long enough to notice.

She charmed them all. The littlest boys and the oldest men. Women liked her, too, he supposed, but the men concerned him most, behaving as though her every laugh and cooing compliment, her every fluttery gesture and graceful turn of toe were an intoxicant. It was true, of course. She was the most intoxicating woman he'd ever known.

As he watched her speak with every villager she encountered, showing unusual deference to the old and sweet affection to the young, he realized it was more than her beauty that enchanted a man. It was her wit, her grace, her kindness. She found joy in small things—gooseberry jam and wilted daisies and a colorful tale told by a woman four times her age.

She laughed readily, often at herself. When the older of the two Starling sisters asked about her reticule, Viola rolled her eyes and said she'd intended it to be a pinecone, as she had a fondness for evergreens. "But as often happens when my fingers wield a needle," she said, "all went horribly awry." Then, she chuckled and waved away the old woman's protests that the work was not unsalvageable. "If it is not," she retorted with a captivating twinkle, "I shudder to imagine work that is."

Now, he walked beside her as an exhausted Amy trailed them across the green. The setting sun painted her ivory skin gold. The light breeze teased the black curls along her delicate jaw. She sighed and bent her nose to sad, wilted daisies. "You have a lovely village, James," she said wistfully.

He'd wanted to speak to her all day, but this was the first time they'd been alone. And now, he had no idea what to say. "Aye," was the best he could manage.

"When I first saw Netherdunnie, I thought it must have been difficult to leave it. Your home. But they are much the same, aren't they? Shankwood and Netherdunnie. Apart from the accents, of course. I imagine you felt a kind of familiarity you hadn't anticipated."

He'd not been able to look away from her for hours, but even so, his gaze now sharpened upon her. "It's true," he replied, surprised by her insight. "I did not expect to like England. I missed my family. The village. But everybody here reminded me of somebody from home."

She nodded, the little white feathers of her bonnet turning yellow in the waning light. "And they needed you here. That is why you stayed."

How did she know? He'd not discussed that time in his life with her. He examined her face, but her eyes focused straight ahead on Shankwood Hall, a stout, gray pile of stone beside a seven-hundred-year-old church. Both sat atop a rise in the center of the village. "Aye. It was."

"You are a good man, James."

"Lass, I ..."

She turned back to her maid as though he'd not spoken. "Amy, I should think supper will be served soon. I must change my gown before dining. Will you inform Mrs. Duckett that I might be delayed? Only a quarter hour or so. I don't wish to cause disruption."

"Yes, my lady."

Wondering when he would have a chance to speak with her alone, he hefted the basket and assorted packages and eyed the distance to the house. He had a minute, maybe two. "Viola, we must talk alone. I have ... things I must say."

Still, she did not look at him, the brim of her bonnet shadowing her eyes. "Perhaps after supper. It has been a lovely day, but most tiring."

Frustration burned from his gut to his nape. "In the village, you had ample time for every man with a set of eyes and a wagging tongue," he gritted.

"Please, James. After supper." She spoke quietly, her tone subdued and flat.

Although his frustration only grew, he bit hard and swallowed it down. For what he had to say, they needed time and privacy. "Very well. I shall come to you in your chamber."

She gave a reluctant nod as they reached the path leading to the front door of Shankwood Hall.

He leaned closer to whisper a final warning. "And I mean to be alone with ye, lass. Ye ken?"

To that, she did not respond, but he was satisfied she'd heard him. He'd never seen a prettier blush in all his days.

❧

SUPPER WAS A LENGTHY AFFAIR FOR SEVERAL REASONS. FIRST, Viola sensed that the staff of Shankwood Hall wished to present their lord and lady with a lavish display of perfection. In this, they succeeded admirably. The long, white-draped table in the oak-paneled dining room was laden from one end to the other with magnificent abundance—roasted pheasant, herb-stuffed pike with a lemon sauce, a lamb-and-potato pie that reminded her of Mam's creation, along with a myriad of vegetables ranging from cauliflower in a creamy white sauce to carrot soup. During the final course, she was gratified to find the cook's talents extended to sweet dishes, as well, with delicious little orange cheesecakes, cherries in brandy, and a decadent raspberry fool. She savored each bite of that dish in particular, for she adored both raspberries and fools, with their juxtaposition of fruit and cream presented neatly inside a glass.

The second reason the meal went on for several hours was that Papa, Georgina, Penelope, and Aunt Marian planned to depart for Cheshire early the following morning, and they lingered over both their meal and the lively conversation, carrying on about innkeepers and the best time of day for catching pike and the renovations to Shankwood Hall that James had implemented over the years. The latter subject piqued Viola's interest, so she asked numerous questions of her husband. How long had it taken to restore the paneling in the dining room? Were the chandeliers new? Had he considered adding draperies to the drawing room? Or perhaps a harp to the music room? After a time, his darkening glower had signaled his annoyance, so she'd stifled her curiosity.

The final reason supper stretched onward late into the evening was that Viola did not want to face James alone. She delayed as long as she could, chatting merrily with the footman who served the wine, regaling Georgina with every detail of her outing in the village, and imploring Papa to tell the story about the time she felt her tooth wiggle and accused Penelope of hitting her while she slept. Whenever a lull in the conversation occurred, she attempted to introduce a new topic. By the time she'd eaten the last of her raspberry fool, Aunt Marian was snoring, Viola had run out of topics, and James looked ready to throttle her. Fortunately, he sat at the opposite end of the table, so even his arms were not long enough to reach her.

By all rights, she should have been exhausted, not having slept more than a minute or two the night before and then spending the day traveling to Shankwood and ambling about the village. But as she kissed Papa's cheek one last time before he ascended to his bedchamber, her nerves sang, her stomach fizzing as though she'd drunk champagne instead of wine.

Now, she stood in her dressing room gowned in a pink peignoir, wringing her cold hands like a nervous ninny. A shiver rippled over her skin, so she moved to the massive chest of drawers on the east wall, retrieved a finely woven white shawl, and tossed it over her shoulders. Then, she took a deep breath, which did not help in the slightest, and opened the door to her bedchamber.

He paced in front of the fireplace. His arms were folded across his chest, one hand covering his lower jaw. He wore only a pair of brown breeches and one of his white linen shirts. She could see a bit of hair peeking out of the opening at his collarbone.

My goodness, he is magnificent, she thought. And he was. Massive shoulders. Thick hair that felt like silk between her fingers. Firm lips that could tease and caress hers until she wanted to absorb him into her skin. Eyes that glowed with heat like a forest burning beneath summer's weight.

He turned. And there were those eyes, devouring her from heated cheeks to bare, chilled toes. The forest was a furnace, a blaze of powerful need. "Viola. Ah, God, lass."

She swallowed, her eyes falling reflexively to his thighs. He was aroused. Very, very aroused. Her tongue darted out to moisten suddenly dry lips. Her belly ached. Her breasts tingled as though he'd stroked them with his long, thick, capable fingers.

Her arms fell away. Distantly, she felt the shawl puddle like a cloud around her feet.

He stalked toward her, his eyes aflame. Then he was lifting her. Kissing her. Taking her lips and giving her his tongue. She clawed at his head, moaning into his open mouth. Heat. There was so much heat. And she needed every bit of it, absorbing his beloved scent into her heart through her skin. Pine and man.

She felt the bed, smooth and plush, rise beneath her back, his hand cradling her head as he laid her upon its surface. Then cool air breathed on her bare legs. He was raising her hem. She could feel his fingers forcing the fabric up her thighs and over her hips. His hands clasped her waist and slid her suddenly downward as he moved to kneel on the floor, putting his shoulders level with her hips. Without a moment for her modesty, he slung her legs over his shoulders and lowered his head between her thighs, holding her hips up like a flask to his lips.

Her hands were still clawed into his hair, so the instant his tongue touched flesh, she formed fists and arched with the bolt of pleasure he wrought with flickering strokes and firm laps. His hands slid down so that his thumbs could spread her folds wide, exposing her more fully to his devilish mouth.

Then, one thumb joined in the play, circling the open bud at her center as his tongue played greedily with her vulnerable opening, dipping inside and torturing her with heat and pleasure and a spiraling, sweet maelstrom that wound so tight, she was certain it could only end in a fiery explosion.

And she was right. She screamed and writhed against him as it burned through her. She yanked his hair and gripped his head with her thighs. But he would not relent. His tongue worked itself inside her, his thumb teasing and stroking until she sobbed and thrashed. Then, the coiling pressure seized in a sharp burst so intense it was nearly pain. It threw her into the heart of the flames, where paroxysms of blasting heat and rippling pleasure buffeted her with breathtaking force. Even then, he did not stop, groaning against her, stroking her gently to expand the cascade, laying open kisses against her inner thighs, her belly.

Strong arms lifted her again, slid her head up so her hips now rested more fully on the bed. Then, with slow deliberation, he clasped her legs behind her knees and tucked her heels on the edge of the mattress. Reaching up, he rid himself of his shirt in a single motion, tossing it to the floor. He unbuttoned his fall, wincing as his fully engorged manhood sprang forward, demanding what it had been promised.

"Viola," he panted, the black at the center of his eyes swallowing the beauty of the forest. "Try tae take me, lass. Please."

She could scarcely think, but she nodded, her hands now fisting in the green coverlet, her legs spread wide for his hips. He towered above her, bending his knees to tuck the head of his shaft against the mouth of her core. She remembered this, the alarming sting of him stretching her flesh. But he needed her. And she needed him. So she concentrated on persuading her muscles to relax.

He pushed. As before, the invasion was uncomfortable. A small, pinching pain formed at her opening, growing as the thicker part of him sank deeper. But it did not compare to the pain of the first time. And, as he slid and stretched and filled her, she blinked at the new sensations.

Of pressure.

Of pleasure.

Of completion.

He filled her so full, she had no room for breath, only him. So, instead, she gasped and gripped him hard, her internal muscles clenching and grasping. He fell forward over her, catching himself on his elbows, protecting her from his weight as he gathered first one leg then the other and wrapped them around his waist. The new angle pressed hard on some mysterious place inside her, sending shockwaves of fiery pleasure through her core.

"Oh, God, James," she groaned, her hands leaving the mangled coverlet to bracket his jaw. She pulled him down into her kiss, grinding her hips upward to take him deeper.

That was when he started moving. Thrusting with slow, heavy motions. Withdrawing one inch and returning two. He was so deep now, she didn't know how he could possibly go any deeper. Except that he did. And his hand was upon her breasts, squeezing her nipples through the silk of her gown. And his manhood was burning her, stretching her, pleasing her in the most astounding of ways.

This was even better than what he'd done with his mouth. This was her husband inside of her, a part of her. She adored him with her hands, trailing her fingers and lips over his mouth and jaw, caressing the muscle that flickered there, relishing how his arms and shoulders shook with the tension of his careful rhythm.

"I must ... I must gae faster now, lass. Bear with me."

Even then, in the moments of greatest tension, he showed restraint. It was why she loved him. One of the reasons, at any rate. There were many.

She kissed that muscle in his jaw again and then squeezed where they were joined and rubbed her hard, sensitized nipples against his chest. His head dropped to her shoulder, and he growled, deep and rumbly the way she liked. She smiled.

He thrust hard, jolting her into a gasp. Pulled nearly all the way out and slid back inside in a long, hard shove. Did it again. And again. She threw her arms around his neck and dragged her mouth along his throat, holding on while he pounded and pounded and pounded. Soon, the friction gathered heat and the pleasure gathered steam and the pressure pressed in just. The right. Way. And she exploded in a showering starburst, the light shimmering behind her eyes to the concussing cadence of James's wondrous thrusts.

His pace quickened, extending the shattering pulses for longer seconds. She sobbed into his neck, stroked his bare shoulders, wanting to give him the same pleasure.

And, in the end, she did.

He roared with it, his muscles going rigid beneath her palms, his hands gripping her hips and pulling free of her, yet pulling her into him as she was filled with his shouts of release, her belly bathed in his seed.

In the storm's wake, her eyes listed, a warm, rich fog of contentment blanketing her as surely as he did. She held him, stroking his neck and back, as the light grew darker, the sounds of his breath in her ear dimming, the sleep she had missed the night before claiming her. Light and sound returned for a brief moment. Just long enough to feel him gather her close beneath the blankets, tucking her into his side and kissing her forehead.

At last, sleep drew its cloak over her, and she dreamed the sweetest dream, one that only a hopeless ninny could conjure—

there, in the darkness, she felt his lips brush her cheek, heard him whisper with heartrending tenderness, "Ye are a bluidy miracle, lass."

Chapter Eighteen

"Winning a woman's favor is the product of abundant charm, appropriate gifts, and avoiding catastrophe. I recommend beginning with the latter, Charles."

—THE DOWAGER MARCHIONESS OF WALLINGHAM to her son, Charles, upon witnessing a most calamitous exchange involving an umbrella, two dogs, a defiled bonnet, and a certain widow.

∽∞∾

"YOU KNOW SOMETHING ABOUT WOOING A LADY, DO YOU NOT?"

Holding his cue with studied nonchalance, Lucien raised a single brow at the question.

James took his final shot, potting both the red and Lucien's ball for a victory.

"Bloody hell, Tannenbrook. Can you not let me win for once? Leave a man a remnant of dignity."

James straightened and plopped the base of his cue on the

floor of Lucien's billiard room with a thud. "Answer my question."

Now, both brows went up, accompanied by a half smile. "I was under the impression you'd already married." He held a hand level with his cravat pin. "Tiny thing about this high. Resembles one of those nymphs from the Greek myths, only lovelier."

James glared at his daft friend before setting his cue lengthwise on the table and folding his arms across his chest.

"Very well," said Luc, tossing his own cue stick in the air, catching it at the base and placing it neatly beside James's. "Wooing. Yes, I know a bit. Why do you ask?"

"I have no facility for it."

"Well, I cannot disagree with you on that point. However, you are spectacular at billiards. Perhaps she will swoon upon seeing you wield your cue."

"I knew I should not have asked ye. Daft sod."

Lucien laughed, shaking his head and waving away James's bristle. "Merely a jest. I am at your disposal. As it happens, wooing is rather a specialty of mine."

The claim was too modest. Lucien Wyatt could seduce a woman with a single arch of his brow. His wife, Victoria, had been his last conquest, and now the man was so mad for her, he scarcely acknowledged other females existed. But that did not mean his skills were for naught.

"I planned to never marry," James began, wondering how much to reveal. "I've not had occasion to court a woman. The marriage to Viola was ... unexpected."

"Ah, yes. Unexpected. I seem to recall only a few months ago, you referred to her as 'nobody.'"

James sighed his frustration, leaning forward to brace his hands on the billiard table. He kept his eyes on the fine brown surface. "I cannot ... She is ..." He swallowed, unable to articulate it in words.

"Everything."

James's head came up, meeting Lucien's dark gray gaze. "Aye," he rasped. And then he could not stop himself. He needed to tell somebody, and Viola refused to permit a conversation more substantive than what to serve for breakfast. "She claims she took one look at me and lost her heart. Pursued me at every bloody gathering during the season. Relentless. God. I thought at first it was some sort of madness."

"Her wanting you?"

"Aye. Then, I felt it, too. But I didna want tae." He shook his head. "I didna want a wife."

Lucien moved to the sideboard, pouring a brandy for himself and one for James. He handed James the glass and leaned a hip against the table. "What changed your plans? Or should I hazard a guess?" This time, he held his glass at the level of his cravat pin. "About this high."

James tossed back a swallow of his own brandy before answering. "Beautiful enough to break your heart. Yes."

"So, now you have her. Wedded bliss, and all that. Why the need for wooing advice?"

"Because I have broken her."

"Peculiar. She appeared in fine fettle upon your arrival."

"She saw another woman kiss me."

Lucien frowned. "What woman?"

"Alison."

Dark brows arched.

"It wasn't as it appeared. I pushed her away. I feel nothing for Alison any longer. It was clear to me that day. Before then, really. But Viola only saw the kiss. She hasn't looked upon me with the same eyes since."

"Have you explained? Apologized?"

James sighed and took another drink, appreciating the smooth, rich heat. It was good brandy. "I've tried. She won't hear it. She even offered to annul the marriage. Or, worse, arrange a *divorce*." He wanted to spit the foul taste of the word out of his mouth. "Like bloody hell. She can have her divorce when I'm cold in the grave, and not a minute before."

"Mmm. For a man who felt no previous inclination toward matrimony, you are rather adamant in your opposition to severing this unexpected union."

James set his glass carefully on the edge of the billiard table. He wouldn't wish to crush it. "She made her choice. If she now suffers regret, that is unfortunate, but I shan't change my mind."

"Still, I wonder if the notion you find most bothersome is that, should a divorce occur, she would then be free to marry another."

James's fist slammed the edge of the table a moment before he could control the impulse. The heavy thud caused Lucien to smirk. James struggled against the fury that had been ignited inside him. A man of his size could not afford to lose command of himself. "She will not marry another. She belongs to me."

"I stand corrected."

"She may smile prettily at every footman and tradesman and bloody lordling within sight of her, but in the end, she is mine."

"Naturally. And it doesn't bother you in the slightest, her smiling at other men."

He began pacing. He'd never been a pacer until he'd met Viola. Running a hand through his hair, James growled the words he wanted to shout. "Aye, it bloody well bothers me."

"There, now, that wasn't too difficult, was it? Admitting one's unreasoning jealousy, I mean."

"I canna abide it, Luc. The way she smiles for others as she should fer me. Ye must help me woo her. Tell me what tae dae."

Lucien sipped his brandy and pretended to ponder. Then, he held up a finger. "First, you must understand what is happening. You are in love with her."

"Nae."

"Yes. Trust me on this point, James. It is better to simply concede that you have taken the fall than to thrash yourself to bits denying the truth. Consider it a glad surrender which will end happily for all concerned."

"It isna true." What he felt for Viola was not the same sort of obsessive preoccupation and wholehearted devotion that Lucien felt for Victoria. James desired his wee bonnie lass, of course. Immensely. And he enjoyed her company, even when she was chattering too much or asking him endless questions. She was a fascinating creature, like a butterfly composed of ever-changing colors. He wanted to take care of her. And he wanted her affection and her laughter and that starlight in her eyes to return. That was all.

"Rubbish," Lucien scoffed. "Do you know how I know? I have plotted the demise of Sir Barnabus Malby approximately four hundred and eighty-seven times. I have dreamed of every conceivable method of that smelly toad's torture and dismemberment. Now, perhaps you would like to understand why this is so."

James frowned at his daft sod of a friend. "Aye."

Lucien's eyes flashed, his jaw tightening in a strangely familiar fashion. "Because Sir Barnabus Malby cannot keep his bulging toad eyes off of my wife's bosom. And if I see him do it again, I shall—" He flexed his fist and appeared to regain control of himself. "Let us say that I understand how *unreasonable* a man feels when he is in love with a woman."

"What does Victoria say about this?"

"She does not know."

Now, it was James's turn to raise a brow.

"Very well, she knows. We do not discuss it. I control my violent impulses, and she rewards me handsomely." Lucien crossed to James and clapped him on the shoulder. "Now, then, we have established that you are in love with Viola."

"She vexes me greatly. And I despise seeing her smile at other men. That does not mean I am in love with her."

"Yes, it does."

"I do not write her bloody poetry the way other gentlemen do. Explain that."

"Describe her to me. Pretend I've never met her."

"But you have."

"Humor an old friend, won't you?"

James pondered for a moment, frowning as he struggled to find the best words for Viola. "She is bonnie and wee."

Lucien chuckled. "Try to reach beyond the Scot side of your vocabulary. What is she like?"

"A butterfly," he muttered. "Bright and fine. The most exquisite of creatures. She is like a butterfly in full color landing on fresh-fallen snow. She blinds you to everything but her." It grew easier, he found, the more he spoke about her. "She has these eyes. They look like the sky, but not an ordinary sky. They're lighter in the center, and at the edges lie rings of darker blue, nearly violet. In between, if the light casts just so, you can see the stars there. Twinkling the way they do around dusk."

Several seconds of silence ticked by before Lucien said, "But you are not in love with her."

James shook his head, more because he needed to clear it than because he disagreed with Luc's sarcasm. "What business have I tae be in love with such a creature, Luc? She is a butterfly and I am Scottish mud."

"And if that were of no import whatever?"

"Ye're sayin' I love the lass."

"That is what I am saying, yes, you bloody obstinate Scot."

James stared into Lucien's eyes and wondered how long he'd known. "When did you—"

"Rotten Row. It was the way you looked at her. Or tried not to, rather. You failed spectacularly, by the by."

James huffed out a burst of laughter, shaking his head in wonder and running a hand over his lower jaw. "In love. Me. Aye, now that ye mention it, I have had a bit of trouble keeping my eyes off of her. Every time she laughs, I have to look at her. Every time I look at her, I want her until the soles of my feet ache. And then, I canna think of anything except—"

"Yes, yes. I know. Not to worry, James. That's what the wooing is for."

James folded his arms over his chest. "When do these wooing lessons begin?"

With a pat of his shoulder and a wide grin, Lucien replied, "They already have, my good man."

VICTORIA WYATT, VISCOUNTESS ATHERBOURNE, WAS NOT AS beautiful as Viola had anticipated, given her husband's dark perfection. While her hair was a lovely shade of golden blond, her features were more pleasant than striking, with the possible exception of her eyes, which were overlarge for her face but a rather unusual color, a balance of cerulean and Saxon green.

However, Lady Atherbourne was extraordinary in every other way. Upon greeting Viola and James, she had glowed with warm welcome, her every word a kindness. Viola had taken to her straight away, enthusing about the elegance of Thornbridge Park and admiring the handsomeness of Atherbourne's heir, Gregory Wyatt, who appeared fond of gnawing his own hand, speaking nonsense, and toddling about the hearth in the opulent blue drawing room. The black-haired infant was shortly to be joined by a sibling if the swelling beneath Lady Atherbourne's azure gown was any indication.

Presently, Viola sipped strong tea and leaned forward to admire the color of Lord Atherbourne's waistcoat. "Your talent is most astounding, my lady," she enthused, shaking her head. "This is one of the finest portraits I have seen. How did you manage to create such a wondrous shade of blue?"

"Ultramarine," Lady Atherbourne replied, smiling with transparent pleasure. "Layers and layers of ultramarine."

Viola returned her smile with an appreciative one of her own. "A labor of love, clearly."

"Indeed, though that is putting it a trifle mildly."

Chuckling, Viola returned to the chair she'd vacated, sipped her tea, and watched as the nursemaid carried a fussy Gregory from the room, pausing to allow his mother a fond kiss. The ensuing silence felt as comfortable as if she and Lady Atherbourne had spent years rather than hours in each other's company.

However, silence gave one entirely too much time to think. And she did not wish to think. Much better to lose oneself in distractions. For example, Viola had awakened earlier that morning plastered atop her mountain of a husband, her nose tickled by chest hair, her thigh brushing a surprisingly robust hardness. He had sighed awake, his hand sliding down her back to her buttocks. "Lass?" he'd inquired after a minute of silence. She'd heard the question—the ominous, looming, difficult problem she'd avoided confronting—in that single syllable. He'd wished to talk. But she had not. So she'd kissed him. Fortunately, lying naked upon one's husband and then kissing his delicious mouth generated a distraction of mighty proportions.

At breakfast, she'd had Papa and Georgina and Penelope and Aunt Marian to see off with tearful hugs and fond farewells. Afterward, James had once again attempted to speak with her, but she had interrupted to suggest they journey to Lord Atherbourne's neighboring estate. He had reluctantly agreed. Then, on the short ride, he had tried again, and she had asked him instead to tell her about how his friendship with Atherbourne had begun. It had been a fascinating tale, even told in James's customary grunting, abbreviated fashion.

"He thought my manner of speech grand," James had

grumbled. "And amusing."

She had sighed, rocking with the motion of a pretty gray mare as they'd wound through a copse of elm trees to the wide brook that divided the two properties. "Your brogue is beguiling, James. Why did you seek to change it?"

He'd cast her an inscrutable look and muttered, "An English earl does not speak in such a way."

"But many Scottish lords do. Lord Mochrie, for example."

He had slowed his mount and waved her ahead as they approached a wooden bridge spanning the brook's swift water. "Aye. They sound nothing at all like a blacksmith's son."

The bridge had creaked and groaned under the weight of the horses, momentarily filling the silence before they crossed to a clearing on the other side. "Lord Atherbourne helped you, then."

"He did. So did his brother, Gregory. Their father, too. Lucien has suffered greatly with their loss."

She had glanced behind her to view the beloved crags and haunted eyes beneath his hat's brim. "As have you," she'd observed quietly.

He'd given a single nod. "Aye."

Now, sitting in Thornbridge's lovely drawing room, Viola noted the differences between Lord Atherbourne's Palladian masterpiece of a home and the gray-stone-and-brown-oak solidity of Shankwood Hall. One was bright and beauteous, the other as stalwart as the earth. Frankly, she preferred the latter.

Her gaze traveled idly from the portrait of Lord Atherbourne to the white marble fireplace, contemplating how unseemly it might be to indulge in another session of lovemaking with James before dinner. Was a wife supposed to desire her husband with such frequency? She did not know, but it was a fact that she did, despite the uncertain state of their marriage.

"I beg your pardon, Lady Tannenbrook, but have you ever considered sitting for a portrait?" The question brought her head around to Lady Atherbourne, who was gazing upon her with an artist's avidity.

"My father commissioned a miniature once, but that was years ago."

The blond woman rose gracefully from the gold damask sofa and moved to the exquisite mahogany secretary positioned between two windows. She returned carrying a large, leather-covered book and what appeared to be two pencils and a penknife. "I hope you will forgive my impertinence," she said, seating herself on the end of the sofa nearer to Viola's chair. "You are quite extraordinary."

Viola laughed lightly. "As it happens, I had the same thought about you, my lady."

The other woman smiled and waved a hand dismissively. "Victoria, please. We are neighbors, and our husbands are the best of friends. I expect we shall soon grow weary of cumbersome formality. Particularly if you should consent to sit for me." Those wide, blue-green eyes sparkled with a pleading sort of zeal. "Please say you will."

Her smile growing, Viola nodded. "Of course. It would be an honor. Just tell me what you require."

Victoria threw open the cover of her sketchbook and tossed aside several pages before apparently finding an empty one. "Nothing more than for you to sit as you are. The light is lovely in here this morning." She sharpened her pencil with quick efficiency, held it up to examine the tip, and nodded. Then, she ran her eyes over Viola's face with such eagerness, Viola began to feel a familiar prickle of discomfort. But it was soon eased by Victoria's grateful smile. "Thank you, Lady Tannenbrook. This will be such a pleasure."

"Viola. And the pleasure is mine." Viola blinked as Victoria began, her hand flying across the page in sweeping strokes. "Your talent is exceptional. I fear my artistic endeavors end rather more abominably."

As she worked, Victoria explained her love for painting

and drawing. "Everywhere I go, my sketchbook goes, too. I cannot resist the impulse to capture what I see. Naturally, from the moment I set eyes upon Lord Atherbourne, I filled pages and pages."

"He is astonishingly handsome," Viola agreed.

"Mmm, yes. Another delight I find irresistible."

"My preoccupation with Lord Tannenbrook is similar. Perhaps there is a nefarious potion hidden in the waters here which transforms these men into objects of fascination."

Victoria's lips pursed. She sent Viola a mischievous twinkle. "A whimsical yet compelling hypothesis. This shall require a long, thorough examination of the subjects in question, I expect." After their laughter subsided, Victoria's eyes turned inquisitive. "How did the taciturn Lord Tannenbrook manage to win your heart?"

Lowering her eyes to the delicate china cup in her hands, Viola replied, "He had no need to win it. My heart was his from the start."

Though his always belonged to another.

Pain flooded her chest, gushing forth from a well she'd covered poorly. Drowning her without warning.

No, no, no. She could not think about this.

He is not yours. You must let him go, Viola. You must allow him his happiness.

The cup began to rattle in its saucer. She set it upon the marble table beside her chair.

I cannot, her heart whispered. *I cannot.*

She curled her toes inside her slippers. She folded and refolded her hands in her lap. She flexed the muscles in her throat and pressed her lips together, biting down until she tasted copper. All to stop the daft, ridiculous tears from erupting in the middle of Lady Atherbourne's elegant blue drawing room.

The scrape of pencil across paper halted. "Viola?"

She mustn't allow the humiliating tears to flow. Mustn't

embarrass herself or James. She shook her head, laughing silently at herself. "I drove him mad, you know," she whispered, her voice a thread. "I called it my Tannenbrook Hunt. Chased him everywhere. Flirted shamelessly. If he were less honorable, I would have been ruined after a fortnight."

There was a clock somewhere in the room. She could hear it ticking.

"But his honor is one of the reasons I love him so."

Her hands distorted, swimming and wavering upon the puce satin of her skirts.

"He is the finest of men."

Her voice distorted, too, twisting and strangling.

"How he must despise me after all I have taken from him. And yet, he protects me still."

A cloth was pressed into her hand. A slender arm came around her shoulders. "Protects you from what?"

She pressed the cloth to her cheeks and mouth, her next words muffled. "I offered to set him free." She dropped her hand and squeezed the now-damp scrap of fabric. "He won't have it. But I must. And yet I cannot." She let forth a sob and covered her face with her hands. "Oh, God. I do not wish to cry. It swells my eyes and gives me a headache."

"Viola, what did he say when you offered to, er, set him free?"

She blew her clogged nose into the cloth, uncaring of decorum. Victoria was seeing the worst possible version of her. What difference would one more indignity make? "He said—" She wiped her nose and dropped her hands. "He refused to hear another word about annulment or divorce. Said even a separation was out of the question. Then he accused me of trapping him."

"Did you trap him?"

"Yes. It is the worst thing I have ever done. He said I'd sprung the trap on us both and that I was caught, too. Then, he said he had no intention of releasing me."

A gentle hand rubbed between her shoulder blades. "Mmm.

Was he, by chance, displaying a bit of temper at the time?"

Viola nodded, dabbing her cheeks with the cloth's only remaining dry corner. "When he is overset, he sounds more Scottish. I had a bit of trouble making out the words, but I had practiced with his family. They were very kind."

"It would appear he is resistant to the freedom you offered. Perhaps that is not the proper course, after all. What do *you* want?"

She did not hesitate, for the answer sprang forth of its own volition. "Him. I want James. I have done from the very first moment I heard how he hoisted a man up by his cravat for insulting a woman he did not know."

"Yes, it was quite a sight."

"You were there?"

"Indeed. Tannenbrook is as honorable as you say. He is deserving of a woman who understands him and loves him with all her heart. Be easy, Viola. I have something for you." Victoria moved away to retrieve her sketchbook. She flipped through several pages before finding the one she sought. Then, she tore the page from her book and held it out.

Viola sniffed and accepted the paper, lowering it to her lap.

"I drew this two years ago. It was a difficult time for Tannenbrook, though I knew nothing of it. All I knew was what I saw. Honor. Loyalty. Strength. And, yes, his stubbornness. Perhaps that above all. I believe being obstinate is his way of coping with all the changes he has had to endure. Changes and losses. There have been many."

The sketch was beautiful. His eyes were shadowed, the furrow between his heavy brows a stark slash of grief. His jaw was pure, hard resolve. But his lips were set with tenderness and the faintest smile along one corner. Everything about it was her James. Her beloved.

Tears came again, this time flowing unchecked. "Thank you," she gasped, clutching the paper to her heart and gazing up at Victoria unabashedly, knowing she looked a fright, knowing she should not reveal so much of herself to a woman who saw too clearly.

"You are most welcome," that woman said, smiling and brushing at a tear of her own. "Now, I cannot tell you what to do, for you must determine your course. But if Tannenbrook refuses to let you go, then it is because he wishes to keep you in his life." She gave Viola's shoulder a final squeeze. "Before you once again decide his fate for him, perhaps you should ask the man what he prefers."

Chapter Nineteen

*"A conversation lacking any form of wit is not impossible,
merely intolerable. This is demonstrated in a fashion similar
to the rising of the sun or the disappointment of mothers.
That is to say, with predictable frequency."*

—THE DOWAGER MARCHIONESS OF WALLINGHAM to Lady
Rutherford upon said lady's expressed desire to be seated at least
four chairs away from Lord Mochrie at any future meals.

HER HUSBAND'S PECULIAR BEHAVIOR BEGAN UPON THEIR
return journey to Shankwood Hall.

With Victoria's help, Viola had managed to cool her face
sufficiently that no signs remained of her earlier upset by the
time James and Lucien returned to the drawing room. Their
visit had ended pleasantly, and Viola had accepted James's
assistance mounting the gray mare.

He'd gazed up at her, his hands sliding from her waist to her legs, his eyes searching her face until she'd wondered if her own eyes were still red and puffy. She'd frowned down at him in confusion. Then, he'd begun smoothing her skirts over her knees. Long, lingering strokes.

"My lord?" the stable lad had queried, still holding James's horse. James had sighed and withdrawn.

Then, as they crossed the bridge onto Shankwood land, he had broken the silence between them with her name. "Viola." That was all.

"Yes?" she'd prompted.

But he'd only shaken his head and grunted before leading them through the wood. When they emerged onto green, rolling pasture, he'd pointed to a trio of sheep in the distance and said, "If they were cleaner, their fleece would be the same color as your skin."

That was when she'd begun wondering if James had imbibed a bit too much brandy.

Feeling raw from her conversation with Victoria, and dreading the conversation she knew she must have with James, she retreated to her chamber upon arriving at the Hall. Carefully, she retrieved the sketch from inside her bodice, where she had tucked it away for safekeeping. She smoothed the folds with the flat of her hand on the dressing table, taking care not to disturb the image. Of James. Just looking upon his square, blunt features made her heart twist and her lower belly heat.

How she loved the daft man.

She tucked the sketch away in the bottom drawer and summoned Amy to help her change into a long-sleeved gown of blue-sprigged, white muslin. She topped it with a bright, coquelicot shawl. Red always added a bit of cheer. Then, she examined her face in the mirror, silently rehearsing the opening lines of her Difficult Conversation with her husband.

James, she would begin. *As you know, I am your wife.*

No. Stating the obvious sounded too much like Penelope.

James, she tried again. *Have you reconsidered the option of casting me aside so that you can marry your first love?*

Her stomach cramped. She could not speak that baldly. She would never make it through the sentence without weeping.

James, she began her third iteration, this time emphasizing persuasion. *What would you require to abandon your lifelong affection for a bloody tall Scotswoman and give your heart into my care? Would a poorly embroidered waistcoat suffice?*

She sighed. A Difficult Conversation, indeed.

By the time she descended the stairs into the south entrance hall, she had settled on a gradual approach. First, she would ask his preference for which day they should have Lord and Lady Atherbourne to dinner. Then, she would mention Lady Atherbourne's admiration for his character. Thereafter, she would inquire about his intention to remain trapped in a marriage with her whilst desiring marriage to another.

She had tucked two handkerchiefs in her sleeve in the event things did not go well. It was a Difficult Conversation, after all.

"My lady," said Mrs. Duckett, entering the small space from the direction of the dining room. "His lordship requests your presence."

Viola smiled at the elderly housekeeper. "Thank you, Mrs. Duckett. Where would he like me to meet him?"

"Oh! I suppose I forgot that part. Now, where did he say ...? Ah, yes. The churchyard."

Blinking at the unexpected answer, Viola repeated, "The churchyard. Are you certain?"

"Indeed, my lady. That is what he said."

Although Viola had her doubts—the housekeeper was very old, after all—she left the house through the south entrance into the courtyard and crossed a wide expanse of lawn toward the stout, Norman-era church a hundred yards away. As she drew closer, she saw that Mrs. Duckett had not misled her, for James stood in the western corner of the churchyard, his backside resting against the stone wall, his arms crossed over his chest. He was still wearing the brown riding coat he'd worn on their visit to Thornbridge, but he had removed his hat, she noted.

He glanced up as she neared, standing straight and running a hand through his hair. "Viola. Mrs. Duckett found you. Good."

She shielded her eyes from the bright sun, realizing she had neglected to don a hat. "I wasn't entirely certain of your message," she replied, passing through the gate and moving to where he stood. "It is not Sunday. Has the vicar requested to meet with us?"

His mouth was set in a flat line, the muscles in his jaw and neck tense. He cleared his throat. "I wish to show you something."

She waited. "Yes?"

He turned his shoulders and waved toward a gravestone in the corner near a small shrub. The cross-shaped marker was covered in moss, crooked and weathered as though it had seen a thousand winters. "This reminds me of you, lass."

"Me?"

He nodded.

She looked again at where he pointed. "This?"

"Aye."

"Well, I ... I don't quite know what to say." It was true. She was utterly nonplussed. "I confess, James, I fail to see the resemblance."

"Its scent is the same. Every time I walk by this corner now, I shall think of you."

She blinked up at him, wondering again how much brandy he and Lord Atherbourne had imbibed whilst playing billiards. "You believe I smell like a grave?"

His brows descended into a frustrated glower. "No. Not the grave, for the love of God. The flower."

Her eyes flared. "Oh! Do you mean this shrub?"

"Aye. It is a peony. The vicar's wife planted it here two years ago." He bent to sift through the leaves, using his fingers to tip upward a broad, ruffled, pink blossom whose petals had begun to wilt and brown at the edges. "I would have plucked it for you, but its bloom is nearly done."

She smiled and stooped to smell the fragrance. Sighing at the sweet, powdery scent, she glanced up at her peculiar husband. "Well, this is most relieving, James. I had begun to wonder if I should request a bath before dinner."

He laughed, the lines of his face relaxing for the first time since that morning. She adored the rumbly, delicious sounds. She wanted him to kiss her. But he did not. Instead, his eyes heated, and he said in a low, shiver-inducing voice, "You smell … good to me, lass. Better than anything else."

Releasing a shuddering sigh, she felt herself blush and dropped her eyes to his hand. His big, strong, capable hand that touched petals with such delicacy.

Perhaps their Difficult Conversation could be delayed for a time. Just long enough for a lie-down before dinner. Or a bath. James's hands could provide critical assistance in either scenario.

"What a fortuitous circumstance, your lordship." The unwelcome intrusion clanged against her heat-softened senses. It was James's estate manager, exiting the church and closing fast, trailed by two younger men she recognized as the oldest Fellowes boys.

"Mr. Strudwicke." James's tone was not hostile, precisely, but she had the sense he'd liked the interruption even less than she had.

Strudwicke and the two boys tipped their hats and greeted both her and James. Then, the estate manager launched into a description of his plans for the upcoming well-dressing festival. Apparently, every year, villagers decorated the well located on the north side of the green with an elaborate array of flowers, seeds, twigs, and leaves, artfully arranged to form images of thanksgiving for the blessings of the land. The custom was an ancient one, according to Miss Starling, dating back centuries at Shankwood.

"Lady Tannenbrook, I daresay, this may be of particular interest to you, as this year's theme is 'She Walks in Beauty Like the Night.' It was suggested by young Mr. Fellowes, here." Strudwicke pointed to the taller boy, who looked to be sixteen or seventeen. "A tribute to her ladyship. And to starry skies, of course. We shall pluck every blue and purple blossom we can find for the design."

Viola gave all three men her brightest smile. "How lovely! That you would choose to honor me in such a way fills my heart with gladness."

From behind her, a shadow moved forward. "Your theme is a poem by a disgraced baron?" James did not sound pleased.

"We—we had hoped you'd approve, my lord," said the younger Fellowes boy, his voice squeaking like rusty hinges. "Miss Tabitha Starling read the poem to us last spring."

"I believed the poem a lot of nonsense until her ladyship arrived, my lord," the deeper-voiced Mr. Fellowes interjected. "Then, I knew Lord Byron must have seen a vision of Lady Tannenbrook, for he describes her—"

"James," barked James, causing to Viola to blink. The oldest Fellowes boy was also called James? And why was *her* James so angry? "Last year, the theme was 'Let the Beauty of the Lord Our God Be Upon Us.' Before that, it was 'Then Shall the Earth Yield Her Increase.' Do you sense a distinction between these and your proposal?"

Seeing red flood the young man's cheeks, Viola tsked. "Well, I think your idea is splendid, Mr. Fellowes."

Behind her, James grunted, muttering something that sounded like, "Splendidly daft."

She ignored her surly husband. "Moreover, I should very much enjoy helping with the arrangements for the festival, if you would find my assistance useful."

"Yes, indeed, my lady," exclaimed Mr. Strudwicke, his droopy, soulful eyes reminding her of Humphrey. "That would be splendid."

"Again with the 'splendid,'" grumbled the ill-tempered man behind her. "Every bloody thing is splendid."

Viola waited until Mr. Strudwicke and the Fellowes boys bid their farewells to turn and glare up at her husband. He was not looking at her, but instead casting a menacing glare at the receding trio. "What in heaven's name is wrong with you?" she demanded.

His eyes dropped to hers. His frown was fierce. "Me? I am not the one quoting rubbish poetry written by a perverted lord."

"No, you are the one being abominably rude to a young man who simply wishes to honor his lord's marriage by paying tribute to—"

"He might as well have crooned about your dewy petal lips. Bloody rot is what it is."

She held up a hand. "I cannot speak to you when you are like this. Perhaps after dinner we will try again, once the brandy has run its course." With that, she pivoted on her heel and stalked toward the Hall, where, one hoped, greater sanity prevailed.

⁘

JAMES DID NOT UNDERSTAND IT. HE'D FOLLOWED LUCIEN'S wooing advice precisely. First, he'd found excuses to touch her, letting his hands linger on her legs after placing her upon her horse. Then, he'd found unexpected ways to compliment her, noting that her skin was the palest shade of cream, like a lamb's new fleece. And finally, he had shared an example of how she pleased him. Lucien had specified that appealing to her senses would enhance the effectiveness of the wooing. That was what had made him think of showing her the peony.

He'd thought it was working, too. Her eyes had gone soft, her lips sweetly parted just before Strudwicke and his pair of randy youths had come upon them to disrupt the delicate process of seducing his wife. Now she was vexed with him, all that warm, honeyed glaze of sweetness replaced with the snap of irritability and decided displeasure.

Bloody hell.

He stomped out of the churchyard, rounding the east side of the house to head toward the village. As usual, her blasted admirers ruined everything. There was nothing for it. He must start the wooing all over again. This time, however, he had a new notion. These small gestures—compliments and such—required eloquence he did not possess. They were better suited to someone like Luc, who had never lacked for a seductive turn of phrase. Words were fleeting and of little substance, in any case. Viola deserved more. She deserved something lasting. Something as beautiful as she was, though that was impossible. Nothing compared to her.

But he knew his wee bonnie lass would approve of his effort, and perhaps it would go some way toward repairing the wound he had dealt her when he'd rejected the gift she had made for him. This sort of wooing might take longer, he supposed. He was out of practice, certainly.

Rounding the corner of the Starling Sisters shop, he strode down a narrow lane leading to a long stone building. Breathing deeply, wondering if he was bloody daft, he entered the workshop he'd constructed fourteen years earlier, ducking past the lintel. He smelled the gritty scent of stone, heard the clinking thud of the mallet striking, and, with a small smile of remembrance curling his lips, felt a sense of rightness settle in his bones.

George Fellowes glanced up, his chisel hovering above a block of limestone. "My lord? What brings you by this old, dusty place on such a fine day?"

It *was* dusty. The fine grains floated on streams of light from the windows. He glanced around at the shop, noting the scarred worktables, the shelves he had crafted alongside George, the tools neatly lined up in a row. Sighing with satisfaction, James grinned at the mason and said, "George, I have a need for stone."

"You—you wish me to make something for you?"

"No. I shall make this myself. I will also require the use of the workshop, for a time. Perhaps a week or so, if it is not too troublesome having me in here again."

George's shaggy brows arched in surprise. He scratched his head with the wrist of his mallet hand, scattering a cloud of dust from the brown mop onto the table and floor. "Of course not. It has been too long since we last worked side by side. What sort of stone are you looking for?"

Pausing to admire a handsome marble round likely destined to top a wooden table, James felt his grin growing. Viola would light up for him again. She would see what he had made for her, and the stars would return to her eyes—he knew it with a certainty he could not explain.

"Something extraordinary, George," he answered finally. "For this, only extraordinary will do."

Chapter Twenty

"I find cleanliness to be an underappreciated and woefully underutilized attribute. Perhaps if you ponder this observation at greater length, and at a greater distance from my current position, you will come to agree."

—THE DOWAGER MARCHIONESS OF WALLINGHAM to Sir Barnabus Malby after said gentleman's third quadrille.

∽∾

THE DIFFICULT CONVERSATION DID NOT HAPPEN THAT afternoon, as James disappeared for hours before dinner, and Viola busied herself consulting with the household staff and familiarizing herself more fully with Shankwood Hall's routines. She would, after all, be its mistress. Provided he chose to remain married to her. And she would not know whether that was the case until she had the Difficult Conversation.

Which, similarly, did not occur that evening, for James entered Viola's chamber whilst she was lingering amidst the scented steam of a bath. He'd sent Amy scurrying and promptly set to work ensuring she was cleaned very, very properly. Thereafter, he'd plucked her dripping form from the water and carried her to the bed, where he'd proceeded to make love to her with breathtaking thoroughness and attention to detail. Those magnificent hands—along with every other magnificent part of him—had done their work well.

Matters proceeded in much the same pattern over the following week, with James waking early and being strangely absent for most of each day, only to return in the evenings to ravish her body until she was limp and sated and sleepy. During meals, they chatted about food and fishing and festivals and all manner of other topics. But not the one thing that might change everything.

A Difficult Conversation, she found, was difficult to schedule when one dreaded the very thought of it.

When it finally did occur, it came at her like a bull charging through an unexpectedly open gate. She was writing a letter to Charlotte, struggling to explain her circumstances without sounding morose, when James entered the sitting room connecting their bedchambers.

She glanced up, noting the odd layer of dust upon his skin, the sweat along the open neck of his shirt. He wore no cravat, no coat. His waistcoat was plain green wool. His sleeves were rolled past thick, muscled forearms.

Suddenly, she wanted to leap upon him. Sink her teeth into those arms. Claw her fingers into his neck. Feel him inside her again.

The need was fierce. Nearly painful in its intensity.

His eyes found her. Heated and burned. "There you are, lass." A half smile curled his lips.

She rose from her chair. Tossed the pen onto the writing desk. Drifted toward him as though pulled by a line. Fisted her hands in the linen of his shirt.

And yanked that delicious mouth down to hers.

He groaned, the sound vibrating against her lips and tongue. She stroked and invaded, pulsing the way he'd taught her. He groaned again. But he did not wrap those arms around her.

"Hold me," she panted, her breath catching as her need caught fire. "I want to feel your hands upon me."

"I am filthy, lass. I don't wish to ruin your gown."

She growled, her fingers digging into the muscles of his chest. "I don't give a blasted fig about my gown, James Kilbrenner. I need you. Now."

He laughed, the sound a sensual rumble that made her nipples peak and her thighs clench. "Demanding little thing, aren't you?"

She tore at his waistcoat buttons, throwing the fabric wide so she could yank the hem of his shirt from the waist of his breeches. Then she went to work on his fall.

"Slow down, lass. There's no need to rush."

"There is every need. My need."

"And don't I always see you well satisfied?"

The third button of his fall gave her trouble, so she resolved the problem by simply reaching inside and taking a firm grip upon his cock. He had taught her the word after much coaxing. He'd been most reluctant to share the term with her, as though coarse language would debauch her any more than the acts his cock performed on a regular basis. Besides, she liked the word. She liked what it described even better.

Now, it was in her hands, exposed to her eyes. All that massive heat and hardness, designed for her. For her pleasure. She bent forward and took him in her mouth, the difference in their heights making it a simple matter.

"Ah, God almighty, Viola." Finally, his hand touched her, but only to cup the back of her head. His hips jerked as she suckled the tip, her hand gripping him at the base, holding him at her mercy. She loved him with her tongue, stroking and circling, finding a sensitive little spot just underneath.

The rumbling roar of her husband's will finally breaking penetrated her consciousness an instant before she felt him take hold of her head and jerk his hips away. Just enough to remove himself from her mouth. Just enough to draw her upward and stare into her eyes with such furious turmoil, she felt it as a pain in the center of her chest. His hands held her cheeks, his fingers enfolding the back of her head. At some point, she realized, he had loosened her hair. She felt the weight of it on her back.

"Ye want this filthy Scot tae soil yer bonnie gown, dae ye, lass? Be very sure."

"I am sure." She groaned. "James. Oh, God. James. I hurt. Take me. Please, I beg you."

In the next instant, his hands were upon her, running over tight, aching nipples. Grasping at rose silk skirts. Tearing her bodice from nape to waist. Then he was spinning her. Forcing the gown down over her arms. Cracking her corset wide open. Cupping her breasts in dusty, capable hands.

She felt his engorged cock pressing against her backside through her skirts, felt his fingers squeezing her wanton nipples. Felt his hot breath and his lips and his whiskery jaw working at the side of her neck. Then one of his arms dropped to her waist. Lifted her out of her skirts. Spun them both. Carried her to the green velvet sofa. Set her upon it sideways with her knees on the cushion, her hands braced on the rolled arm.

He braced himself behind her. Pulled her hips back into his. Ran the tip of his cock teasingly along her drenched folds. Bent over her, squeezing her nipple with his brilliant, strong fingers. Whispered hot in her ear, "Take yer filthy Scot inside ye now, Viola."

He took her in a single, breathtaking stroke, sinking deep and true.

She keened her pleasure, clawing the green twill beneath her fingers, loving the feel of his flesh pounding into hers. Wanting more. Demanding more. Her hand reached back. Grasped a handful of his hair. Pulled him forward so she could turn her head and take his mouth again.

He thrust harder. Faster. Hammered them together with fire and force. Squeezed and stroked her breasts with one hand. Braced the other beside hers, holding himself above her while his hips and his cock took her higher. And higher. And tighter. And then, he was driving her over the precipice.

She seized and screamed and shuddered. Squeezed his ravenous cock with sharp greed and astounding pleasure. She felt his rhythm crescendo, hang suspended for a moment, then he gave one final thrust before pulling free of her body, his slick cock a heated pressure sliding against her skin, jerking and exploding as he broke their kiss to roar his climax. The sound echoed through her skin and bones. She closed her eyes, savoring it. The sound of his pleasure. The scent of pine and sweat and her and James.

Gently, he slumped back onto his heels, gathering her up in his arms and cradling her against him. He sat with her in his lap. Stroked her hair and kissed her neck. "Look what I've done. Bloody hell. Now you're a proper mess." Then he rubbed at a spot of dirt on her shoulder. "I should never have handled you so roughly. I am sorry."

She played with the hand that still gripped her waist, measuring his fingers against hers. That was when she started the Difficult Conversation without even trying.

"Why do you always behave as though I am some pristine creature to be kept safely behind glass?"

His body tensed. A long silence fell. He lifted her and set her gently on the sofa. Then, he rose. Buttoned his fall. Went to the spot where her gown and petticoats and corset had pooled on the floor. Without another word, he left the room, leaving her sitting, stunned and sticky and naked on green twill.

Moments later, he returned carrying her favorite peach dressing gown. He thrust it out to her. She stood to wrap it around her body.

Then she watched him pace the length of the room. Four times. No. Five.

He spun to face her. "Because that is what you are, Viola. Pristine. Beautiful. You are too fine for these hands."

"Oh, that is pure rubbish. I happen to adore those hands. In particular, I adore when they are upon my body. Or inside my body, for that matter."

He ran one of the aforementioned hands through his hair. A bit of dust plumed. "There." He pointed to the dust. "Filthy. I should not be touching you at all. But I am a selfish, greedy, lusty brute, and I cannot bloody well resist."

"You are my husband."

"Aye. But that does not mean we suit, Viola."

All warmth fled her skin. Ice ascended to replace it. She blinked slowly, absorbing what he had just said. Stumbling backward, she collapsed as the backs of her knees hit the sofa's edge, sitting with a soft whump. "Do you …" She swallowed and tried again. "Would you feel the same about Alison?"

He stalked toward her, bending forward and bracing his hands on the back of the sofa to either side of her head, his face hovering inches from hers. "Listen to me, lass. What you witnessed that day was not what it seemed. I went to see her, yes. We spoke. Her husband had died. In a moment of grief, she kissed me. I was surprised for a single moment and did not react. Then, I pushed her away from me."

She watched his eyes, beloved and green. They burned like a forest aflame. "Because you are a man of honor," she whispered.

"No. Bloody hell, Viola. Because I do not want her. I want you. Do you understand? I want you until I cannot bear another moment. Until I hurt in every piece and part, every bone, every muscle, every inch of me. Honor has nothing to do with it." He shoved away. Turned his back to pace half the length of the room from her. Clasped his hands atop his head. And stood that way for long seconds before continuing quietly, "If I were being honorable, I would have let you marry that weak-chinned blighter Lord Hugh."

She wanted to speak. But her heart was squeezing and pounding so hard, she could scarcely take a breath. Finally, she was able to gasp enough air to say his name. "James?" The word was querulous and thin, but it drew him around to face her, his arms dropping to his sides. "You want me?" she confirmed.

"I am not good enough for you, lass."

She shook her head. "That is the silliest thing I've ever heard. You are the finest of men."

He glanced down at his hands. "No. I am—"

"The finest. Of men." She stood. Walked to him. Took his hands in hers. "If you want me, I am yours, James. It is, and always has been, that simple."

⤜∞⤛

HIS WEE BONNIE LASS HAD A SMUDGE ON HER PRISTINE, WHITE cheek. Her hair was in wild, black disarray. Her rose-petal lips were swollen from his kisses.

But her eyes. Ah, the stars had returned. They shone their light up at him, entire constellations of incandescent beauty.

Charlotte had tried to tell him. At the masquerade, when he'd stood watching Viola flirt and dance, when he'd stood burning inside an agonizing hell of rage and want, Charlotte had said all he must do was stop, turn 'round, and let Viola run into his arms. Then she had advised that he take care not to bruise the indomitable Miss Darling, as one never knew when those bruises might begin to matter a great deal.

As usual, Charlotte had been right. But he'd not wanted to

hear it. He'd convinced himself that giving in to his desire for Viola would harm her more than rejecting her. It had driven him to inflict wounds that he was only now beginning to see heal.

Gently, he caressed Viola's precious cheeks with his great, muckle hands, rubbing at the smudge with his thumb. He bent to kiss her brow softly. Then those miraculous eyes. Finally, he kissed her lips, resting his mouth against hers, taking her breath into his lungs.

"You are mine, lass," he whispered. "My wife. I mean tae keep ye, come what may."

She nodded, a tear escaping.

"Dinna cry."

"I am happy," she replied, her voice husky and soft. "I thought you wanted her. Loved her. I knew I had trapped you into marriage, and I thought letting you go was the proper thing to do."

"Now, there is where you went wrong." He smiled and kissed the spot where her tear had fallen, tasting the salt on his lips. "When you pursued me, you didna give a bloody damn what was proper. You tempted and twisted until I didna know up from sideways. That was an effective strategy, by God."

She laughed, the sound a full-throated balm to his soul. "I was determined, wasn't I?" She sighed and stroked his wrists. "Victoria reminded me my mistake had been taking away your choices, and that to leave you before I had asked what you wanted would be to repeat my error. I am glad I listened."

He kissed her again. "As am I, lass. Had you left me, I would have had a devil of a time chasing you. And you would have had a devil of a time being caught."

She raised a brow. "Oh?"

He lowered his voice to a playful growl. "Aye. Locked in here, naked and at my mercy for weeks. All your gowns in wee little tatters."

She laughed, as he'd intended. It was better if she did not

know the seriousness behind his words. Had she left him, he would have chased her to the ends of the earth. He would have done whatever was necessary to keep her.

Fortunately, his wife had both the grace to admit when she was wrong and the courage to do what was right. Not to mention persistence. She had that in abundance.

He drew her into his body, absorbing the sheer pleasure of her softness against him.

"James?" Her voice was muffled and wheezing, so he loosened his hold.

"Aye."

"You are rather filthy, and so am I."

He pulled back, a flush of shame returning. He'd torn her gown. Taken her on her hands and knees—on a sofa, no less. All while covered in dust and sweat. "I'm sorry, lass."

"Oh, I'm not. I was just going to suggest a bath. Do you suppose there is a tub big enough for us both?" Then, his bold, flirtatious, provocative wife rubbed her sweet, tight nipples against him and purred, "I do so admire the way you wash me."

Chapter Twenty-One

"The perception of beauty is, by its nature, subjective.
For example, some may consider your waistcoat a masterpiece,
whilst others have little need for spectacles."

—THE DOWAGER MARCHIONESS OF WALLINGHAM to Lord
Gattingford on a pleasant stroll through the south garden.

∽∞∽

"BLOODY HELL," JAMES MUTTERED AS THE MASSIVE, LIVING
work of art was erected atop the stone well at the edge of the
green. Every year, the villagers built a wooden canvas on a
table-sized frame. They layered the surface first with clay from
a nearby pond, then attached hundreds upon hundreds of
flower petals, leaves, seeds, and any other odd bits that suited
the image they wished to create.

This year, they'd chosen to celebrate the happy occasion of
his marriage by arranging every blue, purple, pink, and white

blossom upon their canvas of mud to form an image of Viola standing beneath a full moon and a skyful of stars—with him.

"My head looks like a loaf of bread," he grumbled.

Viola giggled then shushed him.

"And here we have the magnificent creation," announced the vicar to a rapt audience. "A tribute to Lord Tannenbrook, who has seen fit to grace our village and all the people of Shankwood with a most splendid, virtuous, gracious lady." He gestured to Viola, who inclined her head in acknowledgement. "Lady Tannenbrook, you are a blessing to us all. A gift sent from the heavens to ..."

While the vicar droned on, as vicars were wont to do, James leaned down to whisper in Viola's ear, "Even the bloody vicar, eh? Is there any man who does not worship at your feet, lass?"

She gave a secretive smile and whispered her reply. "There is only one man from whom I seek worship. Perhaps he might consider kneeling at my altar later."

He covered his bark of laughter with a sharp cough. "I'll have you singing God's praises, sure enough."

"... and pray that the fruits of our lady's womb might be bountiful and, by the grace of God, bless Shankwood and its lands with many generations to come."

Loud applause rang out from the assemblage of villagers gathered on the green. James could not determine whether it was agreement or thankfulness that the vicar had ceased droning. Viola, however, had gone strangely still.

"What is it, lass?"

Though she appeared pale to him in the diffuse sunlight, she shook her head and patted his arm to indicate she was fine, subsequently donning her customary smile. Later, after they had greeted the villagers and spoken at length with the vicar, she was still smiling brightly. He could only conclude he'd misread her reaction earlier.

As the crowd dispersed, he leaned down to kiss Viola,

explaining, "I've work I must do. I will see you at the celebration this evening."

She smiled again and nodded. "I promised Victoria that I would sit for her, but I should return well before the festivities begin."

He kissed her a second time. And a third. She chuckled against his mouth and pushed him away.

Trotting the short distance to the workshop, he entered to find it empty. So much the better. He had work to do, and he intended to complete it before Viola returned from Thornbridge. Tonight, his wife would learn just how devoted this particular congregant was to his lady.

He took the greatest care, the work as precise and demanding as he remembered. Every stroke of his fish tail chisel, every fine grate of his rasp, had to be done at the perfect angle to achieve the final effect he desired. Time passed so swiftly, he scarcely noted the waning light. The thunder in the distance. The patter of rain upon glass. All he knew was that, when he glanced up, sheets of water were streaming down the windows, and the cries and laughter of the village children had been replaced with repeating booms and wild gusts.

The sudden squall could cause a delay of the well-dressing festival. He hoped it passed quickly, for Viola had gone to a great deal of trouble to ensure this evening's celebration was a success.

Frowning, he used the light he had remaining to put the finishing touches on his creation. Buffing the last of the dust from the work, he stood back and walked around the table, examining the piece from all angles. It was good work, he thought. He'd never attempted anything quite so intricate before, and for a moment, he felt the warmth of pride sing through his veins.

He glanced around the workshop, realizing he could scarcely see in the low light. He removed his apron and hung it on the peg next to the door before donning his hat and coat.

Then, he went to the table holding his creation, covered it with a bit of canvas, lifted it into his arms, and carried the thing out into the rain.

He was drenched within seconds. "God, what a storm," he murmured to himself, looking up at a roiling, blackened sky. Although it could not be later than five or six, the day had turned to dusk. Thunder rolled heavily. Lightning cracked and spewed its fury across the black.

He hurried down the empty, muddy lane, loping toward Shankwood Hall. By the time he entered through the south hall, he was soaked from hat to boots. Even his face was slick with rainwater, the droplets falling from his lashes with every blink.

"Let me help you, my lord," said Mrs. Duckett, shuffling in from the corridor as he stood dripping on the polished parquet. She took his hat and offered to take the bundle from his arms, but he refused to release it.

"I shall take care of it," he said. "Where is Lady Tannenbrook?"

The old woman blinked and squinted. "Lady ... Why, I assumed she was in the village with your lordship."

He frowned. "She has not returned from Thornbridge?"

"No, my lord."

A prickle of alarm started at the top of his spine.

"Perhaps she elected to remain until the storm passes. That would be sensible. It is a rarity to have such a vigorous downpour as this."

Feeling chilled, he nodded. But his mind was uneasy. He wanted to touch her, to know she was safe.

He carried the sculpture upstairs, placing it upon her dressing table beside the enameled box. With a finger, he lifted the box's lid. The handkerchief was still there, lying beneath a handful of hairpins. He sighed. Perhaps after seeing his gift, she would consider offering him her own creation again. A man could only hope to have a second chance at something so precious.

The door flew open. The youngest footman, a man of forty years named David, was panting, his eyes flared wide. "My lord, you must come quickly. Lord Atherbourne is here."

The alarm he'd felt earlier burst open and unfurled its full, menacing weight along his spine and skull. He ran. He ran as he'd never run before, taking the length of the corridor and the span of the stairs in a mere heartbeat. But then, his heart had stopped the moment he'd seen the look upon David's face.

Then, he saw Lucien. Standing in front of the door. Dripping. Heaving as though he'd ridden pell-mell through this godforsaken storm. Dark eyes caught his when James was halfway down the staircase. They were grimmer than he'd seen them in two years.

Ah, God, no.

Something was tearing at James's chest, clawing and ripping him to shreds. The air around him and inside him froze. He wanted time to stop. He wanted to fall to his knees and beg. He wanted Lucien not to say what he was about to say.

"You must come now, James. I am sorry, but you must."

∾∾

FLASHES OF LIGHT, WHITE AND GRAY, SHONE IN THE DARKNESS. Pain stabbed and pounded. Distantly, she heard the sound of it. Boom and echo. Boom and echo. Boom and echo. Though the sound faded, the pain remained.

It was confusing in the dark. But soon she was engulfed in light. It was morning. Sunlight warmed her hands where they rested upon the oak desk of her sitting room. Dust floated in on a flickering beam, landed upon her fingers and her gown's indigo sleeve.

A letter had come from Charlotte. Viola had tried thrice to write her dearest friend. To explain about James. About how deeply she loved him and yet how she despaired that she must release him for his happiness' sake. Each time, she'd been unable to find the words, even after he had declared his intention to keep her. Now, happily, Charlotte had written, easing her guilt for the lapse in their correspondence.

She worked the edges of the paper between her fingertips and thumb, enjoying the lovely script of Charlotte's hand. Upright and neat, elegant and efficient. Viola's own calligraphy possessed an impatient slant and the occasional wild curl. She'd never mastered elegance in any craft.

Dearest Viola, the letter began. *Perhaps you will think me mad, and perhaps you would be right, but I do believe Benedict Chatham to be the best man I have ever known.*

Viola disagreed on that point—James was finer than all others—but she would concede allowances for Charlotte's obvious infatuation. She sighed and continued reading. Her smile grew as she learned of her friend's recent discovery.

I am with child, dearest. Though, I must tell you, this knowledge constitutes the greatest of joys and the greatest of frights. When one has not a mother of one's own, the prospect of becoming one causes the heart to imagine itself wholly unequal to the task. However, my darling Chatham is over the moon. He insists upon constructing a new cradle for the nursery, despite having wielded neither chisel nor hammer in all his years upon this earth.

Viola smiled again, but her smile soon faded. A child. James had made love to her many times, but if Georgina's descriptions were correct, he had not yet taken the final, critical step to get her—Viola—with child. She'd assumed he sought to give them both time to accustom themselves to their marriage before attempting to beget an heir. Perhaps that was so. But Charlotte's news made her ache inside in a way she hadn't anticipated.

The paper trembled, the words now winking in and out of her sight. Her fingers lowered the letter to the desk and came up to press her forehead. The pain had begun again. She tried to glance out the window, but the light was blinding now, the headache's talons gouging behind her eyes.

Darkness flashed. Then light. Pain boomed and echoed. Boomed and echoed. Boomed and echoed.

She was in James's study now, searching for him. The well-dressing ceremony would begin soon, and they must attend. Her head pained her, but she refused to let such a minor imposition keep her from the event. She spun in the center of the study as she heard footsteps. It was not James, but instead his solicitor, Mr. Gates, an intelligent-looking man who always carried a leather-bound journal in his hand and a pencil in his pocket.

"Lady Tannenbrook," he exclaimed with a broad grin and a nudge of his spectacles. "What a pleasure to see you again. By your expression, I gather you were expecting Lord Tannenbrook."

"Indeed, Mr. Gates, although it is lovely to see you, as well." It was not precisely a lie, but she did feel disappointed. She wanted James. And her head was aching.

"I, too, was seeking his lordship. I have made a discovery which I anticipate will please him greatly."

"Oh?" She did not care, but Mr. Gates was most enthusiastic, so she folded her hands and waited for him to elaborate. She did not wait long.

"His lordship's heir is alive. And, if my research proves correct, he is even now in London."

"His lordship's ... heir?"

"A cousin. As you may know, there was some question about whether the boy had survived, as it appears he changed his name after the unfortunate death of his mother and father." Mr. Gates paused to remove his spectacles, wiping them with a cloth he pulled from inside his coat. "My research had reached a standstill prior to your marriage. I even inquired as to whether his lordship wished to continue the effort. It is well that his lordship insisted, however, for the past three days have seen great strides forward in locating his heir presumptive."

"Insisted? My husband insisted you continue searching, even after we were wed?"

As Mr. Gates plopped his spectacles back upon his nose, a tiny crinkle formed between his brows. "Indeed. Did he not say so? Well, perhaps he felt the matter too uncertain to consider burdening you, my lady. It has weighed heavily upon him, as you know."

She'd known about the search for his heir during the season. She'd also recognized his resolve to complete his self-assigned mission. A man did not subject himself to Lady Wallingham's tender mercies without compelling cause, after all. But she had thought his urgency resulted from his resistance to marriage, for if he never married, he could never produce a legitimate son.

Now, however, he was married. To her. And, yet, he'd asked Gates to continue the mission. *Insisted*, even.

Her headache was worsening, making her stomach roll and quake.

The light wavered and flashed in her sight, blocking out Mr. Gates's nose as though his spectacles reflected the sun's glare into her eyes.

It grew until it flashed, bright and blinding. Then came the darkness. Confusion. She hurt, wanting to whimper. Wanting James.

He was there. They stood together, watching the well dressing. Laughing and teasing one another. The pain in her head was nothing when she was with him. The vicar was speaking. Speaking about wombs and fertility. It made her remember. The yearning joy she'd had upon reading Charlotte's letter. The doubt and confusion introduced by Mr. Gates.

Darkness swarmed again. It was raining. No. Not just raining. Pouring in sheets. In buckets directly upon her and the pretty gray mare. She was returning to Shankwood after sitting for Victoria. Exhausted after hours of pretending not to be in dreadful pain, she had hoped the storm would pass quickly. But it hadn't. Rather than miss the well-dressing celebration that would be held soon, she had ignored Victoria's pleas to wait, reassuring her new friend that it was only a short ride, only a bit of rain.

Now, the flashes in her vision lit up the darkness. The boom and echo, boom and echo, boom and echo became the crack, creak, and groan of wood undermined by a swollen brook. Her horse screamed. Flailed. She was falling backward, sliding. She gripped the horse's mane, clinging with slick, gloved fists. The mare's hooves scraped upon failing wood. Suddenly, they were righted again. Turned sideways on the bridge. Another crack. Another flash. The mare stumbled, her front legs buckling.

And Viola went flying. She hit the water with staggering force, her arms flailing for purchase. Nothing made sense. Water was in her mouth and nose. Cold and merciless, it swarmed. Dragging and shoving. Beating and tugging. Her foot caught something. A stone. She kicked, trying for the surface. Broke free into the air. Spewed and gagged. Sucked in breath instead of muddy water. She fought against the ferocious current, against waters maddened and swollen by the storm.

Soon, her muscles ached and burned. Her lungs ached and burned. Her head ached and burned. She sobbed, watching the bank fly past, kicking her feet to find bottom. At last, she did. Well enough to shove toward land instead of water. She turned her head to look back at the bridge. Splintered wood rushed toward her so fast, she only had time to turn her cheek. The force of the blow was brutal, the pain an explosion of red and gray. Her feet lost their grip. But the curve of the bank caught her again. Everything slowed.

James. She must see James.

Now, her knees knocked into rocks. She clawed and scraped, the pain in her body nothing.

She must get back to James.

Grass tickled her nose. Filled her mouth. Someone was wheezing. She wondered if it was her horse, the pretty gray mare who had tried so valiantly to keep her footing.

Red and gray. Gray and black. Light flashed again. Boom and echo. Boom and echo. Boom and echo.

Then came her name. Viola. Whispered and sweet. Then came the darkness again. But this time, the light did not return.

Chapter Twenty-Two

"We do not create the storm, Humphrey. We merely endure it."

—THE DOWAGER MARCHIONESS OF WALLINGHAM to her
boon companion, Humphrey, in response to his unmistakable
disappointment at the abbreviated nature of their afternoon ramble.

BEHIND HIM, THEY WERE TALKING. LUCIEN AND VICTORIA.

"Do you suppose he would eat something? I could have a tray sent up."

"No, angel. He has no thought but her. I've sent for the physician, but with the storm ..."

Lucien was right. James was not hungry. He was not tired. He was not anything at all.

He stared down at his wee bonnie lass where she lay in Thornbridge's sky-blue bedchamber. Half of her face had swelled and discolored grotesquely. Her beautiful black hair was streaked with mud. He knew from his earlier, panicked explorations that her knees were bruised and bloody, her fingernails torn to the quicks.

The horse had survived. It had scrambled back to Thornbridge, which had sent Lucien out searching. He'd found Viola lying facedown on the bank, one hundred yards downstream from the half-crumbled bridge. Then, he'd brought her back here and ridden like a demon to fetch the man who loved her more than his own life. The man who should have prevented this.

James lowered his lips to her hand, which he had held in his for hours as he waited for her to awaken. To look at him. To speak his name.

A hand gripped his shoulder. "It is not your fault, James." Luc's voice was low.

"Aye. It is. I should have come with her."

"Why should you? That bridge has been there since before you were born. It has withstood flood after flood. You had no way of knowing the weather would turn, let alone that the bloody thing would fail."

"I should have been with her."

"Be reasonable, man. It was an accident."

James shook his head. Luc did not understand. She belonged to him. And he had failed her. It was not the first time he had failed someone he loved.

Lucien drifted away. Time passed as James watched his wife breathe in the golden light of the lamp. Victoria came in to check for a fever and set a plate of bread and butter on the bedside table. "Eat something, James," she whispered, laying a gentle kiss upon his cheek. Then, she was gone, too.

In time, he felt the weight of the day dragging at him, so he rose from the chair, came around to the other side of the bed, and lay down beside his wife, taking great care not to disturb her.

His hand stroked her arm. The uninjured side of her face. He felt for her breath and sighed when the warm, soft air tickled his finger. Then, he moved his hand between her breasts, feeling her heart beat.

He may have slept, because, when he next opened his eyes, it was to see twilight staring back at him.

"James," she murmured, the word distorted by the swelling of her cheek and mouth.

His head now rested upon her belly as though he'd chosen it as his pillow. His hand lay entwined with hers while her other hand gently stroked his hair.

"I love you, lass." The words sprang from him wholly formed and without volition. They were as true as anything he'd ever spoken.

A tear tracked down her uninjured cheek. "Oh, James. I love you more."

"Not possible."

She smiled, but it quickly became a wince. "Perhaps we could argue about it later. My head aches abominably."

He swallowed and sat up, not wanting to cause her any additional discomfort. The light from the window indicated it was morning. Had he slept through the night?

"The physician was here an hour ago," said Viola gently.

Running a hand through his hair, blinking away the fog of sleep, James frowned, wondering if he'd heard correctly. "The physician was here? Why didn't you wake me? Bloody hell, Viola. How long have I been asleep? How long have you been awake?"

She pursed her lips, blinking her single open eye. The other was swollen shut, already sickeningly black. "Hmm, let's see." She held up fingers to count her responses. "Yes. Because you were sleeping so peacefully, and Victoria said you'd been frantic all night. I would guess four hours, based on her recollection of events. And approximately two hours, though I might have dozed sporadically."

"What did the physician say?"

She stroked his arm. "I have bruising and soreness which

will pain me for a week or so. He focused mainly on the injury to my face. After the swelling subsides, he will be better able to assess whether there are any fractures or damage to my eye, but for now, he sees no indication of either. He suggests laudanum for the pain and a good deal of rest. Oh, and kisses. Many, many kisses."

It should ease his mind. She was awake. Injured but breathing. Talking. The physician had seen her, and she would heal.

He still felt frantic. Vibrating like a plucked string. Torn apart by visions of her wee, dainty bones being cracked in her fall. Her wee, dainty cheek being slammed by debris. His wee, dainty lass being drowned and taken from him forever. He wanted to hold her in his arms, but he couldn't risk hurting her. He'd done enough of that already.

Rising from the bed, he began pacing. "From now on, wherever you go, I go."

"Don't be silly."

He pointed a finger at her. "Heed me well, Viola. I'll not countenance another incident. You may wish to traipse hither and yon on a whim, but I am responsible for your care. Me. You will do as I say. You are my wife."

"Precisely. Your wife. Not your child."

His feet stopped in the middle of a sky-blue carpet.

His child. Not his child.

Something was crushing his chest. His hands moved to his hips. A force bent him forward. Buckled his knees. Right there, upon an ornate carpet in front of his wife, he broke open with a grinding groan. Sound faded until it felt eerily like he was drenched with rain and kneeling in mud beneath a grove of willows.

"Ah, God, I canna bear it."

Bedding rustled. Whispered. A breeze scented with rainwater and peonies brushed him. She was there, standing when she should have been lying, her hands upon his face.

"What can't you bear, my love?" she asked softly.

"Tae fail ye the way I failed my son."

Her hands and body stiffened for a moment. Then, she drew his head to her chest and wrapped his neck in her arms, cradling him to her. Helpless to stop himself, he encircled her tiny frame, clutched her softness with all the desperation he could not suppress.

"Tell me about your son, James."

IT WAS A SIMPLE STORY, REALLY. HE'D BEEN A BOY IN LOVE with a girl. Then, he'd become an earl. One year later, he'd returned home, only to discover his girl, Alison, had married another. Also in that time, she had given birth to his son, who had died days after taking his first breath.

The babe had been weakened by a fever. It had been a difficult birth lasting two days. Alison had barely survived, herself, and had never borne another child.

And Viola's beautiful, honorable husband believed himself responsible. For planting his seed before taking his vows. For leaving to become a "bloody English lord." For not marrying Alison or taking her with him or bothering to return for an entire year. But, most of all, for not knowing his son. Not holding his son. Not saving his son.

He'd told no one. Not his mother or sister or best friends. He had carried the guilt and shame of it alone as though that would keep his son with him.

Viola held her husband tightly, her chest aching worse than her head. She rocked them together, trying to soothe him in whatever way she could. Laying a kiss upon his head, she said over and over, "You did not know. You are not to blame, my love. You are not to blame."

He couldn't hear her, it seemed, for he only clutched her tighter and fell silent. In time, she persuaded him to lie down with her, and they slept.

Upon awakening, Viola found her headache had lessened, and James was already making arrangements to transport her back to Shankwood. Victoria helped her into a fresh, borrowed dressing gown and fed her a bit of tea and a biscuit or two.

James lifted her into his arms, climbed with her into the Atherbourne coach, and held her tightly in his lap for the entire, quarter-hour journey. He then carried her into the house, up the stairs, and into her bedchamber. He did not release her until he laid her upon her bed, drawing the plain, green coverlet over her, kissing her temple, and murmuring, "Sleep, lass."

When next she awakened, Amy helped her into a bath that James had arranged in front of the fireplace. She sighed upon sinking into the hot, fragrant water. Moaned as the miscellaneous aches, stings, and oddly sore, previously unknown muscles in her arms and shoulders eased. Amy washed her hair clean of the mud from the brook, lathering it twice and rinsing with pitchers full of fresh water. After a while, Viola noted the girl's uncharacteristic silence.

"Amy? Is everything all right?" She still had swelling in her lips, which made her speech a bit less distinct, but the words were clear enough to be understood.

"Oh! Yes, my lady."

"You are very quiet."

"Er—yes, my lady."

"Why is that?"

"His lordship mentioned your head pains you greatly, and that I should not chatter on like a bloody magpie whilst you recover from your injuries. Begging your pardon for the vulgarity. I am quoting his lordship."

"That is both very thoughtful of him and very rude."

Amy did not reply.

"Amy, where is his lordship now?"

"In his study, I believe. Shall I fetch him for you?"

Viola sighed, leaning back against the tub and absorbing the water's soothing heat. She did not yet have the strength for her next Difficult Conversation with James. "No. I shall find him later."

"Very good, my lady."

After her bath, she felt much refreshed, donning a simple white muslin gown, sitting on the edge of the bed, and letting Amy brush and plait her hair. Finally, she was ready to face herself. She had not yet glimpsed the damage, and she dreaded discovering just how hideous she looked.

"Amy, would you be so kind as to bring me a mirror? There is one in the top drawer of my dressing table."

The girl scurried away and returned in seconds, holding out the small, silver hand mirror.

"Here you are, my lady. If you're certain, now."

That did not sound promising. Taking a deep breath, Viola closed her one functioning eye, raised the mirror into position, and then silently counted to three. On the last number, she opened her eye. And slumped. She was hideous. It was not worse than she'd suspected, but neither was it better. The entire left side of her face was swollen, particularly her eye. It looked as though she'd stuffed her eyelid full of stones and lard and sewn it shut. Similarly, her cheek and jaw were puffy and distorted. And the colors. She groaned aloud. Black and blue and red. Even a bit of green and yellow.

"I am monstrous," she moaned. "How can you even look upon me, Amy?"

"Oh, it's not so bad, my lady. My great Aunt Sophie took a tumble down a set of stairs once. That was much worse. You're just a bit puffy is all."

"That is kind of you to say, but it is not true. I have seen dead, bloated fish more attractive."

"Well, if you like, perhaps I can do something different with your hair."

Viola stood, holding the mirror out for Amy to remove from her sight. "Anything. Yes. Let us try a new coif. Perhaps it will serve as a distraction."

Amy followed her into the dressing room. As Viola approached the oak dressing table, she noted an oddly shaped object resting on its surface, right next to her box of hair pins. She slowed as she drew closer, blinking to be certain she was seeing clearly, as one of her eyes was swollen shut and the other had recently been subjected to a glimpse of her own face. But the object did not disappear.

It was slightly less than a foot in length, perhaps half that in width and height. It appeared to be made of stone, but a most extraordinary stone it was. The base was a swirl of browns from nearly black to pale fawn. Its form was that of a rough-hewn hand, fingers fanned and cupped like a shell, the thumb a branch outstretched. Inside the dark hand's palm, resting with wings poised as though ready to take flight, was a butterfly. This part of the sculpture was as bright as the hand was dark, an exquisite palette of blue and green and white and red—even a bit of yellow. Every small detail of the wings was carved with loving precision. Every surface of the tiny creature had been polished until it shone mirror bright.

The piece as a whole was astonishingly beautiful, the butterfly an exquisite work of art.

But her favorite part of all was the hand. It was *his* hand. She recognized it instantly, even though he'd formed it to resemble wood or mud, with jagged cuts along the base.

"Amy," she said softly, struggling to catch her breath. "You may fetch his lordship now. Tell him not to delay, for I must see him immediately."

"Yes, my lady."

She worked to compose herself while she waited, rehearsing what she would say in this new Difficult

Conversation. She ran her fingers over the curves of his hand, missing the heat of his flesh. She thought of all the ways to say what was in her heart. To ask the questions she must hear him answer. In the end, she elected to keep things simple. As he'd once said, he was a simple man.

When he entered, it was as a bull bursting through her dressing room door, his eyes afire. "What is it, lass? Are you ailing? Bloody physicians don't know a bloody thing."

She stood with her backside propped against the dressing table, her hands braced on the edge to either side of her hips. "I am well enough, silly goose. I simply have a question or two."

He halted three feet away, his shoulders squaring, his brow furrowing. "What questions? Why are you not lying in bed where you belong?"

"I shall do that later, provided you join me."

Blinking, he dropped his eyes to her bosom then raised them to her face as though he'd been caught ogling by an alert chaperone. "I—I am not tired."

"Mmm. Neither am I." She smiled. "Now, then, that settles our plans for later. About those questions."

He was back to frowning. "Viola, I am meeting with Gates and Strudwicke. Can this wait? You are supposed to rest. And take laudanum, if I remember correctly."

"One of my questions pertains to Mr. Gates."

"He is my solicitor."

"Yes, I know."

"Has he been mooning over you, too? Bloody hell, lass, must you enchant every male within—"

"He mentioned yesterday morning that he'd made progress in the search for your heir."

Silence.

She waited.

"And?" he said.

"When did you decide you would never have another child, James?"

He froze. He looked as though she'd swung a giant iron pot at his face and connected soundly. "When I saw his grave," he rasped.

"This is why you did not wish to marry. Why you resisted marrying me. Isn't it?"

His chest was working as though he'd sprinted across the green. For a long while, he simply gazed at her, his eyes tearing her apart. "Aye."

"I want children, James."

More silence.

"Your children, specifically. I was reminded of this yearning early yesterday morning, when I learned Charlotte is with child."

His eyes lowered to stare at his boots.

"Does this matter to you?"

"Of course it matters." His voice was sharp, his eyes rising to her, fierce and anguished. "It is why I resisted you. But I made a vow, Viola. To my son."

"You made a vow to me, too. And yet, without speaking to me about it, you have done all you can to prevent me conceiving a child." She recalled the strange sheath he had used only once. "Even on our wedding night. The French gift."

"Letter. French letter."

"Your son's death was not your doing."

"Aye, it was. I should have—"

She continued, needing to say this as clearly as she could before falling apart. "Just as my accident was not your doing."

"Viola."

"You are not God, James Kilbrenner. You are not a king. You are not even Lady Wallingham. You are a man." A tear escaped her hold. "The finest of men. But still, just a man."

He blinked, his brow furrowing. "I am responsible. You are mine to protect. So was he."

Frustration burned inside her belly, rising up and nearly choking her. "I want you to ask yourself this question: If it had been me whom you loved in Netherdunnie. If I had been your lass, and you were leaving for England, do you suppose I would have simply accepted it? Or do you suppose I would have followed you?"

His nose flared, his head shaking. "I wouldna ever hae left ye. I couldna."

She smiled, her eyes filling with tears, distorting the light. "And I would not have *let* you leave me. I would have chased you to England or to the other side of the world. Because when a girl loves a boy as much as I love you, she does not give up. She does not let go. She does not marry another. She does not conceal a man's son from him until it is too late."

"Alison paid fer her sins, lass. What has been my punishment?"

She shook her head. "You have punished yourself every day since then. And now, you are punishing me, too."

The color left his skin. He blinked slowly once. Twice.

She spoke softly, knowing she must say these things and knowing they would hurt him and wanting to stop. But she had no choice. Just as she had refused to let him go, she now refused to let him punish them both forever. "Consider whether you would wish to deny Alison the chance to bear another child. Or me to bear my first."

Now, his breathing was shallow. Fast. "I—I wouldna."

"No. You wouldn't. Because you are a good, honorable man."

His brow crumpled. "I wish ye tae be happy, lass. That is a' I ken."

"Do you want children, James?"

He swallowed. Ran a hand over his lower jaw. "I dinna deserve them."

"But do you *want* them?"

He stacked his hands atop his head and began pacing. "I dinna want tae fail again. Them or ye." He stopped and faced her, dropping his arms to his sides. "Ye are tied tae me now. I tried tae let ye gae, lass. I couldna."

She swallowed, squeezing the edge of the table, trying desperately to keep her muscles from taking her across the floor to him. "I forced your hand."

He laughed, the sound dark. "Nae. Wallingham gave me a way oot. I think he knew I wouldna take it, but I could hae. I wanted ye sae damn badly. An' I took what I wanted. Soiled ye wi' my great, muckle hands. Even though ye deserved better."

"There is no one better," she said, her voice growing thin through a tight throat. "Do you want to have a child with me, James? I should like an answer, please."

He took a deep breath and closed his eyes briefly before they landed upon her with a fierce green fire. "Aye," he gritted. "Wee little lassies. With black hair and eyes full of stars shinin' fer me alone."

She could wait no longer. She ran to him. Leapt upon him, her arms grasping at his neck. He wrapped her up, lifted her, taking care to cradle her head gently. "I love you so much," she gasped into his neck. "So much."

"I love you more," he said, his voice rumbling through her blood and bones.

"Not possible," she whispered.

Chapter Twenty-Three

"True love is a foolish notion. However, if it will persuade the intractable to at last see reason, then by all means, let foolishness reign supreme."

—THE DOWAGER MARCHIONESS OF WALLINGHAM to Lord Tannenbrook during a discussion of Lady Tannenbrook's much improved embroidery skills.

HE'D MEANT TO RESIST HER. MEANT TO KEEP HIS HANDS FROM stroking that beautiful skin, cupping that curvaceous backside. Meant to give himself time to absorb the new shape of his heart, a shape molded by Viola's dainty, determined hands.

But as usual, his wee bonnie lass—and his lust—had other ideas. She washed over him with gale force, clinging and making the sweetest hitching sounds as she ran kisses along the underside of his jaw.

"Kiss me," she demanded through gritted teeth.

He buried his face in her neck and gripped her tighter against him, his cock surging against his will. "I dinna wish tae hurt ye—"

"You won't. Now, please, James. I need you. Your tongue. And your fingers. And your—"

Chuckling and shaking his head, he marveled at the tiny woman who managed to turn him inside out. "Weel-a-weel, lass." He lifted her into his arms. Carried her into her bedchamber, setting her down beside the green bed. He grunted at the sight of it. "We must change this room. It doesna suit ye."

"We will discuss décor another time, James Kilbrenner. For now, I wish to feel your hands upon me."

He gritted his teeth against the surge of heat generated by her sweet demands. "I am tryin' tae—" He stopped, struggling for better control. "I am trying to slow down, Viola. If you continue to push me, I cannot be as gentle as you need."

She grasped his hand, cupping it to the right side of her face, leaving the injured side exposed. "I am ugly, aren't I?"

"Bloody hell."

"Can you love me like this? I am almost as hideous as one of my embroidered reticules."

He shouted his laughter, the sounds ringing out before he could contain them. It was a kind of release. But then, his lass had always been able to make him smile. From the very first.

"Will your flesh harden?" she queried. "I do not wish us to have awkwardness between—"

He answered her question with the simple expedient of grasping her hand and bringing it to the front of his trousers, right over his astoundingly appreciative cock.

"Oh," she breathed. "That is lovely."

His breathing quickened at the feel of her fingers caressing him. "That's one way tae put it, I suppose."

Not one to exercise patience when there was an alternative, Viola sat on the bed and began lifting her skirts, a tempting, mischievous smile playing about her lips. Her ivory legs, inch by inch, revealed themselves. Then, he was looking at the sweet object of his obsession, cloaked in a tuft of glossy, damp, black silk.

"Ah, God, lass."

She simply refused to let him delay, pushing him past all his boundaries, making him want her light too much to dwell in the dark.

He slid his palms up her thighs then back down, hooking behind her knees, pulling her hips toward him, stepping between her legs. Her scent was lush and rich and dark. Peonies and woman. His Viola.

Her head tipped back on her lovely neck. He used one of his hands to grip her there, his thumb moving across her jaw to the side of her lips he could caress without causing her pain. Her tongue darted out. Her mouth sucked him in.

He groaned, the heat and scent of her rushing through his blood like a brushfire. "Take me out," he commanded.

She smiled around his thumb and went to work on his fall. Those dainty fingers with the torn nails ripped at his buttons. Then the greedy little things clasped him at the root, squeezing firmly. He gasped and groaned at the pressure. The pleasure. "Ah, God."

Her tongue circled his thumb, her mouth suckling as her hands stroked his cock to even greater hardness. He hadn't thought it possible.

"Ye are a miracle, lass," he panted, feeling as though his head was going to burst into a thousand tiny bits if he did not sink inside her soon. He pulled his thumb from her mouth, grinning at her little grunt of annoyance.

Then, he moved it down to the sweet center of her, where honey had pooled to beckon him with its sleek invitation. He stroked the way she liked, soft and slow in subtle circles around her firm little nub. Her entire body jerked. She threw her head back and moaned his name.

He grinned wider, feeling her soften and swell, watching her hips writhe against his hand. "That's right, my bonnie Viola. *James.* An' no other will ever see ye like this. Now, lie back and take this filthy Scot inside ye."

She did lie back, but she took umbrage at the latter part of his demand. "You are not filthy. You are wondrous."

"If ye could see what is in my heid right now, lass, ye wouldna say such a thing."

"Oh. That sort of filthy. The sort I enjoy immensely."

He tucked the head of his cock against her lush core, throbbing and pulsing with the lust that had only grown as they'd learned and explored one another. He'd been waiting for it to diminish, but it hadn't. Just one more thing about Viola he'd been unable to predict. He sank inside her tight heat, keeping the circling pressure upon that tiny nub, swollen and glistening. She took him more easily now, with none of the discomfort of the first few times, but her sheath was still tight as a fist. It clenched and milked him as her head rolled back and forth, her arms stretched out to her sides, gripping handfuls of green twill.

He fell forward, bracing himself over her as he pumped his hips against hers. Savoring every inch of their union, he gave her long, slow strokes of his cock, pleasuring his wife for the sheer joy of seeing the shiver in her skin, hearing the choking cries from her throat, feeling the grinding of her hips between the coverlet and him.

Tiny warning ripples seized around him as her moaning, gasping cries increased, he let her have more of his fire, slamming her harder, changing the direction of his thumb. Suddenly, she tightened and squeezed upon him, sobbing and undulating with explosive ecstasy. Her beauty shook him. Forced his own crisis to crouch tightly in his lower spine. His ballocks and cock were painfully weighted and heavy with need. He lowered his head to nuzzle her bare throat, suckling a bit of her flesh into his mouth, teasing it with his teeth while increasing his tempo. He wanted to expand her pleasure. He wanted to draw this out so that he would never have to leave her intoxicating heat.

Then, he felt her hands upon his face. Stroking his lips tenderly. Running her fingers over his brow in soothing little passes. "You don't have to release inside me, you know," she whispered. "We have time. Take what you need, my love. Whatever that may be."

Her heat caressed him. Her love shone up at him. Her hands held him steady.

And everything he'd been afraid to envision with her—kissing her beneath a summer moon, lying with her in a cool, dark bed when her head pained her, listening to her laugh at Miss Starling's preposterous tales, and yes, watching her belly swell with their child—all coalesced inside him. The vision grew and glowed until there was no more room for the darkness that had kept it contained. It was a miracle. It was unstoppable.

Finally, he stopped fighting and let it take him.

And released everything he had—his joy, his love, his essence—inside his beautiful wife while she whispered her pleasure and her love in his ear.

Afterward, they lay together for a long while. He'd removed his coat and cravat and waistcoat. Tossed aside his boots. Settled on the bed to draw her into the curve of his body. She was holding his hand and kissing each finger, one by one.

"Are you certain, James?" she said.

"Aye."

He watched her lips curve in a smile. "I found what you made for me. It is the most beautiful thing I have ever seen."

Frowning, he recalled placing the sculpture on her dressing table. "I intended to give it to you yesterday. Before ... before the storm."

"My favorite part is the hand."

He grunted. "Daft woman. I made it to resemble mud."

"I know. But I don't know why."

"Because that is what I am."

"And you see me as a butterfly?"

"Aye." He nuzzled her temple, savoring the warmth of her. "I never knew how dark and cold it could be in the mud until a wee, bright butterfly landed upon me and refused to depart."

"I love you, James." Her voice was distorted by tears, but he judged them to be happy ones.

"And I love you, lass. Now, I must ask one small favor."

Again, she kissed his hand. "What is it?"

"I am in need of a handkerchief. But it is a very particular one. Ye see, I was a great, muckle fool and tossed it away when I should have kept it tucked right next to my heart. It has a wee purple fish in one corner. Have ye seen it, by chance?"

She turned her head to gaze up at him. "Oh, James. It is not very handsome, you know."

He leaned down to kiss her gently. "I know, lass. But no other will ever do."

Epilogue

*"Those who heed my advice end happily. Those who
ignore it suffer mightily. I should think this
would be obvious to you by now."*

—THE DOWAGER MARCHIONESS OF WALLINGHAM to her son,
Charles, during a rather fractious discussion of matches and
meddling and mothers who only desire to hold a grandchild before
being too weakened by old age and infirmity.

∽⧜∾

December 2, 1818
Shankwood Hall, Derbyshire

"SHE IS CONVINCED IT IS A BOY," VIOLA SAID, GRINNING DOWN
at the letter in her hand. "He will arrive in spring."

Warm, firm lips caressed the nape of her neck. "Mmm.
Perhaps you could embroider a wee woolen cap for the bairn,

lass. The lad surely could use one for the Northumberland winters."

Reaching up to stroke James's hard, delicious jaw, Viola chuckled. "I think you may be overestimating Charlotte's tolerance for mediocrity."

He covered her hand with his, drawing her palm to his mouth. His touch sent tingles shimmying across her body, even though it had been mere hours since he'd last made love to her. "You are the furthest thing from mediocre that I can imagine," he whispered. "These hands have wrought miracles."

She leaned back into his arms and closed her eyes briefly, savoring her husband's strength and heat. "I may have improved a bit in my efforts at stitchery, James, but I would hardly call it miraculous."

Rumbling a deep laugh, he nibbled her ear and glanced over her shoulder at the letter. "How does Lady Rutherford fare?"

"She has formed a rather alarming friendship with Lady Wallingham, but apart from that, she sounds ... blissful."

He must have heard the thread of wistfulness in her voice, because his arms tightened around her waist, drawing her deeper into his body, surrounding and steadying her with every breath. "It will come for us, too, lass." His big, strong hands flattened over her belly. "Ere long, it will come."

She smiled softly and turned her lips to his jaw. "Do you think so?"

"I have an Inkling, I do."

Sniffing, she neatly folded Charlotte's letter and placed it on the writing desk—the *new* writing desk in her newly refurnished sitting room. James had not relented until she'd replaced every drapery, every chair, every inch of green twill with lighter, more curvaceous, and decidedly more feminine décor. Naturally, she had refused to similarly transform their shared bedchamber, although she had added a number of lovely, embroidered pillows to soften the square, oak furnishings and plain twill coverlet. "You may laugh, but my Inkling has served me well. It led me to you, did it not?"

He hummed his agreement before giving her neck one final kiss and releasing her to withdraw a letter of his own from the pocket of his blue wool coat. "I have a letter, as well, lass. From Lady Wallingham."

Her eyes widened upon the expensive, folded paper, the dark-red, embellished seal, the bold, flowing script. "Do you suppose ...?"

He waggled the thing between his fingers. "We must open it to see." For entirely too long, he stood, staring at her, his eyes roving her face, running down to her belly, pausing at her breasts.

She began to wonder if he was deliberately delaying. "Well, open it, James!"

"Sae impatient ye are, my wee bonnie lass."

"Yes, I am. You may ogle me later. For now, I am dying of curiosity."

Looking as though she had denied him a delectable treat, he sighed. "Weel-a-weel." Then, he loosened the seal, unfolded the paper, and began reading. Silently.

"Aloud, if you please."

He smiled, his green eyes twinkling with a mischief she adored. Playfulness had been too rare in her husband's life. Her heart soared to see him this way, glowed at the knowledge of his happiness.

Clearing his throat as though preparing to announce the queen's entrance, he shook the paper and began reading. Aloud. *"Lord Tannenbrook. I do apologize for the delay in addressing your recent inquiry, but I have been most preoccupied of late. You should know that my dear, dear son has waged a ceaseless campaign on your behalf. Had the sound of his pleas not been overwhelmed by the cacophony of his wretched attempts to woo a certain widow, perhaps I might have responded sooner. Alas, a woman of my years must accept her limitations.*

Regarding your cousin, Elijah Kilbrenner, I am happy to inform you he remains corporeal on this earth. According to his grandmother, he was taken in by a kindly man after the deaths of his parents. The boy was instructed in several trades, including chimney maintenance and pocket inspection. Needless to say, he elected to be called by a new name as the questionable nature of these trades requires. I believe you may be acquainted, as he currently resides in London."

James stopped, a deep furrow developing between his brows. Viola waited, blinking between her husband's face and the paper at which he glowered so fiercely.

"Well?" Viola demanded.

"The man's name is Reaver. Sebastian Reaver."

Now, Viola was the one frowning. "Should that mean something? Who is he?"

Green eyes came up to hers. "He owns a gaming hell off of St. James. A rather notorious one. Before Rutherford married Charlotte, he frequented the place almost exclusively."

Her brows rose. "Oh, dear. It is a club for scoundrels, then."

James nodded and dropped his eyes back to the letter. "She goes on to explain further her reasoning for withholding the information from me." He chuckled. "She says, *'Now you understand why I was loath to burden you with the knowledge of your presumptive heir's identity. There is only one sort of man less deserving of your title than a Scottish stonemason. And that is Sebastian Reaver. But, now that Lady Tannenbrook is with child, I don't suppose it is any longer a worry, for you shall soon have ...'"*

He raised his head. Green eyes caught fire. "You—you are ..."

Filled with the luminous weight of the knowledge she'd carried for more than a fortnight, she gave him her happiest, watery smile. "With child. Yes. Your Inkling was right, after all, my love."

The paper fluttered to the floor. His arms came around her. Lifted her. Spun her about until she was dizzy and bursting with a joy she could not contain. And all the while, the captivating sounds of his laughter rumbled and boomed. She kissed his beloved mouth. Cradled his beloved face in her hands.

He stopped spinning long enough for her to catch her breath. "Bloody hell, you told Lady Wallingham before you told me?"

Viola chuckled. "I believe she guessed. Lady Atherbourne says the dowager has numerous, mysteriously knowledgeable sources in Derbyshire. I simply confirmed her suspicions. I intended to tell you this morning, but you distracted me."

"Why did you not tell me sooner, lass?"

She could hear a thread of sadness in her own voice when she answered, "We had been disappointed before. I wanted to be certain."

His lips caressed hers softly. Tenderly. "I love ye, Viola."

She grinned. "And I adore my Scottish stonemason." Laying a gentle kiss upon his brow, she held him to her and whispered the truth of her heart. "For he is the very finest of men."

More from Elisa Braden

It's far from over! There are more scandalous predicaments, emotional redemptions, and gripping love stories (with a dash of Lady Wallingham) to come in the Rescued from Ruin series. For **new release alerts and updates**, follow Elisa on Facebook and Twitter, and sign up for her free email newsletter at **www.elisabraden.com**, so you don't miss a thing!

Plus, be sure to check out all the other exciting books in the Rescued from Ruin series, available now!

THE MADNESS OF VISCOUNT ATHERBOURNE (BOOK ONE)
Victoria Lacey's life is perfect—perfectly boring. Agree to marry a lord who has yet to inspire a single, solitary tingle? It's all in a day's work for the oh-so-proper sister of the Duke of Blackmore. Surely no one suspects her secret longing for head-spinning passion. Except a dark stranger, on a terrace, at a ball where she should not be kissing a man she has just met. Especially one bent on revenge.

THE TRUTH ABOUT CADS AND DUKES (BOOK TWO)
Painfully shy Jane Huxley is in a most precarious position, thanks to dissolute charmer Colin Lacey's deceitful wager. Now, his brother, the icy Duke of Blackmore, must make it right, even if it means marrying her himself. Will their union end in frostbite? Perhaps. But after lingering glances and devastating kisses, Jane begins to suspect the truth: Her duke may not be as cold as he appears.

DESPERATELY SEEKING A SCOUNDREL (BOOK THREE)
Where Lord Colin Lacey goes, trouble follows. Tortured and hunted by a brutal criminal, he is rescued from death's door by

the stubborn, fetching Sarah Battersby. In return, she asks one small favor: Pretend to be her fiancé. Temporarily, of course. With danger nipping his heels, he knows it is wrong to want her, wrong to agree to her terms. But when has Colin Lacey ever done the sensible thing?

THE DEVIL IS A MARQUESS (BOOK FOUR)
A walking scandal surviving on wits, whisky, and wicked skills in the bedchamber, Benedict Chatham must marry a fortune or risk ruin. Tall, redheaded disaster Charlotte Lancaster possesses such a fortune. The price? One year of fidelity and sobriety. Forced to end his libertine ways, Chatham proves he is more than the scandalous charmer she married, but will it be enough to keep his unwanted wife?

WHEN A GIRL LOVES AN EARL (BOOK FIVE)
Miss Viola Darling always gets what she wants, and what she wants most is to marry Lord Tannenbrook. James knows how determined the tiny beauty can be—she mangled his cravat at a perfectly respectable dinner before he escaped. But he has no desire to marry, less desire to be pursued, and will certainly not kiss her kissable lips until they are both breathless, no matter how tempted he may be.

About the Author

Reading romance novels came easily to Elisa Braden. She's been doing it since she was twelve. Writing them? That took a little longer. After graduating with degrees in creative writing and history, Elisa spent entirely too many years in "real" jobs writing T-shirt copy ... and other people's resumes ... and articles about giftware displays. But that was before she woke up and started dreaming about the very *unreal* job of being a romance novelist. Frankly, she figures better late than never.

Elisa lives in the gorgeous Pacific Northwest, where you're constitutionally required to like the colors green and gray. Good thing she does. Other items on the "like" list include cute dogs, strong coffee, and epic movies. Of course, her favorite thing of all is hearing from readers who love her characters as much as she does. If you're one of those, get in touch on Facebook and Twitter or visit **www.elisabraden.com**.

27297893R00167

Printed in Great Britain
by Amazon